MW00941909

populatti

JACKIE NASTRI BARDENWERPER

TAUTOG
PRESS

Copyright © 2014 by Jackie Nastri Bardenwerper

All rights reserved. Published by Tautog Press.

No part of this publication may be reproduced, stored in a retrieval system, or transmitted in any form without written permission from the publisher. For information regarding permission, write to Tautog Press, Attention: Permissions, P.O. Box 5032, Greenwich, CT 06831.

Tautog Press
P.O. Box 5032
Greenwich, CT 06831
www.tautogpress.com

Cover and inside images by iStockPhoto.

This is a work of fiction. Any resemblance of characters to actual persons, living or dead, is purely coincidental. The author holds exclusive rights to this work.

The publisher is not responsible for websites (or their content) that are not owned by the publisher.

For more information:

www.populatti.com

Populatti

ISBN-13: 978-0-9907858-0-4

ISBN-10: 0990785807

*To Heather and Lauren,
for then and now.*

populatti.com

lululivi: 96%

Approved Members: 23
Pending Applications: 4
Access Denied: 45

POP REPORT: Another week down at Golden Hill High! All you popsters out there, watch out. Phones will b blowin up at 5 w tonite's invite courtesy of our very own CelebSammy. Happy Friday! ~ Crys

COMMENTS:

EVAbeautiful *posted at 3:26 p.m. ET May 9:* whoa livi, what happened to your nose today? ever heard of clearasil? we have standards to maintain, remember?

celebSAMmy *posted at 3:16 p.m. ET May 9*: happy sweet 16 baby, can't wait to party like a rockstar!

jake *posted at 3:12 p.m. ET May 9*: happy birthday livi!

BiancaSpeed *posted at 3:02 p.m. ET May 9*: val, u think u can take me???

Tarable *posted at 2:55 p.m. ET May 9*: lookin sexy livi! good luck w ur permit test!

ValieGal *posted at 2:49 p.m. ET May 9*: anyone need a ride tonite, lemme know!

CHAPTER ONE

"What's up with Eva's comment?" I asked, pointing to the Populatti.com homepage. "Is she really trying to start something with me on my birthday?"

Tara stretched out on my bed with the May issue of *Vanity Fair*.

"Nah, I wouldn't look into it," she said.

"Um, it's kind of hard to ignore," I said. "Do you think she's still angry about that suspension thing?"

Tara shook her head. "Livs, that was a year ago and the way I heard it, you tried to help her. My guess is she's still angry she got rejected from Pop so many times before finally getting in."

I sighed, thinking back to Eva's honor council meeting last fall. Maybe I'd been too hard on her. But then, I'd tried to convince the board that extra Physics help would be a more productive punishment than a suspension. It wasn't my fault Golden Hill had a zero-tolerance cheating policy.

I twirled a wisp of hair before turning back to Tara. "I don't know, it feels related. Why else would she start bashing me the minute she gets into to the group?"

"Probably because you're friends with Crystal," said Tara. "And tonight you're the center of attention. My guess is you're guilty by association."

"Maybe," I said. "Crystal is the one who started the vote-against-Eva campaign."

Tara laughed. "If there is one thing that girl doesn't like, it's people copying off her tests."

"Of course," I said, smiling. "How else is she supposed to be first in the class?"

"Not by helping a cheater. So, feel better?" Tara asked.

"Maybe a little. Though the whole thing still bothers me. I mean, my nose. Is it really that bad?" I swung my chair away from my desk and stared at Tara.

"Livs, your zit is tiny. I can't even see it from here," she said, without really looking.

I brought my palms together, then swung them back to my sides, placing them in front of my thighs.

"I hope you're right," I said. "You know, usually I wouldn't care but a Sweet 16 isn't like any other Friday, you know? Tonight I have to be perfect."

Tara groaned. "Livs, how many times do I have to tell you? You're fabulous. Your approval rating has never dipped below 90%. You are the full embodiment of what Populatti is all about."

I frowned, thinking back to the days a few years back when I was anything but fabulous. But, knowing that Tara was not privy to that information – I never spoke of my days before moving to Golden Hill unless absolutely necessary – I just smiled, telling her she was right. Of course I was overreacting.

"So tell me, how did Eva finally get into Pop anyway? I don't remember another vote, and I can't imagine anyone not respecting Crystal's wishes," I said, reaching for my bottle of Hoodoo Voodoo nail polish.

"Matt asked her out," said Tara. "Significant others get automatic admission, remember?"

"Oh. Right," I said. "Crystal couldn't have been happy about that."

"Nah, but rules are rules. Even the founder can't change them without consensus."

I nodded, though the truth was after over a year of Populatti many of its rules still eluded me. Like why there were so many loopholes. All they did was help people like Eva, who should not have been a popster no matter who she was dating. Not that her résumé didn't match that of a popster, because it did – long golden hair, impeccable taste in clothes and makeup, a talented artist whose paintings peppered the Golden Hill halls. But cheating off Crystal should have ruined her chances. It seemed wrong that she should now have access to our secret world.

"You want some?" I asked, waving around the gooey wand of nail polish.

"No thanks. Fuchsia is not a redhead's best friend," said Tara.

I nodded. We both knew that even if redheads could wear fuchsia, which they couldn't on account of pink always looking tacky with red except for maybe on Valentine's Day, Tara would never be the type. It would clash too much with her freckles and textbooks. Hot pink and AP Chem? No thank you.

After fanning my nails dry, I returned to my iPad, willing another comment to bury Eva's at the bottom of the list. Yet the page popped up unchanged. I debated signing into Crystal's administrative account and removing it from the site, but with Crys unaware I'd snagged her password when she forgot to lock her computer during gym class, I decided against it. Signing into Crystal's account was a major violation of the rules. Something, unlike Eva, I respected. And besides, members had been terminated for much less.

Like Rachel Herval, when she tried to dye her hair blond and turned it orange instead. Within two hours, her approval rating had plummeted to 42% and she'd been dropped from Populatti. Not put on probation, not given a warning. No 'it's okay honey, we'll give you a few hours to get to the hair salon.' Nope. Just booted that very day and forced to reapply for membership. Which wasn't easy since the emergency dye job left her looking like a skunk. Two months later, her ends were still orange and she'd missed every social engagement of the summer.

Which was why even with my approval rating hovering around 94%, it was hard not to worry. With Populatti, members could be kicked out at any time. All it took was an approval rating below 50% or a member calling a termination vote where the majority of the group voted against the accused. Meaning that even the most trivial comment could lead to disaster.

"So much for divine intervention," I said as the comment reloaded on the screen.

"Quit worrying," said Tara. "It's your birthday. You're supposed to be having fun. And getting ready for your party, which is going to rock."

"I hope so. You have any idea what Sammy has on the agenda?" I asked.

As the social director of Populatti, Sammy had a knack for planning parties. Her love of neon-colored paper goods ensured there were always decorations to match the theme. Though it was her master social calendar, complete with detailed scheduling info on members and parents, that separated Sammy from the amateurs. Thanks to her meticulous research, there was never trouble finding a parent-free party venue. Pasta night at the Rotary Club meant Tara's house was open. Clambake season on Cape Cod guaranteed that Jake would be hosting. Since Sammy's parents visited relatives in September, she owned Labor Day.

And because cold weather parties were rare – it wasn't as much fun to hang out by the beach or chill in someone's backyard once Golden Hill turned into the arctic tundra – my birthday had become an even bigger celebration. Falling on May 9th, my birthday marked the unofficial start of Populatti's summer season.

Without any hints from Tara on the night's plans, I amped up my grilling and tried to look desperate. Protocol was that Sammy announced the party locations just a few hours in advance. The practice was supposed to keep nonmembers from crashing our parties and creating crowds that would attract attention. But it also made selecting the appropriate attire difficult.

"Please, a hint here? It's my party," I said.

Tara smirked. "All I'll say is that Sammy had five popsters offer their houses, but I have no idea which she chose. Guess you'll have to wait until 5:00 along with the rest of us."

"In that case, I better hit the shower. Mom's planning a big dinner tonight," I said, trying not to look too excited in front of Tara. Even in Golden Hill, it wasn't every day that a popster was handed the keys to a brand-new car and I didn't want to rub it in – even if I did have to pull straight A's and volunteer at the hospital on weekends for an entire year to earn it. It was still a touchy subject, especially since Tara's car had been purchased used from her crazy cat lady of a neighbor who had decided that even gliding down the street in a Prius was emitting too many harmful fumes. And while the Prius did suit Tara better than most cars on the market, every now and then Sammy or Crystal or I would come across a tuft of orange fuzz or a dried-out crumb of cat food that would remind us of her vehicle's checkered past.

"Good luck with dinner and I'll pick you up at 7:00," Tara said. She laughed under her breath as her lips curled into a smirk, the face she made whenever she felt uncomfortable.

I wondered what bothered her more, the fact that I was getting a new car, or that it was an ozone-killing SUV. With my party just hours away, I decided it wasn't the time to ask.

"I'll try to be ready," I said, steering the conversation away from my parents. "That is, if I can find a suitable outfit. Three hours is cutting it close."

Tara laughed, her face softening. "I'm sure you'll manage. And don't worry about Eva. As soon as she and Matt break up, you know Crys will have us vote her out."

"Can't wait. Let's just hope this is the last of her comments."

"It will be. Now go make yourself gorgeous and don't forget to pack a bag. You're ours for the whole night, and as much as I love you, I don't feel like sharing a toothbrush."

"Why not? I floss every day."

"Still doesn't make it sanitary."

I followed Tara down the curved staircase that led to our two-story foyer, a dramatic entryway that was by far my favorite feature of our house. As Tara grabbed her miniature size-6 shoes and headed to her car, I waved goodbye, then headed upstairs.

Once in my room, the shower beckoned. The house was empty so I plugged my iPod into the sound system and turned up the waterproof speakers in the bathroom. Then I picked up a towel and tried to forget about Eva's comment. Unable to do so, I instead replayed the previous year's honor council meeting in my head. How I'd recommended Eva take a zero on the test she'd cheated on and commit to a month's worth of extra help. How obviously that would be more beneficial if she was struggling than to just issue a suspension. But then I remembered the other student representatives acting like I'd just committed treason. A zero and extra help? For cheating? Apparently it didn't send the right message.

Unfortunately for Eva, the faculty reps had

agreed, sentencing her to a full week of in-school suspension. But I had tried. And that was a year ago. Could Eva still be looking for some sort of payback? Or was she angry about something else? The randomness of the comment bothered me. But then, even compliments about my appearance often got to me. It was one of the after-effects of my hellish middle school years in Boston, before we moved to Golden Hill. Back then, everyone called me Drumstick because of my skinny calves, meaty thighs and propensity to raise my hand with a little too much excitement when I knew the answer to a question. Which happened to be all the time. Sometimes I still had nightmares I was back there riding the bus home from school, slumping low in my seat and trying to pretend I didn't hear the muffled clucking and laughter coming from the rows behind me.

Moving to Golden Hill had saved me from a high school existence as Drumstick. Who knew what would have happened if my dad hadn't left Boston Children's Hospital for a great job at Yale-New Haven? Certainly my legs hadn't changed much, even if they were a little thinner. Only the town had, which was a good thing because here in Golden Hill, a tiny dot of a town located right outside of New Haven, Connecticut, I wasn't Drumstick. I was Livi Stanley, known more for my long blonde hair and bubbly personality – and seat on the honor council, of course – than my legs. Though really it was my friendship with Crystal that had saved me. Because Crystal was the founder and creator of Populatti, the social network that ruled Golden Hill's social life.

Meaning that really there was little to worry about with regard to my membership status. While Crystal claimed she'd never fudge numbers to save a member, she could if she wanted to, and no one would ever know. Crystal was the only one who knew how Populatti's mysterious approval ratings worked – she once said it was some combination of the number of "high fives" members received for their most recent posts, plus their profile's total daily pageviews – and she alone had the power to change the system at any time. Seeing as none of us four founding members had ever seen ratings below 90%, I often wondered if she'd changed the formula in the past. But then, since we had all been pretty well-liked since Crystal launched the site last year, maybe there had never been a need.

Hopefully there wouldn't be a need now. With Eva being a new member who was already on shaky ground with Crystal, I knew the odds of her comment gaining momentum were small to miniscule. Further diminishing the odds was the fact that I'd secured my place on next year's honor council during the election last week. Meaning most popsters wouldn't want to anger me and risk a harsher punishment if accused of a rule infraction – not that I'd ever think of abusing my power, especially since I had my sights set on quashing real crime one day as a prosecutor.

And none of that took into account the unimportance of Eva's comment in the first place. Zits were fleeting. A part of everyday life. Nothing even close to "Drumstick." Feeling a little steadier, I took a deep breath and reached for the body wash. One comment was not enough to ruin a party.

After steaming my skin to look like one of Tara's dehydrated apricots, I slid out of the shower and threw on my pink fluffy robe. It was almost 4:30, giving me just 30 minutes before Fiesta Stanley began downstairs. This left no time to view Sammy's 5:00 invitation and venue reveal before getting dressed. It was one of the pitfalls of having doctors as parents. Given the chaos of their schedules, every minute of family time was sacred. So much so that even my phone was not allowed in the dining room, even though their work phones were exempt. While I understood that a crisis with a patient could be more important than counseling Sammy through a wardrobe meltdown, wasn't calming a spastic friend good for her mental health? Despite repeated arguments, my parents were not convinced.

So without knowing the party's location or theme, I entered my walk-in closet (another perk of leaving Boston – closet space in the suburbs was much more luxurious) and began thumbing through my wardrobe. There was the pink and black dress I'd bought the week before, my favorite jeans-and-tank combo, and the cream-colored tunic I'd been dying to wear with a pair of leggings and high sandals. After trying on what became a growing heap in the back of my closet – thirty minutes didn't leave time for folding – I settled on a sleeveless pink tunic, paired with shiny silver leggings that looked like leather pants but felt like yoga pants, and had just a wide enough seam running down the side to make my thighs look almost thin.

The outfit screamed rock and roll more than my usual prepster look, but rock and roll seemed more appropriate than understated chic, given the occasion. Tonight I was going all out. So I grabbed a bag of Velcro rollers and rolled them into my damp hair. Concealer and blush came next, followed by a thick layer of black eyeliner and glitter mascara to frame my eyes. As the mascara dried, I flipped on every light in the room and stared in the mirror. My pimple was just a blur, like a light mark on an airbrushed photo. And my thighs? They were as well hidden as my days as a middle school misfit. Breathing deep, I hit the dimmer switch and took one final look. This time my zit disappeared. And my legs looked inches longer. Perfect. All I needed now was a party locale with decent lighting.

With ten minutes until dinner, I sprayed some volumizer over the rollers and began blow drying my hair. At 4:57, with my hair a mess of tight curls that would be ready for brushing after dinner, I grabbed a black hoodie, zipped it up to my chin to hide my shirt, then booked it to the dining room.

Downstairs, candles and pink plates adorned the table along with a huge arrangement of calla lilies and orchids. A basket of bread stood at each end along with dollops of heart-shaped butter. I relaxed into my chair and made a mental note to thank Lona, our cook and housekeeper, for the gorgeous display.

Lona was the well-oiled machine that kept our family running. With a knack for design and a degree from a real culinary institute, Lona was in high demand. Most nights she wasn't with us, she was off catering parties and special events. A side job Mom thought should become her main one, but that I hoped never would. Because over the past five years, no one had been there for me more than Lona. Lona was the one who gave me hints on what to wear on my first day of high school. Who taught me the ins and outs of living in a small, tight-knit beachfront community. Who always remembered that calla lilies were my favorite flower and that shaped butter tasted better than cubed. Things Mom and Dad just never seemed to care about. Their crazy schedules made sure of it.

As I waited at the table for my parents, my phone buzzed in my purse. It was 5:00. Sammy's invite was here. With no one around to enforce the no-phone rule, I shuffled away from the table and grabbed my bag off the banister. If Mom and Dad can be late, then I can check my phone, I thought, already forming the excuse in my head as the message loaded.

Club Dash, b thereee!!!! it said.

"Yes!" I said, skipping across the foyer.

The party was at Brandon Dash's house. It didn't get better than this. Not only did Brandon have stunning blue eyes and these full pink lips that I'd been dying to kiss for years, but he lived in the most hooked up house in Golden Hill. Three floors of pure heaven with a huge kitchen and a game room that included a dance floor. It was the kind of house that I thought only existed in the movies until we'd left Boston. Not that the Boston suburbs weren't filled with big houses. They were. But there, we'd lived crammed into a three-bedroom townhouse. In downtown Boston, big houses weren't part of my everyday life. Not like now. In Golden Hill, many of the houses towered over the trees. Most didn't qualify as mansions – from what I'd heard most of those existed to our south in towns like New Canaan and Darien – but they were impressive nonetheless. Mom called them charming, having fallen for the classic New England architecture on first glance. And I had to admit, the sleepy roads were a nice change of pace from the honking horns of our previous life. Our street looked like a New England postcard, lined with ancient oak trees, whose branches leaned in just enough to create a summer canopy that shaded our extra wide, meandering street. Stone walls replaced the sidewalks we'd grown up with. Fences covered in climbing roses and gardens filled with dahlias, cosmos, and snapdragons sweetened the air, so different from the exhaust fumes that had perfumed the back patio we had tried to call a backyard. Golden Hill looked like it was built for winter nights by the fire and summer days spent on the beach. Here, kids played outside. They walked to the beach, collecting scallop shells and quahogs and jingle shells along the way. It was a place that honored the old, while embracing the new.

Our house was a perfect example of this. Built only twenty years back, it had large closets and level floors and all the modern conveniences our townhouse had lacked. Yet from the outside, its wooden siding and stone foundation blended with the older colonials lining the street.

And that is what made B-Dash's house so unique. Because B-Dash's didn't blend. His house was all flash.

My face flushed as I sat back down at the table. The last time I'd ventured to Club Dash, I had started a karaoke contest that had ended with Sammy singing the entire Madonna *Like a Prayer* album from start to finish. During her performance, Crys had gone so crazy dancing that she'd snapped both her stilettos. Then when she refused to walk across the yard barefoot, Sammy had to swoop in and carry her over her shoulder just to get her into the car. And that was back when Brandon was dating Chloe. Something told me now that he was single, things would be much more interesting.

Confident that my outfit was the perfect choice for a night at Club Dash, I fought the urge to call Tara and ask what she was wearing. My restraint paid off as the front door of the house opened and Mom, along with my two little brothers, piled inside.

"Livi, honey, we're back," Mom said.

The voices of Chris and Charlie, the terrible twins, echoed through the halls.

"Happy birthday, Livi," they said in unison before dropping their bat bags in a heap next to the table. Chris was wearing his dusty brown baseball glove as a hat and Charlie's face was smeared with white powder. I brought my hand up to his chin and wiped off a layer of sugar.

"You guys have a good practice?" I asked, eying Mom in the doorway. She was talking away on her phone, heading back towards the foyer. Her voice sounded strained, concerned.

Not in the mood for more doctor talk, I turned back to the twins.

"Livi, check out Charlie's finger," Chris said in his girly voice. "He cut it opening the Fun Dip. It's disgusting!"

Charlie waved his finger in the air. His expression was somewhere between a smile and a grimace. As the blood trickled out of a small jagged opening on his knuckle, his bottom lip began to quiver.

"Chris, go grab the first aid kit," I said, pulling out the chair next to me. "Charlie, sit down and tell me about your practice. Don't look at your finger. It'll help, I promise."

As Charlie told me about his day, Chris ran back to the kitchen, returning a second later with a milk crate stuffed full of Band-Aids, Ace bandages, gauze pads, IVs, epinephrine shots and a million other things most normal households never thought to stock. With Dad being the king of the Children's ER, it was no surprise that we had a mobile medical unit stashed in our pantry next to the Carr's water crackers and multi-colored Gold-fish.

After retrieving Band-Aids, Neosporin and an antiseptic cloth, I cleaned Charlie's finger and wrapped it up tightly. "Okay, cut's gone, you can uncover your eyes."

"Thanks Livi," said Charlie as Mom reentered the room.

"Boys, I thought I told you to wash up before dinner," she said, not even noticing the remnants of our emergency procedure. "Bring those bags to your room and wash your hands. You never know what's lurking in those batting cages."

"Fine, we're going." They shuffled out, bat bags and first aid kit in hand.

"Hey baby, happy Sweet 16," Mom said as the room cleared. She was coming off a marathon shift at the hospital and I hadn't seen her in two days.

Her hair stood high on her head in a greasy knot. Tendrils of honey blonde clung to the side of her face, glued in place from two days' worth of sweat and worry.

"You have a nice day?" she asked.

I nodded.

"Good. Now about dinner." Mom looked away as the words slipped out of her mouth.

For a moment her drooping eyelids and iodine-stained hands made me want to tuck her into bed for some much needed rest, but the impulse passed quickly.

"Your dad's in another emergency surgery and I just got off the phone with Mrs. Olson. She's gone into labor early and I have to get back to the hospital as soon as I can."

"Okay," I said, following her eyes to the butter hearts.

"Lona did a marvelous job, didn't she?"

"I guess."

"You still going out tonight with the girls?"

"Yeah, Tara's picking me up at 7:00. We're having a slumber party at Sammy's."

"That's right. Why don't we celebrate tomorrow then? We can have a birthday lunch."

I sighed. Here I'd applied my makeup two hours early for nothing. "Sure. Maybe after I get my driver's permit and we pick up the car," I said, forcing a smile.

When we moved from Boston, part of the deal

was supposed to be that Mom would work a little less so there would be time for things like birthday dinners. But the new practice she'd joined was even more overcrowded than her last one. Meaning that hijacked events were nothing new. And that I was lucky to have the imminent arrival of my new car to cancel out the disappointment.

"Shoot, the car! I was supposed to call about that last week." Mom brought her hands to her temples and began kneading her forehead. "I forgot to tell them we wanted to pick it up on Saturday. I don't know if it'll be ready."

My mouth dropped. "Are you serious?"

"I'm sorry, honey, I'll call first thing in the morning and check. I'm sure if it's not ready tomorrow, we can get it on Monday."

I breathed in deep and prepared to scream, before nodding in agreement. It was after five o'clock on a Friday. The dealership was closed. My dreams of pulling up to driver's ed on Sunday in my silver Ford Escape were fading, and no amount of whining would make them reappear.

"So we still might be able to get it tomorrow, right?" I asked, trying to save my good mood.

Mom smiled. "I'm sorry honey, I really don't know. But if it doesn't work out, maybe we could go shopping or something."

"I don't know," I said, folding my arms over my lap.

Mom was trying and I knew I should accept her

invite, especially since she was offering one of her rare days off to just me and not Dad or the twins. Yet right then, as much as I wanted to say 'yes,' I found myself shaking my head. Even though I knew it was childish, sometimes I just wanted her to see that I was upset. And that she couldn't make it better with a new pair of shoes.

My phone rang in the foyer as Mom and I sat at the table in silence. Without thinking, I jumped up to retrieve it.

"Livi, get back here. You know the rules," Mom said.

"But we're not eating!"

"Yes, but we're talking."

"Of course." I sat back down as Chris and Charlie pounded down the steps. Their faces were clean, but a layer of dirt was still visible under their nails, yet I was too tired to insist they scrub them clean.

As the twins sat down, Mom turned to me, determined to finish our conversation. But before she could speak, Lona walked in with a tray of chicken parmesan. The tantalizing scents of bubbling mozzarella cheese and tomato sauce caused Mom to reconsider. Instead of making more promises we knew she might not keep, she closed her mouth and served the boys an ample portion of chicken and sauce.

Once the boys were settled, Mom said goodbye and headed back out. I was a few steps behind her.

As her car door slammed shut, I grabbed my phone and listened to my voicemail. It was Sammy, chattering on about logistics. I sighed. Dinner was off, my car was MIA, and I had a zit the size of Minnesota invading my nose. But Brandon Dash's was on. And Brandon's house always had good lighting.

populatti.com

lululivi : 92%

Approved Members: 23
Pending Applications: 4
Access Denied: 45

POP REPORT: Another week down at Golden Hill High! All you popsters out there, watch out. Phones will b blowin up at 5 w tonite's invite courtesy of our very own CelebSammy. Happy Friday and stay beautiful! ~ Crys

COMMENTS:

BrandontheGREAT *posted at 7:32 p.m. ET May 9*: happy bday livi, can't wait to c u!

celebSAMmy *posted at 6:38 p.m. ET May 9:* you rock sista. See you tonitee

ValieGal *posted at 6:14 p.m. ET May 9*: happy birthday livi! tonight is gonna b great!

celebSAMmy *posted at 6:01 p.m. ET May 9:* you better watch it eva. Zits go away, comments are remembered...

EVAbeautiful *posted at 4:26 p.m. ET May 9*: whoa livi, what happened to your nose today? ever heard of clearasil? we have standards to maintain, remember?

CHAPTER TWO

"Livi, let's go!" Tara yelled from downstairs. She'd barreled through the front door ten minutes ago and was growing impatient, even though the wait was nothing new.

"Come up for a sec. You have to see this," I said.

"Oh, fine. I'm coming." Her feet pounded on each step with a thump. She must be wearing her skinny jeans, I thought, knowing that the tighter her jeans, the less responsive her kneecaps.

I stared at my iPad as Tara entered, unable to move my eyes from the latest Populatti comments. So far no one was talking about Eva's comment, thank God. But the bigger development was B-

Dash. He'd wished me a happy birthday. And said he wanted to see me. On my birthday. Despite Eva's talk about my pimple. This had to mean something.

"What are you doing?" Tara asked.

"Brandon. He commented. He wants to see me."

"I know. I saw it before I left."

"And you didn't call me?"

"I didn't want to be late and I couldn't find my Bluetooth."

"That is so lame. Like the cops are gonna pull you over for a ten-second conversation."

"Talking to you about Brandon is never ten seconds."

"Fair enough. But since you've seen it, what do you think?"

"That he's being nice. You two are friends, you know."

"But it could mean more," I said, my voice climbing higher.

"I guess."

"He didn't comment when it was Sammy's birthday, and they're just friends too. See, I checked." I opened the adjacent Web tab where I'd saved the archived comments page. "Jake wrote, and even Matt, but no Brandon."

Tara groaned. "Stop obsessing. Let's head to the party and maybe you can have a real conversation with him instead of cyber stalking all night."

"You are so not fun," I said, jumping out of my chair.

"God Livi, what are you wearing?" Tara shrieked as I shed my oversized Golden Hill High t-shirt and reached for my pink tunic.

"What? I didn't want to wrinkle my outfit when I sat down."

She spun around as I threw my shirt on over my head. That was Tara all right. No joint toothbrushes and no nudity. Even though my zebra striped bra covered more than my string bikini.

"You decent?" she asked a few seconds later.

"Yes, Tarable, all is covered."

"Thank God."

Tara stretched her back as we headed for the door. Her jeans were glued onto her long, thin legs, making her look like one of those double popsicles with the two sticks peeking out of the bottom.

"You sure this top's not too tight?" Tara asked as we reached her Prius.

"Of course not. You look hot." I tried to remember what Tara had been wearing before she'd thrown on her coat. When nothing came to mind, I decided to play along. With Tara it was always the same. Tight jeans and a loose tank top that she always thought was too clingy. Sometimes I wished she'd just get over the fact that she had an awesome body and quit trying so hard to hide it. It wasn't like anyone was going to hold it against her. Even if I was a teensy bit envious of her slender thighs and stellar curves.

After readjusting the mirrors on her car and

flicking on the fog lights, Tara put the car into gear.

"Are we picking up Sammy and Crys?" I asked, reaching for the radio.

"Nope. Sam's mom dropped them off earlier."

"Does Sammy have any idea who's coming?"

Tara shrugged. "I assume most of the popsters will be there. Maybe Christian too. Crys says he's the most promising of all the new recruits."

I swayed back and forth to the music. "He's the new guy from Greenwich, right?"

"Uh-huh."

"Is he cute?"

"You sit next to him in English class."

"Oops, I didn't realize that was him. His body is smoking."

"He plays lacrosse."

"Looks like we have to start stalking the lacrosse field."

"Aren't you into Brandon?"

"Doesn't hurt to have a backup plan."

"Maybe not, but leave Christian out of it. He's mine."

I choked on a drop of melon lip gloss as Tara turned onto Brandon's road. Tara was so quiet, so organic. She always dated artists and musicians and more dignified men. This was the first I'd heard of her pursuing an athlete.

Tara seemed to read my mind. "Christian's into photography. You'll have to check out his stuff. Pretty amazing."

My lips curled at the admission. Tara and her artists. "You better put in a good word with Crys then to make sure he gets approved."

"I will, and you talk him up too. Don't let on that I like him or anything, just that he's a cool guy. Maybe you can get Brandon's vote. It could be a good excuse to talk to him."

My hands tingled. "Now that's a plan. Though you could just pull an Eva and ask him out. Seems that buys you automatic admission these days."

"Stop it. No more Eva talk. She made her comment and now it's over, okay?"

"You sound like my mother."

"Then you get the message. You look hot, your zit is nonexistent, and tonight is going to be great. Which reminds me, we have to keep an eye on Crys. You know her and Jake. We don't want any more dance-offs."

"Agreed," I said as Tara parked the car.

We walked toward Brandon Dash's front steps and opened the door without ringing the bell. While I wished we could announce our arrival, it was protocol to park down the block and enter the house quickly when attending a popster event. Sammy would have you believe it was so nonmembers couldn't find the party, but we all knew the unspoken truth. Golden Hill was a small town without much real crime, leaving a whole police force full of muffin-top cops with nothing to do but bust every teen party they could find. So far we'd been lucky.

Sammy, Crystal, Tara, and I hadn't been involved in a single raid. Though if it hadn't been for Crystal's mom taking us to Boston last spring to visit colleges – Crystal is a computer genius from a family of mad scientists who insist she go to MIT – we also would have matching citations from Golden Hill's finest.

Inside the Dash residence, the first floor was quiet. The only hint of a party was a note directing guests downstairs. Tara and I bypassed the staircase and walked into the living room, one of the "off-limits" areas where we knew no one would go snooping. We left our purses and coats behind the grand piano and snuck out of the room. Before heading downstairs, Tara and I picked up a marker and each placed an X over our hands. It was lame, but again, popster protocol. While drinking wasn't prevalent at Pop parties, it did happen. So, to ensure no one drove drunk, only those that marked their hands with X's were allowed to leave. And if someone with an X picked up a drink, he or she lost the privilege of driving home. Not that Crystal, Tara, or I ever touched the stuff. As the founding members of Populatti, we had too much on the line to be careless. Drinking would mean relinquishing control and potentially damaging our image. So for us, Shirley Temples were about as wild as we got. But then, Sammy was a founding member too and every now and then she definitely let loose. And okay, Crys and Tara had a couple of times as well.

Yet still I always kept my word. As an elected member of the sophomore honor council, I'd signed a pledge and planned to stick to it. Though following through was actually pretty easy given that my doctor parents had done a good job exposing me to the types of accidents and conditions alcohol could cause. After a lifetime of listening to their lectures, drinking had lost a lot of its luster. Not to mention that by even attending parties with alcohol, I knew I was already letting them down. Something I hated doing, but saw no way around unless I was willing to give up my friends and Populatti. Which was too scary to think about seeing as Sammy and Tara and Crystal were the first real friends I'd had since my days as Drumstick. Hence the compromise. And even though there were times I felt left out of my friends' illicit exploits, dripping with danger and sophistication, I was okay knowing my hands would always be marked.

After branding ourselves with marker, Tara grabbed my arm and led me to the back staircase. The thumping bass tickled my eardrums as we descended lower. At the foot of the stairs, a cool breeze greeted us. I rubbed my hands against my naked arms and looked around for Brandon. But the room was totally deserted, despite evidence of some aggressive party prep. Like the pink streamers hanging from the chandeliers, and disco ball that had been hung in the center of the room. And the red cups scattered across the bar top, along with a bottle of Ocean Spray Cranberry Cocktail and pile of tiny pink umbrellas. Even the stainless steel fridge was raring to go, its shelves now a bottomless pit of sodas. And that wasn't all. The dance floor, a small patch of hardwood usually hidden by some fancy wool rug, glistened from a fresh coat of polish. Two leather couches lined the edges of the room, finishing the party-perfect scene. Yet in front of us a pair of outside doors swung open, explaining the breeze. And potentially, the lack of guests.

"Where is everyone?" I asked, walking toward the doors. "I thought Sammy said 7:30."

"Oh, I got a text on the ride over. They ran out to get some..."

Before Tara could finish, Sammy and Crystal ran through the doors each holding a side of a gigantic pink cake. It was shaped like a purse, with sugar buckles and candy zippers. Painted in the center was a block of purple lettering that said "Happy Sweet 16 Livi!"

"OhmiGod this is perfect," I screamed as Crystal and Sammy placed the cake on top of the bar. "I can't believe you did this. It's freaking awesome!"

"Glad you like it, girl. It was all Tara's idea," said Sammy.

"You did this? Even with your hatred of pink?"

"I told you we had to be on time tonight," Tara said.

"And to think I thought it was just for party prep!"

Tara laughed. "We thought it'd be fun to have some time to ourselves before everyone arrived."

"I couldn't agree more," I said, hugging Tara.

Crystal started cutting the cake and handed me the first slice. It was one of my favorites, pumpkin spice cake with cream cheese frosting. I had no idea where anyone would be getting pumpkin in May, but decided not to ask. Knowing Crystal and Sammy, they'd probably taken Tara's idea and gone to some cake designer in New Haven who imports pumpkins from Brazil or Africa, or wherever it is that fancy cake stores procure out-of-season produce.

After inhaling a slab of cake and two candy zippers, I turned to see Brandon and Jake stroll in from outside, cases of soda in hand. I brought my hands behind my back and headed to the stereo, hoping to look busy as they finished stocking the fridge.

I counted to ten as I began to check out Brandon's playlist, refusing to look up or say hi to Brandon first. Seeing him walk in may have been the highlight of my night, but I didn't want him to know it. So instead I began scrolling through his music, looking for something party appropriate. Keeping with the tradition of all Golden Hill baseball players, Brandon preferred classic rock over real party music. He claimed classic rock could unite people of all types and ages in a way that Jay Z just couldn't. While I did see the logic of his reasoning when applied to public events, for our parties it just seemed flawed.

"Crys, did you bring your music?" I asked as I scanned Brandon's list of artists. Bob Dylan, The Eagles, and Bruce Springsteen. What was he doing, trying to put us to sleep? I pulled Brandon's iPod out of its dock and placed it in a cabinet next to a bunch of movies.

"Here you go, everything's covered. Put on the playlist named 'Livs.'" Crystal handed over her million gigabyte iPod and I connected it to the player. A minute later, the room filled with the beat of my favorite song.

"Thank God. Who let Brandon near the music anyway?" I asked.

"Ladies, it is my house," he said from behind me.

I jumped, biting my lip in the process. Ignoring his entrance had worked.

"Sorry Brandon, I just thought our guests might like something a little more current." I tried to smile like it was no big deal, even though everyone in the room knew we'd had this argument before.

"Good thing no one's here then. Sammy told everyone but you to get here at 8:00, giving us exactly five minutes until the party begins." He yanked out Crystal's iPod, fished out his own, and turned up some awful ballad sung by an old man with a serious congestion problem.

I pretended to slap Brandon's back and retreated to the bar to stare from afar. As I took in Brandon's green polo and just tight enough jeans, Sammy handed me a cranberry with Sprite complete with pink umbrella.

"Ah, finally, just what I need," I said, starting to relax. But the feeling was short-lived.

"Girls, I need you *now*," said Crys, running toward the bathroom.

I turned to Sammy, who shrugged. "Guess we better go."

Together, Sammy, Tara, and I filed in to join Crys.

"Look at my shirt, already soaked," she said, pointing at what appeared to be spilled Coke.

I looked down at her tank top and wondered why she was so worked up. Sure, I'd be angry if it was my shirt, but Crystal's top had an intricate design, making it almost impossible to see the stain.

"Can you believe Jake? What a klutz, spilling on me before the party even starts," Crystal said as she blotted the spot with a hand towel. "Though it was the perfect way to get the four of us alone before the party."

Sammy and Tara then held hands and squealed as Crystal rummaged through a bag she'd stashed under the sink, pulling out a small bundle.

"What is going on?" I asked, catching a flash of glitz.

"We're crowning our princess!" Sammy yelled.

"Tonight it's all about you, girl," said Tara.

Crystal ripped off a layer of tissue paper, un-veiling a bright silver and pink rhinestone tiara with a number 16 on top. I pretended to cringe, hoping it wasn't too obvious that my shirt was the perfect shade of pink to match the rhinestones.

"You knew this was coming. It's tradition," said Crystal. She jumped up onto the sink and placed it on my head.

"I thought maybe you forgot."

"Like that would happen," Tara said. The nightmare of her own Sweet 16 crowning must have still haunted her. The pink. The glitz. The attention.

I adjusted the tiara in the mirror and smoothed out my hair so that a few strands still fell in front, framing my face. "How does it look?" I asked.

"Fantastic," said Sammy. "Let's just hope it gives you better luck than Crystal."

"It couldn't get much worse," I said, remembering her Sweet 16 beach bash. Crys had insisted on a beach party, then let Jake bury her in a cesspool of sand and muck, ruining her white eyelet halter dress.

"Hey! That party was awesome," said Crystal, running her hands through her silky black hair. "It's not my fault I always get into trouble."

"True. Though if you want some real trouble, I suggest you pop one of these," said Sammy, waving around a beer while pulling down the hem of her zebra print mini skirt.

"No thank you. Now let's go mingle," said Crystal, opening the door.

In the few minutes since we'd entered the bathroom, Club Dash had come alive with party guests and music. Someone also had swapped out the light bulbs on the chandelier with colored bulbs, giving the room a hazy cave-like feeling that reminded me of being underwater. A group of well-sculpted guys was congregating around the drinks, and a couple girls I didn't recognize were dancing.

"Who are they?" I asked Sammy, pointing to the newcomers.

"New members," she said. "I know I voted for the girl on the right, but I don't remember the other."

I looked at the girls again, wishing it wasn't so dark. "Huh, I guess I must've voted too, but the one on the left, she really doesn't look familiar at all."

"That's Bianca. You know, the softball star," said Crystal, catching the end of our conversation.

"I forgot we voted her in," I said, as her application came to mind. Plain face, no makeup, little style. She wasn't a typical Populatti member, but they said she pitched like 100 mph and had a real chance of getting the team to States. And apparently a lot of her friends were popsters, which had helped her application.

"Time for a refill?" asked Crystal, interrupting my thoughts.

"Sure," I said eying my empty glass. But before

I could finish, a hand swooped down onto my head and snatched my tiara.

"Hey! Stop it, that's mine," I said, spinning around.

Brandon held his hand over his head and grinned. "You want it back?"

"Obviously."

"Then how 'bout a dance?"

"With you?"

"I don't see anyone else."

"I'll think about it," I said, my palms tingling.

Ever since Brandon had broken up with Chloe, I'd been dying to get his attention. Now that I had it, I didn't want to appear desperate.

"Suit yourself," he said. "Though something tells me Sammy will be pretty pissed off if she doesn't see this on your head."

The smell of cherries filled my nostrils as he bent in closer. I took a step back and licked my lips. "How about you give me some of what you're drinking and I'll let you take me to the dance floor?"

He handed over his cup and I took a sip. Cherry Coke. My favorite.

"I got it just for you," he said, grabbing my hand.

For the next hour, nothing else mattered but Brandon Dash's hands. The growing slick of drinks covering the dance floor, the whirring music and wails of botched lyrics, I was oblivious to it all as Brandon brought his palms up to my cheeks and then down to the small of my back. His muscled arms held me close enough that I could see the hairs on his ear lobes and smell the Lacoste cologne Chloe had gotten him last Christmas. As the music pulsed on, I said a silent thank you to Crystal for putting together the world's perfect playlist. Each song was hotter than the next.

Somewhere between song fifteen and twenty, the tips of Brandon's fine brown hair began to curl from the beads of sweat lining his forehead. I ran my hand through his hair and smiled. Brandon brought me in closer and grabbed the back of my neck. He looked into my eyes and smirked before leaning in. I raised myself up onto my toes, ready to meet his lips. But as I readjusted my weight, I felt myself slip. I tried to steady myself by grabbing Brandon's shoulders, but it was too late.

Instead of kissing Brandon, I was lying face down on the dance floor.

"Oww!" I tried to get up before anyone could see me sprawled out on the floor like some newbie at yoga class, or worse yet, like a chicken. But when I jumped up, I slipped and fell backwards, this time into a mound of something wet.

"Whoa, are you all right?" asked Brandon. He peered down at me in a daze, as if he was scared that if he moved me, I might break.

I stood up and dusted myself off. Not sure what I'd fallen into, I was hopeful the long tunic would hide it. Once back on my feet, I draped my hands around Brandon's neck and tried to finish what we'd started. The crowd was still swaying around us. The lights were still shining purple and blue. My tiara was still in place. No one had seen me fall, and all was right with the world. That is, until Brandon brought his hands around my waist. I wasn't sure who screamed first, if it was Brandon or Tara, but either way, it seemed that just as I worked up the courage to lean back in toward Brandon's shining lips, he was pushing me back, farther away.

"Livi, what happened? Oh my God, we have got to get you out of those pants, like now," Tara screamed. She grabbed my wrist – which was floundering, searching for Brandon's now missing hand – and pulled me into the bathroom.

"Thank God no one else saw this. It looks like you're wearing half your cake back there," Tara said as a cackling voice cut her off.

"Happy Sweet 16, Livi," said Eva. "I've heard of smashing your face into a cake, but never your..."

Tara slammed the door before Eva could finish.

"What is that girl's problem," I said, trembling.

"Don't worry, she's just jealous," said Tara.

"I don't know. She's acting like she's mad about something," I said as I stripped out of my cake-covered leggings. "If she keeps this up, we are going to be forced to retaliate."

"That's probably what she wants. To give her a way to start a fight with Crystal," Tara said, pulling a chunk of purple fondant out of my hair.

I turned to the mirror and readjusted my tiara. "You think?"

"Definitely. And don't worry, rumor is Matt's already thinking about dumping her. But I guess her parents are going out of town soon so he figures he'll take one for the team. Could be a good place for a party."

"Like we'd ever set foot in her house."

"It could be a good way for revenge."

"Yeah maybe," I said, both of us knowing I'd never do anything that could land me in real trouble.

Tara laughed. "Now, get to the good stuff. What is going on with you and Dash? That was intense out there."

"Aw honey, I'm just getting started," I said, breaking into a dance.

Tara's face flushed red. "Cut it out, you're as bad as Crystal."

I kissed her cheek then spun back to the mirror. My tunic, which had miraculously survived unscathed, was long enough to function without the pants. But that meant exposing my unshaved thighs and sandpaper-dry knees.

"This is awful," I said, shaking my head.

"Livs, you look awesome. Totally gorgeous. No one out there's going to even notice. It's so dark there's like zero visibility."

"But Brandon. What will he think?"

Tara chewed her lip. "That you had to improvise. And that you look practically the same."

"Promise?"

"Of course."

Buoyed by Tara's confidence, I decided to give it a try. And ten minutes later, I was back on the dance floor, ready to resume my place with B-Dash. Only he was off in a corner now, a swarm of girls closing in. The group included the two softball players from earlier, along with Eva. I contemplated finding Sammy and reconnecting with Brandon later, but decided against it. There was no way I was going to let B-Dash out of my sight again.

"Hey there," I said, pushing my way into the group next to Brandon.

"Livi, where'd your pants go?" asked Eva. "Are you a stripper now too?"

I held my breath as my eyes darted around for a rock I could crawl under, before remembering what Tara said about Matt. Eva's time in Populatti was already limited.

"Sorry, you must have the wrong girl," I said. "I'm the one who makes people follow the rules, not break them."

One of the softball girls smiled. "Oh yeah, you're on the council! Is it true you're going to be voting about off-campus lunch privileges?"

I nodded, trying to regain my composure. "Think so, but probably not 'til the fall."

Eva rolled her eyes, then disappeared into the

crowd.

Relieved by her retreat, I draped my arm around Brandon.

"Miss me?" I asked.

"Of course," he said. "Hey, did you know that Bianca here can throw a softball like 100 mph?"

"Yeah, I heard," I said.

"Isn't that awesome? She challenged me to a throwing contest."

"Cool. But don't girls throw underhand?" I asked, turning to Bianca. It was the first time I'd seen her close up, and even in the dim blue lighting, it was apparent she wasn't well-versed in the makeup department.

"Yeah, that's how we pitch, but I can throw overhand too. I've been clocked at over 65."

I looked back and forced a smile, wishing I'd paid a little more attention to the twins' baseball games so I knew exactly what she was talking about. But sports had never been my thing. After years of running up and down soccer fields and basketball courts and never touching a ball, I'd finally accepted my fate. My coordination was nonexistent. I was not an athlete. Words were my thing. Writing especially. Something told me Bianca would not be impressed.

And she wasn't, especially when just seconds later a group of guys ran across the dance floor, knocking me off balance once again, my stiletto falling right into the meat of her sneaker.

"Ahh, watch out," I said, catching myself on her shoulder.

Bianca jerked her knee up towards the ceiling. "Oww!"

"OhmiGod. Sorry, are you okay?"

"Yeah, fine," she said, rubbing her foot. She brought her gaze to Brandon, and I could tell she was looking for some attention, some glimmer of recognition that would confirm that she should stay and talk, but Brandon just patted her shoulder and told her to walk it off, his smile never wavering.

Bianca bowed her head. "Well, I guess I should find some ice. And we should probably get going. See you later, Brandon," she said without acknowledging my presence.

She probably thought I'd fallen into her on purpose, I thought with a sigh, hoping she wasn't off to start more rumors. But then, how could anyone fault me for being clumsy? For a moment I debated running off to help Bianca find some ice, but then my eyes met Brandon's. And at that moment, I couldn't help but feel relieved to see Bianca walk away.

"Guess she's postponing our throwing contest," he said.

"Good," I said, stepping closer. "Because you're busy now anyway."

"Really?"

"Uh-huh."

"And why is that?"

"Because we're not done dancing." I started leading Brandon back to the dance floor.

He stopped me mid-step. "I hate crowds."

Then B-Dash slipped his hand onto my back and led me toward the basement wall, putting one arm above my head for support. As I fiddled with my empty hands, he leaned in and kissed me. Hard. His lips tasted sweet and syrupy from the Coke. His cheeks felt rough like a pumice stone against my hot cheeks. After a minute, he pulled away and put both arms around me, holding me closer.

"So am I forgiven for changing your music?" I asked, breathless.

"This is a lot more fun than fighting."

I brought my hand to his cheek and laughed. We met halfway this time, both of us leaning in, and in an instant his lips were tickling mine, his eyelashes so close I could see the way they curled up towards his brow. And for a moment I wasn't thinking about Eva or Bianca or my MIA parents or any of the other million texts and messages that seemed to crowd my life. All that mattered was B-Dash. That he had chosen me. On my Sweet Sixteen.

We stayed in that corner, my thoughts lost in a hazy, dreamy trance, until my cheeks felt raw. By the time I looked up, the crowd had thinned. Eva was gone, and so was Bianca. Crystal was sleeping on one of the leather couches, with Jake sitting by her feet. Tara and Sammy were missing.

Brandon turned to me and narrowed his eyes. "You want to crash here tonight?"

I took a step back, surprised.

"I mean, I'm here all alone with my parents away until Sunday. I would ask Jake but he has something lame to do tomorrow with his parents."

My mouth felt dry and itchy, despite the cranberry juice I'd been chugging all night. I'd wanted Brandon for some time, but as a boyfriend. Not catch and release. Staying over was way too serious for night one. Or night twenty for that matter. Suddenly, I wondered if I'd sent the wrong message back on the dance floor.

"I should check with the girls first. Looks like we missed quite a party," I said, changing the subject.

The floor was covered with a layer of crushed and shredded red cups and cake bits, creating a slipping hazard even more dangerous than black ice. Someone had spilled the cranberry cocktail, and it had congealed down the side of the mahogany bar. Tiny fruit flies were swarming around the sink and congregating next to the tiny pink umbrellas, where Sammy had put out a plate of cut lemons and limes.

I bent down to pick up a pile of trash, but Brandon stopped me.

"I've got our cleaning service coming in the morning. I'll pick up some of the cups when I get up, and they should be able to handle the rest."

I nodded, hoping he didn't think it was weird that I'd tried to help. Of course there'd be a cleaning service. This was B-Dash's after all. I walked over to Crystal and shook her awake. She opened her eyes until they formed two glassy half moons of hazel.

"You have fun, Crys?" I asked.

"Yea, it was great. Now let me sleep."

I turned to Jake. "How long did she make it?"

"Until an hour ago. Which is pretty good considering she usually can't stay up past 10."

I grinned. "I appreciate the effort, Crys."

"Anything for you, darling."

The last group of guests was walking over to Brandon to say their goodbyes. After determining I knew none of them well enough for a goodnight kiss or hug, I resumed my search for Sammy and Tara. Crystal and Jake hadn't seen them in hours, and after a careful inspection, it appeared they'd vacated the basement.

"You sure you didn't see them leave?" I asked Jake again.

He shook his head.

I folded my arms across my chest as Brandon came up behind me. "Maybe they went upstairs."

"And leave the party? Seems unlikely," I said.

"It's worth a shot."

I grabbed Brandon's arm, still nervous to be going upstairs with him in any capacity, but before we reached the staircase Tara and Sammy came stumbling into the room, a bag of doughnuts in hand.

"Crystal, Livi, let's go. We have to leave now," Tara yelled.

Crystal sat up on the couch, still groggy. Sammy ran over to Crys's outstretched hands, pulled her up, and threw her body over her shoulder. I shook my head. No matter how many times I saw Sammy's superhuman strength, I was still impressed.

"Here, take one and go grab your pants and coat. It's already 11:30," Tara said, handing me the doughnut bag.

After grabbing my leggings from the bathroom, I looked up at the clock hanging over the bar. Was it really 11:30? I shuddered as the hands came into focus. It was more like 11:45. "Geez, how'd it get so late?"

We began hustling up the stairs with Brandon and Jake close behind. On the first floor, I threw down the doughnut bag and ran into the living room to retrieve my coat and purse. Brandon followed me, his hand outstretched.

"You never answered me. About staying over," he said, reeling me in. "All of you can if you want. Actually really you should, especially since it's past 11. Technically, you can't drive. You know, it's just Connecticut State law you're playing with," he said, this time pointing at Tara.

I held my breath as my stomach churned. Never before had I simultaneously hated and loved the

Connecticut State graduated license program. Not that Tara seemed to have the same conflict.

"Sorry, but we are supposed to sleep at Sammy's," she said, her voice booming. "And I can assure you the wrath of our parents will be much worse than any ticket if we do get stopped. And besides, with my flawless driving, there will be no reason to pull us over."

"Aw leave it to Tarable to spoil all the fun," said Brandon as we shuffled out.

I looked back one last time at the open door, hoping for some final comment or invitation for a date or phone call the next day. But all I saw was B-Dash's smile grow smaller and smaller as we reached Tara's Prius and piled in. And before I could even rehash and analyze the night's events, I felt my eyelids close as the whir of Tarable's hybrid motor rocked me to sleep.

populatti.com

lululivi : 93%

Approved Members: 23
Pending Applications: 4
Access Denied: 45

POP REPORT: last nite wuz wild. as always, the best part was the dance floor. Hope you all had fun ☺ ~ Crys

COMMENTS:

EVAbeautiful *posted at 11:34 a.m. ET May 10:* so did anyone else see livi fall into a pile of cake last nite?

ValieGal *posted at 10:00 a.m. ET May 10:* thanks Brandon for anotha awesome nite!

Tarable *posted at 8:05 a.m. ET May 10:* tell that to crystal

celebSAMmy *posted at 8:00 a.m. ET May 10:* no more cranberry juice. Like ever.

BrandontheGREAT *posted at 7:32 p.m. ET May 10:* happy bday livi, can't wait to c u!

celebSAMmy *posted at 6:38 p.m. ET May 10:* you rock sista. See you tonitee

CHAPTER THREE

Afraid I was hallucinating, I reread the comment that had just loaded on my phone as I dropped the egg that had been meant for my bowl of cookie dough onto the floor. Could it be? Could Eva be causing trouble again? I let out a loud moan, thankful no one was in the house to hear it. And even more thankful Eva hadn't snapped a picture or video of my fall. At least the trip to the DMV had been a success, I thought, picturing my shiny new learner's permit as I grabbed a paper towel to sop up my mess. Sure, it was annoying that Mom and Dad had bailed again and asked me to catch a ride with Tara, but at least I'd gotten there. The trail to freedom blazed ahead.

As I finished up the cookie dough and threw it into the fridge to cool – the plan was to make sugar cookies in cute shapes to thank the girls for the amazing birthday party – an engine rumbled outside. It was too loud to be Tara's Prius, and it was still too early for the twins to be back from baseball practice. I ran to the window. Could Dad have secured my car? Maybe skipped out on his afternoon shift to give me my first driving lesson? All signs pointed to probably not. So it wasn't surprising when my visions of a glistening Ford Escape were replaced with Sammy, fumbling to shut the rusted driver's side door of the "Beast." The ancient Suburban shook as Sammy gave it a hard kick, then headed for the house. She was wearing skintight yoga pants, a lime green sweatshirt, and a sweatband that matched. Her long hair was swept into a tilted ponytail, and her skin glowed orange. She looked like she'd stepped straight out of one of the '80s exercise videos Mom used to watch when I was a kid.

The doorbell rang before I could clean the flour off my hands. Sammy didn't wait for me to answer.

"Livi darling, where are you," she said.

"In the kitchen, what's up?" I yelled.

"Everything, as usual."

She skipped into the kitchen, then opened the pantry, grabbing a bag of Cheetos and Cherry Coke. She handed me the soda, then dug into the chips.

"Whatcha doing?" she asked.

"Making cookies. Supposed to be a surprise," I said. "Dough still needs a few minutes in the fridge. Wanna help me make the icing?"

"Girl, you shouldn't have," said Sammy, already reaching for the sugar. "Though I'm glad I caught you when I did. The frosting is the best part."

"It's even better with company," I said, pouring two cups of powdered sugar and a few tablespoons of milk into the mixer. "So what have you been up to this morning?"

"Hmm, let's see. After you and Tara left, I drove Crystal home, went to the gym, did a yoga class, and got sprayed. You know, typical Saturday routine. Gotta stay beautiful."

Her voice sounded upbeat and perky. Her eyes looked clear and rested.

"The gym? After last night? Sammy, you are a freak."

"What can I say, I thrive on sleep deprivation and adrenaline."

"I'll say," I said. Ever since I'd met Sammy, she'd been able to function on no sleep, stay strong without ever lifting a weight, and make conversation with a goldfish. She was the craziest girl I'd ever known.

"So about last night," she said, plucking a water bottle from her purse. "What was going on with you and B-Dash?"

"I dunno, seemed like a pretty typical night to me," I said, adding some vanilla to the icing. "Wanna taste?"

Sammy dipped her finger into the icing, then stuck it in her mouth.

"Tastes amazing," she said. "Though if you thought last night was typical, you're crazy."

I blushed, thinking of B-Dash. "Well, okay so me and Brandon..."

"Exactly. You and Brandon. I've never seen two human beings lip locked for that long in my entire life, and I've seen some pretty wild stuff."

I let out a small laugh, then looked down at the frosting. "I guess we made out a little."

"More than a little. Because of you guys, the party cleared out way earlier than normal."

"No, it couldn't have been that bad," I said, thinking back. "We kissed a little, and then..."

"Yeah?"

"And then the party ended."

"Right. Because of your make-out sesh."

"Oh God," I said. "I think I'm going to be sick."

Sammy smiled. "Now Livs, don't get all dramatic. It's not the worst thing I've seen."

I cringed. "Did everybody notice?"

"It was pretty hard to miss. Though you should be thanking God that corner was in a serious shadow."

"Guess I wasn't thinking. Or, uh, was focusing more on Brandon."

Sammy smirked. "Good old Brandon. Talk about a lucky birthday, huh? How many years you been into him now?"

"More than two," I said, my stomach fluttering.

"So then, spill. Is he a good kisser?"

My legs began to shake. "Hey, didn't I answer this already last night?"

"Last night you were so tired I didn't get any details."

"Well then you're not getting any now," I said, placing the icing into the fridge next to the cookie dough.

"All right, all right. But it is super exciting, so if you ever want to talk about it..."

"I'll let you know, okay?"

"Deal. Though there is something I want to talk to you about," she said, sounding more serious.

"Yeah sure, what's up?"

"Well, you know I am thrilled that you got to hang out with Dash and all, but you might want to take it a little easy next week. Maybe try not to draw any attention to yourself."

"Um, okay. Why?"

"My phone has been blowing up all morning with comments about your little stunt with Bianca."

"Bianca?" I asked, thinking back to our short conversation the night before. "What stunt? Who's talking about me now?"

Sammy sighed. "No one's talking about you, just commenting on what happened."

"And what happened? I only talked to her briefly."

"She's telling peeps you broke her toe."

I brought my hand to my mouth, smearing powdered sugar onto my lips. "OhmiGod, my fall. That really hurt her? You sure I broke her toe?"

Sammy shook her head. "No, not yet. Val said she's waiting on x-rays."

"Oh God, I hope I didn't ruin her softball career."

"I don't think the toe should affect it. Val was pretty worked up though."

"I feel terrible, it was such a stupid accident. I didn't mean to hurt her. Or upset Val. I didn't even know they were friends."

"They play softball together."

I thought of Val and nodded. Val was a quieter girl with short, frizzy black hair and the kind of eyes that could always put me at ease. She wasn't one of my best friends, but I'd always liked her. Somehow that made upsetting her worse.

"Was Val even at the party last night?" I asked.

Sammy shook her head. "Bianca called her afterwards and filled her in. So now Val's telling everyone that you like severed Bianca's toes."

Sweat dripped down my arms as Sammy's voice grew softer.

"And I'm sure you've seen that Eva started talking about your cake fall early this morning," Sammy said. "I gotta say, it's really not so good. You gotta watch it. The last thing we want is for this to escalate into some kind of termination talk."

My mouth dropped on the words.

"Whoa, wait. Who said anything about termination? Isn't that a little extreme?"

My eyes darted from side to side as I threw the dirty mixing bowl into the sink and tried to process the information. Sure, maybe I had been a little careless kissing Brandon. And I had most definitely been a klutz, falling not once but twice in one night. But termination? For a few minor slip-ups? My stomach churned as thoughts of Rachel Herval again popped into my head. Maybe I wasn't as safe as I thought.

"Look, no one's talking about termination now," said Sammy. "But it's not premature to think about it. That way we can make sure things with Bianca, Val, and Eva don't get worse."

"But there is nothing going on with Bianca or Val," I said, feeling my face grow hotter. "My falling on Bianca's toe was an *accident*. And I still don't have a clue why Eva's freaking out on me. I thought maybe it could be that honor council stuff, but this seems a little harsh for that..."

Sammy sighed. "I know, I know. And I agree with you about Eva. Whatever's bothering her has got to be bigger than that suspension thing," said Sammy. "But honestly this situation with Bianca might be worse. Even if it was an accident, it doesn't look good. Especially since she told Val you fell into her because she was talking to B-Dash."

"It was a coincidence, honest," I said. "Though I

think she was angry that I got Brandon. She seems to have a thing for him."

Sammy shook her head. "Contrary to popular belief, not everyone is obsessed with Brandon. And even if she does like him, you need to remember he's not exactly yours. You got him for a night. There's a big difference."

"Obviously I'm hoping it leads to a relationship," I said, leading Sammy to the living room couch. "I was actually thinking about stopping by the baseball field later. He told me he was pitching in today's game, so I thought I could, you know, cheer him on."

Sammy opened her water bottle and poured it over my head. "Girl, you have got to cool down! Brandon Dash may be gorgeous, but he's a player. And believe me, right now you are in too much trouble to get tangled up with a player."

"You jerk!" I said, bringing my hands up to my dripping hair.

"Hey, it may not be pretty, but it's the truth. You know we all love Brandon, but if you go prancing around that field today, you're setting yourself up to be used."

I folded my hands over my chest and worked my lips into a pout. Sammy had never deigned to saddle herself with a boyfriend – despite the fact that there was always tons of interest – and I didn't see how she was in a position to give advice. But at the same time, Brandon's wish for a slumber party was alarming. And pretty much in line with stories I'd heard about him using and then ditching other girls. I decided that this time, I'd have to trust Sammy's judgment, especially since as much as I wanted to see Brandon, I knew deep down I'd never show up without an invitation. And without Sammy's buy-in, there was also the problem of securing a ride.

"So what are you doing for the afternoon?" I asked, trying to change the subject.

"Apparently making sure you don't go near Brandon."

I sighed. "You know as well as I do that I'd never follow through. But seriously, B-Dash isn't the same as before," I said. "He dated Chloe for like an entire year before dumping her and that was because she cheated on him."

"True, but he's been a revolving door ever since. And don't forget that the only reason he was even interested in Chloe was because she ignored his advances for months. Judging from the performance you two gave last night, you're gonna have to give him the cold shoulder for at least a few weeks if you even expect to have a chance at a legitimate relationship."

"But Sammy, we're different," I said, my voice wavering. "Brandon and I've been friends for years. We always talk and bicker about music and stuff."

"True, but last night was so public. That at least warrants no contact for the rest of the weekend."

"Now you sound like Tara. At least I didn't go all narcoleptic like Crystal."

"Yeah, but she's the creator of Populatti, remember? She can't get kicked out. No one else knows how to operate the site."

I didn't know why Sammy had to bring up the termination idea again, but figured if she thought it was a legitimate concern, I should probably play it safe. Even if it sounded ridiculous.

"I guess I can hold off on calling Brandon 'til Monday. But what if he calls me before then?"

"Look. If Brandon Dash calls you this weekend, then you my dear, are a goddess and have my blessing to do whatever you want with him."

"You mean it?"

"Yeah, sure. Now get dressed. I told Crystal we'd be over at 2:00 to bust her from SAT prep and it's already 2:30."

"But what about my cookies?"

"Finish them tomorrow. I'll act surprised if you bring them to school on Monday."

I smiled, happy to be free from Sammy's lecturing, as I raced upstairs to find a respectable outfit that didn't include my favorite sweatpants. After scanning my closet, I settled on a pair of boot-leg jeans and a light blue tank with matching cardigan. Dressing in seconds, I then gathered my wet hair into a ponytail and walked into the bathroom to wash my face. If Crystal was doing SAT prep, that meant her 4'11" mother would be hunched over the kitchen table, looking over the shoulder of her tutor, and questioning every word he said. I could hear her already, drilling Crys on the scientific method, mocking her reading comprehension skills, telling her that a 2340 would never be good enough for MIT, and ranting about how no self-respecting Lim had ever gone anywhere but MIT.

Sometimes I wished I could take Mrs. Lim aside and show her the brilliance that was Populatti, because if she could understand the skills her daughter possessed, she'd realize that MIT was going to be child's play. Crys was going to be like that kid who developed Facebook in his dorm room. No one doubted that one day she would run the world, or at least create something to navigate it. But for the next two years, Mrs. Lim still had control. Populatti had to stay hidden, and all plans for world domination were on hold. Not that I minded. It gave me two more years to display my undying love so that when Crystal made it big, she wouldn't forget to drag me along.

"Livi, almost ready?" Sammy called. I tied the laces of my pink sneakers and headed down the stairs. Sammy was still sitting on the couch, now sandwiched between the twins who'd turned on some video game and were racing each other around a virtual track.

"Wanna go?" I asked.

"Yeah, sure. Bye boys. Great to see you guys

again," said Sammy.

Charlie pouted. "Please don't go, Sammy. You can play the next game if you stay."

"All right, but just one," she said, without waiting for my response.

I shook my head and popped into the kitchen, hoping to find Lona. I'd been wanting to talk to her all day, but she'd been busy vacuuming every time I'd seen her. Sure enough, this time she was there, chopping and dicing ingredients for dinner.

"Hey Lona," I said. "I'm going to head out for a bit. Mind watching the twins?"

"Of course not, that's why I'm here," she said, engrossed in her chopping.

I nodded, then stepped over to the counter.

"Thanks again for last night," I said. "The food was amazing. The flowers too."

"Of course, honey. I'm glad you enjoyed everything. And that I could find your flowers," she said, chuckling.

"Well I hope it wasn't too much trouble. It made my night."

"Then it was worth all of it," she said, looking up.

"Thank you," I said. I leaned in for a hug, feeling my throat tighten as Lona put down her knife and wrapped me close.

"You don't have to thank me for anything," she said.

"But I do. For more than you know," I said, my

voice a whisper.

Then I tiptoed out of the kitchen, wiping my eyes before heading back to Sammy. I was okay with Lona seeing my tears – I wanted her to know how much dinner meant to me, especially after Mom and Dad bailed – but Sammy was a different story. She wasn't one to get all sappy and I didn't want her asking about what was going on. She wouldn't understand.

An eruption of laughter greeted me in the family room as Sammy crashed her virtual car into a virtual tree.

"That's it, this game is rigged," she said, throwing the controller.

The twins rolled around laughing as Sammy shook her fist at the TV.

I laughed back, wondering how some people could be so good with kids, while others were not. It was like certain people were born with this gene that taught them to be patient and welcoming, and others were just deficient. Like me. Every time I was near the twins all I could see were their dirty little hands and endless strings of baseball games that seemed to require all of Mom and Dad's free time. But Sammy? She didn't see any of that. In fact, she could keep the twins entertained all day just like she was one of the guys. And she enjoyed it. For a moment I wondered if she'd make a good backup babysitter before thinking better of it. Kids may have loved Sammy, but parents didn't. Because

Sammy's idea of a good time involved dancing on the furniture and jumping in mud puddles. A far cry from the coloring books and play dough I remembered from babysitters of yore.

After a ten-minute drive across Golden Hill, Sammy directed the Beast into Crystal's circular driveway. A fleet of Mercedes was parked under a massive carport along with a green and brown Subaru that looked like it belonged in Vermont, or some other place where cars with big tires and odd color schemes were considered stylish.

"Looks like Oliver's here," Sammy said, trying not to laugh as she adjusted her backpack and headed toward the front steps.

"Ugh, why is it that Ivy League boys are so granola?" I asked, running my hand over his weathered Dartmouth sticker. "He's never any fun."

"Probably 'cause most of those schools are in the freaking arctic circle," said Sammy. "I think it freezes the fun gene."

"Then we better pick colleges that are somewhere warm."

"Stanford or bust," she said, referring to her dream of jetting off to California.

"Works for me," I said as Sammy rang the bell.

Before the chime stopped ringing, Mrs. Lim was at the door.

"Hello girls, can I help you?" she asked. "I'm afraid Crystal's busy with her SAT session now, but I can tell her you stopped by. Or, she should be free around 4:00 if you want to come back then."

I looked down at my watch. Was her SAT prep really four hours long? That was longer than the Academy Awards, and the Academy Awards were long.

"I'm so sorry to interrupt," said Sammy. "Crystal promised to help us with this problem set for Physics. Livi and I have been struggling, and we know she's got such a knack for this stuff..."

Mrs. Lim's face lit up at the mention of physics. "I see. In that case why don't you girls head up to Crystal's room, and I'll send her up as soon as they find a stopping point. They were working on a practice test, but Crystal can always finish tomorrow. More physics sounds like a good idea actually. Never can study too much for that AP exam!"

We bolted up the staircase before Mrs. Lim could change her mind. It wasn't the first time we'd used the homework story, and I was worried she was starting to catch on. Mrs. Lim was a scientist after all. Her whole job was to disprove theories. I feared it was only a matter of time until she asked why Crystal never partnered with us in class, or why Sammy and I never seemed able to make it to the science fair.

In Crystal's room, Sammy pulled a copy of *Vogue* out of her backpack and flung it at my chest.

"Some reading material for you, dahling," she said. "By the way, I forgot to ask you. Where on earth is Tarable this afternoon?"

I looked up from a waxy photo of some scary thin cheerleader wearing a pair of purple suede pants I was sure would never be popular. "She's with her mom shopping or whatever. I guess she was overdue for some bonding time."

"That's right. Second weekend of the month. It's their thing."

I tuned Sammy out as I came across an article about how applying eye shimmer to the outer rims of your eyes could make them look less puffy. It said to apply white powder in the inner corners and then brush it out underneath the bottom lashes.

"Huh, I wonder if this works," I said. "It says putting white eye shadow in the corners of your eyes can make you look more awake."

"Try it out." Sammy dug into her backpack and produced a small compact. "Here, catch," she said, throwing it across the bed.

In usual Livi form, I missed the toss and fell off the bed trying to reach the tumbling eye shadow. After retrieving it from beneath the dust ruffle, I walked up to Crystal's mirror and slid over a stack of heavy science books for courses I was sure they didn't offer at Golden Hill.

"Does Crys really read these in her free time?" I asked as I held up a copy of *Advanced Web Design*.

"Judging by Populatti, I'd say yes. Did you see the video news feed she added the other day?"

"Yeah, but I didn't realize it was all so complicated."

As Sammy turned back to her magazine, I stretched out my wrists and popped open the eye shadow, ready to add eight hours of sleep to my face. But as I brought the sponge applicator to my skin, the opening notes of my favorite song began blaring from the bed.

"Hey Livi, your phone," said Sammy. She grabbed it from the bed and wound up for a throw.

"Girl, don't even think about it." I dropped the eye shadow and raced towards her.

Just then, Sammy screamed. "Oh no, change in plans. You cannot answer this. I repeat, let it go to voicemail."

"Wait what? Who's calling?" I asked, wrestling her for the phone.

By the time I pulled the phone out of Sammy's killer grip, the ringtone had started its second loop. With seconds to go until the voicemail kicked in, there was no time to look at the caller ID. So I swiped open the phone, rolled off the bed, and said hello in my most official-sounding voice. Based on Sammy's reaction, I half expected to hear Eva or my mother or someone else I didn't want to talk to like Bianca, not that I had her number programmed. But instead of hearing any of the voices I was expecting, I was greeted by the deep voice of Brandon Dash. My mouth dropped. Had he actually called me during daylight hours? Less than 24 hours since I'd left his house? Maybe I am a goddess, I thought, as I smoothed out a wrinkle in my shirt and tried to act like I was (a.) not surprised that he had called, and (b.) not about to start shrieking like some ten-year-old girl at a Justin Bieber concert.

"Hey, Brandon, good to hear from you. How was your game today," I said after regaining a modicum of composure.

"All right, I played well but we lost in the ninth. Anyway, it was good to see you yesterday."

"Yeah, the party was great," I said, biting my nails.

"Glad you had fun. You know, my parents are still away," he said.

"I remember you mentioning that."

"I still have some Cherry Coke left too."

"Is that so?"

"Yep, though I'm afraid I don't have any more of Crystal's music, so you may want to bring yours along."

"Bring it along? I didn't know I was coming over." I saw Sammy glaring over the cover of her magazine.

"Do you want to?"

"Is anyone else gonna be there?" I asked, trying to keep Sammy from hearing anymore. I knew there were no Pop events planned for the night, but there had been plenty of times when Sammy, Tara, Crystal, and I had hung out with Jake and a few others. Often those nights were more fun than the parties.

"I was thinking this time it could maybe be just us," he said.

As I debated what to say next, Crystal entered the room praising Sammy for busting her out of hell. "I swear, my mom is the ultimate tiger mom. I mean, can she be more stereotypical? It's a miracle she never made me play the violin, though I swear if I had better hand eye coordination, then..."

Sammy motioned for her to shut up, which she did, but not before I lost my train of thought. It didn't help that a second later Sammy was giving Crystal an instant replay of my end of the conversation. Not wanting to miss a word of Brandon's, I opened the door and booked it across the hall to the bathroom, then turned on the fan.

"Livi, you still there?" Brandon asked.

"Sorry, the signal must have gone out for a second. But yeah, tonight sounds great."

"What time are you free?"

"Whenever," I said. My parents hadn't called all day so I figured our family dinner was still off, and the twins had some sleepover so I was free from babysitting. And while Tara and I had talked about catching a movie, I figured she'd understand. I mean, this was Brandon Dash after all. How often did a guy like Brandon ask me out on a date?

Well, okay, so I had dated a few baseball players before, but that was not the point. Because they were just normal, everyday guys. The kind that wore their baseball hats even in the winter and didn't cut their hair unless it was three inches too long. Brandon was nothing like those guys. No wads of gum or faded graphic t-shirts. His hair was always cropped short, with just enough bounce to hint at his natural curls. He never wore a baseball hat unless he was on the field. And graphic tees? Not Brandon. His southern-debutante-turned-yankee mother would never have allowed it. It was nothing but polo shirts for little B-Dash. Which, of course, was probably what made him so absolutely irresistible.

"So how about I pick you up at 7:00? Maybe we can grab some dinner, then hang out for a bit," he said, bringing me back to reality.

"Seven o'clock, okay, sounds perfect. I'll see you then," I said, then hung up the phone and turned on the sink faucet. After dousing my face with water, I flipped off the bathroom fan and wobbled back to Crystal's room.

"Okay, spill girl," Sammy said as I reached the doorway.

"Don't leave out a single detail," said Crystal, a pen and notebook already in hand.

"It's not a big deal. Notes aren't necessary."

"But it could be perfect for Populatti's new Popurazzi feature. I can see it already. LuluLivi and BrandontheGreat spotted together at Watcher's Point. Love is in the air."

"Geez, you sound more like a romance writer than a scientist. What happened to using Populatti to get into college?" I said.

"I just thought it could use some sprucing. You

know, to keep it fresh."

"I doubt this is newsworthy," I said as I began to visualize the feature. "We're just gonna hang out tonight. His parents are still out of town, so I guess we'll get some food and watch a movie or something."

"Oh. My. God. This is beyond newsworthy. This is like grade-A gossip," Crystal said.

"Livs, are you sure you should go?" asked Sammy. "After last night it could be too much togetherness too fast. You don't want to scare him off or anything."

"She won't scare him. He called her, remember?" said Crystal.

Sammy folded her legs like a pretzel and scooted closer. "Livi, I know I told you if he called this weekend it was a good sign, but doesn't the fact that his parents are gone make it sound like he just wants to hook up?"

"Since when is kissing someone a crime?"

"And what if he wants more?"

"Well Livi Stanley is a PG-13 prude."

"Which is why you really shouldn't go to his house alone. You know his reputation."

I tried not to fidget as my nerves started to get to me. "Even so, this could be the only chance I ever get with him. Besides, it's not like Eva or Bianca are gonna be there to report me to the Populatti police."

Sammy sighed. "Whatever then, I give up. It's

your life."

"So do I have your blessing?"

"As long as you promise you won't do anything stupid. And that you'll call if you need backup."

"Of course," I said, before jumping onto Crystal's bed, a fit of laughter already bubbling in my throat. Because we both knew how much I liked B-Dash. And how hard that would make it to ever call for backup.

populatti.com

<u>lululivi : 92%</u>

Approved Members: 23
Pending Applications: 4
Access Denied: 45

POP REPORT: Saturdays are for....mani and pedis! Stay beautiful popsters! ~ Crys

COMMENTS:

BiancaA *posted at 6:02 p.m. ET May 10:* suree c ya there!

ValieGal *posted at 5:26 p.m. ET May 10:* anyone up for watcher's point tonight?

celebSAMmy *posted at 4:32 p.m. ET May 10:* no, but your underwear were red!!!

EVAbeautiful *posted at 1:42 p.m. ET May 10:* at least I wasn't puttin on a show on the dance floor

Tarable *posted at 12:00 p.m. ET May 10:* I remember that. funny stuff.

celebSAMmy *posted at 11:39 a.m. ET May 10:* yea so? didn't u split your pants open in chorus last year in front of like a million pple?

EVAbeautiful *posted at 11:34 a.m. ET May 10:* so did anyone else see livi fall into a pile of cake last nite?

CHAPTER FOUR

"I can't believe you're canceling. What happened to tonight being just the girls?" Tara yelled into the phone.

"I figured you'd understand. We are talking about Brandon Dash," I said.

"That's what you said about Nick last month," she said, reminding me of one of my more unfortunate dates.

"Nick? Come on. His hair looked like he dumped a bottle of mousse on it every morning."

"But you did go out with him."

"For like a second."

"It was long enough for you to blow off a girls' night."

"Yes, but that was just because I needed a boy-friend for Homecoming and he was the best option. I couldn't alienate him before the dance. Come on, Tarable, please don't be mad. This is different. It's B-Dash," I said, my voice growing higher. "You know, the guy I've been drooling over since like the first day of eighth grade."

"I know. It is a big deal. And I'm happy for you, really. It's just that...oh never mind."

"No. What?" I said. It wasn't like Tara to hold back.

"It's that, well, Brandon is gorgeous. And he's a lot of fun as a friend. But something about him just always leaves me a little, I dunno, unsettled, I guess. And it's not just his reputation as a player. More that I can't read him. I never know what he's thinking."

I breathed in deep as I found myself nodding my head. Because of course Tara was right. Brandon was impossible to read, flirting one minute then going cold the next. But then, wasn't a little mystery a good thing?

"Look, I know Brandon is a little cool at times, but Chloe dated him for a year without a problem, and I've wanted to date him for a long time now. So I think I need to take my chances."

"You're right, you do," she said. "I just don't want to see you hurt."

I smiled into the phone.

Tara groaned. "And I don't want to go see our

vampire movie with Sammy, or worse yet, Crystal and Jake. You know they'll just laugh at me all night."

"Yeah, I know. They are seriously lacking in the romance department."

"And that's why I love you, Livs. Not many would see vampire slaying as romantic."

"And not many friends would be so cool about me bailing on another girls' night. So thanks," I said.

"You're welcome just as long as you call me and report back every detail as soon as you get home. Oh and try not to make any more public scenes, okay? Last thing we need is more comments on Populatti."

"Agreed on all fronts," I said, before loosening the grip on my phone.

An hour later, I was dressed and ready for my date with Brandon Dash, thirty minutes ahead of schedule. While usually I didn't like getting ready early on account of the twins usually spilling something on me or knocking me into a pile of grime, tonight I was too nervous to wait.

After settling on a casual jeans and polo look, I descended the stairs just as the twins stampeded out of the house and into their friend's minivan, which was set to deposit them at some sixth grade sleepover. Relieved to have the brat pack out of my hair, I waltzed over to the couch just as the door opened again. I popped my head over the couch as

Dad floated into the foyer, looking like he'd just won a Caribbean cruise.

"Happy birthday, Olly," he said, using the nickname he'd come up with for me back when I was a zygote. I got up off the couch and greeted him by the door. Before unbuttoning his coat, he grabbed my arms and twirled me around the foyer. My feet glided across the tile as he put down his briefcase and pulled me back toward the door. My mouth opened and I squealed, happy to see Dad in such a good mood. It was rare to see him really laugh.

"I'm so sorry I wasn't here last night," Dad said, his smile growing as he let me go. "But I have no more shifts for the rest of the weekend and I told the attending I'm not to be bothered tomorrow."

"Nice," I said, already tasting my father's peanut butter waffles. They were his Sunday specialty. "Is Mom off too?"

"As long as no more babies decide to be born. Though I was thinking maybe you and I could have some father-daughter time. You know, test out the new wheels?" He reached into his pocket and pulled out a glittering set of keys.

"OhmiGod the car! You got it!" I screamed, grabbing the key ring from his hand.

"It's all gassed up and ready to go. You have your permit with you?"

"Yeah! OhmiGod I can't believe it!"

"Well, start believing because it's yours, just as soon as you get your license, that is. So how about it? Ready for a quick spin around the block?"

I bolted out into the dark before answering, drenching my socks in a puddle before reaching the driver's side door.

"Hey, not without your shoes," Dad said behind me.

I turned back, threw on my sneakers, then again ran out the door.

"This is amazing," I said, running my fingers over the cool tan leather seats. The car was even more beautiful than I remembered from the lot. Even in the dark, its silver paint glistened and the chrome wheels sparkled. Catching the beams of light from the house floodlights was a roof rack with the special attachment Dad had ordered for our skis. As I envisioned Tarable and me cruising up to Okemo Mountain, my hands drifted toward the radio. Again, the car did not disappoint. There was a hookup for my iPod and speakers lining the front and back. I set the radio to Z-100 and cranked the volume, making a note to jack up the bass when Dad wasn't in the car.

"You ready to take her out?" Dad asked.

"Yes! Let's go!" I said, adjusting my mirrors, then pulling the car out of park. The car lurched forward then stopped as my foot came down hard on the brake. I'd only practiced a couple times in parking lots with Dad last summer, but never on the roads. I felt my back stiffen as I reached the end of the driveway.

"Okay, that's it. Now put your foot on the gas, just like I showed you in the Chevy," he said.

With Dad as my copilot, I clung to the steering wheel and guided my foot to the gas. Then I flipped on the turn signal and pulled out onto the street, just like a real licensed driver. Ten minutes later, the drive was over, my knuckles were tingling from my grip on the wheel, and the car was parked in the garage connected to our house.

"You did fantastic, honey," Dad said, once inside. "You handled that stoplight like a pro."

"Thanks. For the ride and car. And for getting it today," I said.

"You're welcome. It was the highlight of my year. Though now I'm afraid I will be expecting chauffer service whenever I need a ride."

"Anytime." I kicked off my sneakers, replacing them with my pink ballet flats. It was almost 7:00, and the only thing that could drag me away from the Escape was supposed to arrive any minute. As if on cue, the doorbell rang just as I finished flexing my toes.

"Wonder who that could be?" Dad asked, walking to the door.

"It's for me. I forgot to tell you, I have a date tonight."

"Oh, okay," he said, his voice falling.

I looked down at my feet, wondering why my first, and potentially only, date with B-Dash had to fall on a night when my friends and family seemed to need me more. "I can cancel if you'd like me to stay home," I said, already envisioning Dad sitting in the family room alone, remote and burned popcorn in hand.

"No, of course not," Dad said. "We'll do something tomorrow. Oh and tell Nick to pop in. Always like to say hello before you head out."

"Dad! Nick and I broke up like two months ago. Tonight I'm going out with Brandon," I said, my cheeks burning. Dad wasn't around much, but when he was, he loved nothing more than playing bouncer with my dates. The wrong piercing, or handshake, or even smile was grounds for date refusal. Something he found to be highly entertaining. And I found to be miserable.

"Oh," he said, rubbing his eyes. "What happened to Nick? I was all right with that one."

"I don't know," I said. "He wore too much hair mousse?"

Dad raised his brow. "All right well, tell Brandon to come in then. Wouldn't hurt him to say hello either."

I nodded, then swung open the door and invited Brandon inside. Lucky for me, he was looking his finest, his piercing-free, dad-friendly face shining almost as much as my new silver car. After passing inspection with even higher marks than his predecessor – he received a firm handshake but no broken bones or red finger imprints – we buckled ourselves into Brandon's car and headed out to cruise the strip.

The strip was nothing more than a short stretch of the Boston Post Road that housed a number of strip malls, fast food joints, and fancy restaurants that my parents sometimes went to when their schedules gave them both a night off. I sat at the edge of the seat and fiddled with my seatbelt as we pulled onto the main road. Brandon had mentioned getting dinner, but had never said where. And he hadn't asked for my opinion either. Again I thought of Tarable and her comments about Brandon's elusiveness, and then of Sammy's remarks about Brandon ushering girls through a revolving door. Was his not asking for my input a bad sign already? Should I have just stayed home with Dad or gone out with the girls? Or was I being paranoid and silly, my thinking blurred by the blood pooling in my feet as I tried to make sense of how it came to be that I was finally sitting next to B-Dash?

I wasn't sure, but hoped it was the latter. I looked out the window and tried to think of the different restaurant options as Brandon filled me in on his day. Of course there were the fast food staples like McDonald's and Burger King, but there were also those restaurants that were more in between, like Chili's and TGI Fridays. I knew enough not to expect a three-course meal or anything, but I was hopeful he'd choose somewhere with a waiter.

After driving by a few glowing drive-throughs, my stomach began to stir. A few more blocks and we'd be up by the Outback and then Applebee's, which wasn't my favorite but did have a chocolate brownie dessert that was to die for, not that I'd ever order it when I was out with Brandon. Yet before I could even visualize the Applebee's menu, we were zooming past it. The restaurants and stores were further apart now. The road was growing darker.

"Where are we going?" I asked when we passed the last Starbucks in town. We were in the next town over now, and having just gotten my driver's permit, I wasn't as familiar with places farther away.

Brandon shook his hair out of his eyes. "I was thinking pizza if that's cool. I know a pretty good place."

"Pizza, sure. That works," I said, relieved that he had at least sort of asked for my input. I held my breath and tried to decide where pizza fell on the list. It had to be above the fast food joints, but was it better than Applebee's? I wasn't sure. I thought about checking in with Tara or Sammy, but given their lukewarm support of the date in the first place, I decided to pass. And I knew I couldn't ask Crystal. For all her brains, she just couldn't keep a secret. Everything I told her always made its way back to Jake – or Populatti.

"Did you hear about Watcher's Point tonight?" Brandon asked as we passed a sign welcoming us to New Haven. We were more than a few towns over now, which I took as a good sign. Even if pizza was cheap, gas was not.

"Yeah, I saw a comment on Populatti," I said.

"Some of the guys were thinking of going. You interested?" said Brandon.

"Isn't it still a little cool for the beach?"

"They were planning a bonfire."

"Even so."

"Why don't we skip it and just go back to my place then? I told Matt and Eva I'd let them know if we were around anyway. Both their parents are around and they're looking for somewhere to hang out."

Of course, I thought, leave it to me to shoot down the option that would have kept me out of trouble.

"Huh, maybe Watcher's Point wouldn't be so bad after all," I said.

Brandon laughed. "Lemme guess. You're not too thrilled with Eva's Pop posts. Well I wouldn't take them too seriously. You know everyone always posts crazy stuff."

"I know," I said, surprised he'd been so quick to pinpoint the reason for my hesitation. "They were annoying, but no big deal."

"Good. Then why don't we wait until after dinner to figure out our plans. See where everyone is then."

I nodded, my throat too dry to form more words. And before I could think much more about a night pretending to be Eva's friend, something I still wasn't sure I could pull off, Brandon had the car parked and was motioning for me to follow him toward a small glowing window on a busy commercial street. Sirens wailed a few blocks over. Trucks and vans crowded the gas station on the corner.

"You sure we should be eating here?" I asked.

Brandon grabbed my hand and pulled me forward.

"Are you kidding? The pizza here is amazing. You've never been?"

I looked up again at the sign. Modern Apizza. It didn't ring a bell. Though apizza was code word for New Haven-style pizza, which was both famous and intoxicating.

"If it's so good why couldn't they get a better building?" I asked, my mind drifting to New Haven's cozy center near Yale. Or to Wooster Street, the apizza capital, where my parents would sometimes take us for a pie from Pepe's or Sally's or one of the other famous places dotting the cherry tree-lined neighborhood.

Brandon opened the door to the restaurant and led me inside. "Livi, this place is a landmark. I can't believe you've never been."

My eyes watered as they adjusted to the dim lighting and the huge crowd of kids hovering around the entrance. "What's going on? There's like a whole little league team in here," I said.

Brandon grabbed my coat, then put our name on the list. "Don't worry, it's worth the wait."

His deep voice helped my shoulders relax as I gazed up at the large hand-painted menu hanging on the wall. I was out to dinner with B-Dash, after all. Did it matter where we went? Even going to McDonald's would have been news.

We waited in line for about 45 minutes before getting a table. As it turned out, the wait was worth it, even if the wafting smells of pizza along with Brandon's constant pokes were driving me crazy. Because when we finally got the pizza, it was sublime. The crust was crisp and thin with a thick layer of mozzarella oozing off each slice. It tasted less like pizza and more like some new type of super food.

"OhmiGod, how did I not know about this?" I asked, as I reached for my third slice. I was breaking all the rules now, eating mass portions in front of Brandon and not even blotting my mouth between bites.

"I told you it was worth it."

"You win. I'll never doubt you again."

"Is that so?"

"Uh-huh," I said as our phones both buzzed against the scuffed wooden table.

Brandon got the text first.

"Looks like Watcher's Point is off," he said. "Guess it was too cold after all."

"Really?" I said, the butterflies back in full force, although the news was not a surprise. Even if it was May, real summer nights were still a month away.

"Wonder where everyone's gonna go then," I said.

"Whatever, not our problem. We'll just chill with Matt and Eva. It'll be fun."

"Right," I said as the waitress approached our table. I was pretty sure a night with Eva would be anything but fun.

After Brandon picked up the check, further signifying that this was in fact a real date, we headed back to his place. The drive seemed much shorter now that I knew where we were going, and before we could even start a real conversation, we were standing on his doorstep.

Inside, the house sparkled, just as spotless as it had been on Friday before the party. It was like the party had been nothing more than a dream. Except that if it had been a dream, then I most definitely would not have been following Brandon into his kitchen.

"We really under-ordered tonight," Brandon said, reaching for the fridge. "It's a crime to leave that place without leftovers."

I nodded, embarrassed to admit I was still hungry.

"Good thing I've still got leftovers from last night." He opened up the fridge and pulled out a cardboard box adorned with the Modern Apizza logo.

"Wait, you ate there last night too?"

He nodded. "It's my favorite. I'd eat there every day if I could."

I ran my teeth over the edge of my lower lip so that it couldn't move upward. He'd taken me to his favorite restaurant. Could it get any better? Forget Applebee's, he'd let me in on his secret pizza lair when he could have just taken me to some generic chain or drive-thru. I tried to act disinterested as he pulled out two slices and closed the fridge. Better he doesn't know I'm onto him, I thought as we dug in.

A minute later, the pizza gone, I reached for my stash of gum. After depositing two slabs under my tongue, Brandon popped the last piece into his mouth and took me into his arms.

"Now, where were we?" he asked, lowering his head to mine.

"I think we were right here." I reached up to his lips.

"That's about right." He picked me up into his arms and carried me to the living room couch.

The next fifteen minutes were a blur as he laid me down onto the fluffy couch cushions and began kissing me with even more intensity than he had the night before. Every touch felt like a shock, as if he were brushing a live wire across my skin. It felt fun. Dangerous. And invigorating in a way I'd never felt before. Sure, I'd dated other guys, but never had I felt anything like this. And never had I cared enough about anyone to make out for such an extended period. I closed my eyes and let my mind drift as Brandon kissed my cheeks, then worked his way back toward my mouth. *This is it,* I thought. *This is happiness.*

But no sooner had I thought those words, than I felt Brandon's hand gripping my shirt. Surprised, my muscles tensed and I tried to guide him away, back to my mouth, to the kisses, to our perfect moment. But he just laughed and pressed on further.

Too shocked to speak and too scared to ruin the moment and risk losing Brandon, I tried once more to guide his hand away.

Again he laughed.

And I gritted my teeth, angry at myself for being so naïve and unprepared. For not listening to Sammy or Tarable or all the evidence before me that clearly stated that B-Dash was a player. I tried to think of a clever way to extricate myself from the situation, but my thoughts were too jumbled to form a coherent plan. I blinked fast and hard, hoping to rid my eyes of the tears already welling. How had I let this happen? I was supposed to be confident, carefree Livi. Not some tear-stained doll.

Memories of Drumstick and a decade of unimportance rushed into my mind as I fought to find my voice.

Trying to sound flirty yet stern, I started. "Hey, maybe we should…"

But my words were lost as Matt and Eva

strolled into the room.

"Hey Dash, you here?" said Matt, peering over the side of the couch.

"Shoot," said Brandon, jumping up. "Wasn't expecting you yet, man."

He took Matt's arm and ushered him into the kitchen, leaving me with Eva.

I grabbed my shirt, bunched up from all of Brandon's pulling, and pulled it back over my waist.

"Huh, interesting," said Eva. "Never pictured you a Dash girl, Livi. But then, it fits with your trend of stealing boyfriends."

A chill ran down my spine.

"And what does that mean?" I asked, my mind racing. I'd only had a few boyfriends and I certainly hadn't stolen them away from anyone.

"Just what you think," she said. She stared down at me, judgment shining in her eyes.

"Well I think you're mistaken," I said. "I haven't done anything wrong."

"Maybe you haven't," she said.

"Then what is your problem?"

"Just because you haven't broken any rules doesn't mean you're innocent," she said.

I tilted my head, unsure about what she was getting at. Then I thought back to Bianca and the toe. Was she telling people I'd stolen Brandon from her now too?

"God, is this about Bianca?" I said. "Because

Dash and her are just friends. I didn't steal him away or anything."

"No, you just broke her toe."

"Turned out it wasn't even broken!"

"Whatever. Close enough."

"No, it's not," I said, blinking away a siege of unwelcome tears and reaching for my phone. It was definitely time for backup.

"You need to get over yourself," said Eva, staring me down.

"And you need to watch it. Because you and Matt aren't exactly the perfect couple. Meaning that if you're not careful, our paths might not be crossing for much longer."

I stared right back at her, hoping she'd realize that Matt was the only thing keeping her in Populatti.

But Eva seemed unfazed. "You're right, they might not. But I can guarantee that it won't be for the reason you're thinking."

Brandon and Matt entered before I could respond.

"Sorry again, Livi," said Matt.

"So, you ladies want to watch a movie?" said Brandon.

I smiled, then shook my head. "I'd love to but my dad just texted. He just got called into the hospital and needs me to watch my brothers."

"Oh, okay then," said Brandon. "Let me drive you home."

I breathed deep and let my shoulders roll back, shocked by how good it felt to have an escape plan. "No need," I said. "I already texted Sammy and she's on her way."

Brandon opened his mouth just as the shining headlights of the Beast appeared in the drive.

"Sorry to run out, guys," I said back to Matt and Eva. "Thanks for dinner, Brandon. Guess I'll see you Monday at school?"

"Yeah, sure. And I'll call you later," he said. "We've got some unfinished business to take care of."

I nodded, then let him kiss me on the cheek before running out into the night.

populatti.com

lululivi : 93%

Approved Members: 24
Pending Applications: 3
Access Denied: 45

POP REPORT: Good morning popsters! As you all know, today we've officially approved Populatti's 24th member! Looks like Christian's passed the first test, but can he partay? Stay tuned for Friday, details to follow tomorrow at 5! ~ Crys

COMMENTS:

Jake *posted at 1:26 p.m. ET May 12:* congrats, man. Can't wait to get after it manana

Tarable *posted at 1:00 p.m. ET May 12:* so does this mean I can finally see the pics you took in art class last week?

BiancaA *posted at 12:00 p.m. ET May 12:* welcome christian! Thanks for the help in photography today

BrandonTheGreat *posted at 8:45 a.m. May 12*: good to see another guy in this joint – welcome!

celebSAMmy *posted at 6:30 a.m. ET May 12:* congrats coop! welcome to the club!

ValieGal *posted at 6:01 a.m. ET May 12:* and then there were 24!!! Yaaay Cooper!!

CHAPTER FIVE

Tara pushed my hand off the mouse and guided the cursor to the upper right corner of the open web browser.

"Do you want to get us expelled? Those librarians check everything," she said as the Populatti home page faded into the great beyond.

"What did you do that for? I was gonna clear the history," I said.

"That's what Noah said right before he got busted for changing his Biology grade last year."

"He broke into the online grade book. I'm just visiting a website. You know I'd never risk anything that would break the honor code. And besides,

Crystal has encrypted this thing to death. There's no way you could even tell what the site is without entering a password."

Tara didn't look convinced.

"Sorry, but this is an emergency," I said. "I had to see if those comments Eva left last weekend were off the front page yet, which they are, thank God. It's not my fault phones aren't allowed during school hours."

"Just because the comment is gone doesn't mean everyone will forget what it said. I fear the damage has been done," Tara said as she pulled up a site about Robert Frost. "We're working on a poetry project if anyone asks."

I reached for my book bag and grabbed my anthology from English. "Here, at least now it's believable," I said, placing it next to the keyboard.

Tara kept working with the mouse until a series of poems filled the screen.

"You don't think anyone's gonna take Eva seriously, do you?" I asked as Tara finished. "I mean, she doesn't make any sense. And what she said to me about stealing B-Dash from Bianca? It's crazy. How can anyone believe anything she says?"

Tara shook her head. "Eva sure is one to blow things out of proportion."

I frowned, thinking back to the nasty fight that had broken out on Populatti late Sunday night, with Eva insisting I was not Populatti material because I'd hooked up with B-Dash and all Dash girls lacked respect for themselves. This had infuriated me, first because Brandon and I were not just hooking up – we were on a date, hello – and second because the scene she'd walked in on looked way worse than it really was.

Luckily, the fight had ended when Brandon posted some long epic about how he has so much respect for women and what Eva saw was a big old nothing – yes, he actually used the word 'women' though I was pretty sure we were girls – but still, even after the resolution, I felt uneasy. Because truth was, that night Brandon had been trying to push my limits, a fact I still hadn't felt brave enough to tell the girls. I wasn't sure which image I wanted people to see, or which was truer. Was I a bold and fearless popster or a straight-A honor council prude? I wasn't sure.

My hands shaking with uncertainty, I pulled a Cherry Coke from my backpack.

Tara plucked it from my hand and threw it back in my bag. "What has gotten into you today? No drinks in here, you know the rules."

"Yeah, but I need to calm down."

"Then you don't need more caffeine."

"Please?"

"No."

"Can I have some of the sugar cookies I gave you? I know you have some left."

"I thought they were a gift."

"They are. But they'd help calm me too."

"Too bad they're also on the banned list."

"You are so not fun today."

"Just breathe deep. The period ends in 15 minutes."

"But I'm thirsty and hungry and you still haven't answered my question. Do you think people will believe Eva? Or did Brandon's comments help? No one thinks I'm a Dash girl, do they?"

Tara frowned. "The comments helped, but after the way you guys carried on at Friday's party, I'm afraid Eva looks more believable than she should. You are going to have to cool it this weekend until this whole mess blows over."

"Wait, people are *still* talking?" My throat grew itchier as my Cherry Coke craving grew stronger.

"I haven't heard anything more since Tuesday, but Sammy heard some of Bianca's friends talking about it in Gym."

"This is ridiculous. Why is Eva acting like such a jerk? I mean, it's been a year since that whole suspension thing."

"I know. Though I still think Eva's just insecure. Don't worry, I'm sure this will fade away soon. Just don't do anything stupid."

"Like start a termination vote against Eva?"

The words slipped out before I could stop them. Yet saying them felt good. Like a relief. As if I was finally acknowledging what I'd been thinking all along.

"Livs, you better not," said Tara.

"Why? We all know that Crystal hates her anyway," I said, liking the idea more and more.

"Yeah, but everyone loves Matt. No one's gonna vote out his girlfriend. Not even Crystal. Especially since your behavior Friday night was so questionable."

I frowned, wishing for once Tara didn't have to be the voice of logic. "But it was my Sweet Sixteen! And it was B-Dash! How did a little kissing get me into so much trouble?"

Tara shook her head. "I don't know, but we need to be smart about this. You just lay low and we'll figure out our own way to get back at Eva. Promise."

I nodded, unconvinced.

Tara looked behind her back for the librarian, then cleared the web history just as the bell rang out across the scratchy intercom.

We darted out of the library and headed to English, my last – and favorite – class of the day, and the only one us four girls shared together.

The halls were buzzing with bodies, the thick air clinging to our faces as we reached the staircase leading up to the English wing. May was the beginning of the sweaty season, as Sammy called it, when the temperatures were hotter in the school than out. I wiped my forehead as we cut through the crowd, wondering if the air quality would ever improve.

Golden Hill High was a sprawling two-story

building which had been built in the 1990s with every feature imaginable. It was a testament to the top test scores which had convinced Golden Hill taxpayers that high school kids needed a turf football field, state-of-the-art Chem lab and separate gymnasium and auditorium for athletic events and school plays. But twenty years later, the building was overstuffed with students and rife with problems. Last year a water main had blown, taking out the auditorium for the entire spring semester. The year before that, there'd been a siege of killer mold from a roof leak. Today, the town claimed the building was fine and up to the challenge of the well-documented overcrowding, pretending that stuffing hundreds of extra students into the halls didn't create new problems like sweaty air, for which the school had no purification system. But then, given Golden Hill's reputation as a town with a chart-topping high school, it was no surprise the administration liked to downplay our problems.

We reached the classroom as the bell chimed, giving Tara and me just enough time to scoot into our seats and wave hello to Crystal and Sammy. With seating done in alphabetical order, none of us sat close to one another, though it was a relief just knowing they were there.

With everyone seated, Ms. Tilfry walked to the front of her desk, then sat down on top of it, facing out. "Good afternoon, class. I assume you are all refreshed and ready to learn on this fine Thursday afternoon?"

I laughed under my breath with the rest of the crowd as Ms. Tilfry crossed her legs. One of the younger teachers, Ms. Tilfry wore black leggings, a long batik shirt and a wide headband over her auburn curls. She had a bohemian vibe I had always admired, especially since she always looked so comfortable, even when her outfits were a little strange. It was like she really didn't care what we thought of her. Hard to believe, but refreshing, especially since I couldn't imagine ever straying from the looks outlined in *Vogue*.

"All right then, I am going to dive right in," said Ms. Tilfry, her red moccasins dangling on the tips of her toes. "As you know, we've been talking a lot about *The Grapes of Wrath* and how Steinbeck used the novel as a means of social and political change. It was through the eyes of the Joads that many Americans first learned about the scale of hardships affecting families during The Great Depression. One of the most powerful aspects of this novel is its rawness, which really created a firestorm when it was published. Remember, this book was burned and banned before going on to win the Pulitzer Prize. This was neither merely a novel nor a history book, but a real, live social commentary."

Ms. Tilfry waved her hands as she talked, her voice rising and falling with excitement, as if she'd just discovered the book for the first time.

"Following Steinbeck's example, I have decided

that for your end-of-year project, we are going to create our own social commentaries. Only instead of writing more stories or essays, this time we are going to use the most popular medium of today. Video. Now I've broken this class into four groups. There will be sixteen other groups across the grade. Each group will be responsible for creating a ten-minute video that tells a story that also sheds light on an issue you feel strongly about. These videos can include both fictional and nonfictional elements, as long as they focus on telling a story, just as is done in *The Grapes of Wrath*."

Excited murmurs broke out on the mention of shooting video, a welcome change from the usual writing.

Ms. Tilfry smiled, as if she'd anticipated the response.

"Topics do not have to be school-related, but they do need to be approved by me before you begin. Once your topic is approved, you can start work on the script. All completed projects will include a video, script and expository essay explaining the main message and rationale of your video. I've got a whole packet explaining the assignment here, but before we go through it, I'd love to take any general questions?"

"Can we pick our own groups?" asked Chloe.

"No, I've already got your groups right here," said Ms. Tilfry, pointing to our packets.

"Will we get to watch each other's videos?"

asked Sammy.

"Of course! In fact, part of this will include a contest, where student votes will help determine the best video in your class."

"But what about the best video in all the classes?" asked Crystal. "You said all your classes were doing this, right?"

"Uh, yeah, but I think we're just going to stick with viewing videos from your period."

"Oh, but Crys you're right, it would be so cool if we could watch everyone's in a group class," said Sammy. "Or better yet, we should plan a film festival where we can walk the red carpet and get all dressed up and..." Sammy's voice climbed higher and higher as she fanned her face with her hands.

Ms. Tilfry laughed. "Wow, it's so great to see so much enthusiasm, Sammy. You know, I hadn't thought about a film festival, but it's a cool idea. Let me check with Principal McCafry and get back to you. But maybe we can plan a special viewing, see if we can get the auditorium for a Friday night?"

"Yes, that would be amazing," said Sammy.

The chatter intensified as Ms. Tilfry handed out the information packets. It seemed the class was split on the film festival idea, which wasn't a surprise seeing as Sammy had most likely just signed us all up for another night of school. But then again, it would be an opportunity to get dressed up, and maybe it would lead to a Pop after-party as well. It was hard not to see the brilliance in Sammy's thinking.

"Okay everyone, now if you turn to page two, you'll see I've outlined the groups..." Ms. Tilfry's voice faded as I flipped the page and started scanning through the list of names. As she'd said, there were four groups, each with four people. Skimming the names, I first found Crystal's, neatly typed next to Sammy's. Tara was in the next group with her new boy crush Christian.

After running down the list twice, I found my own name toward the bottom of the page. I was with Jake, a good sign since Jake was just about as smart as Crystal. I began to smile, pleased with my assignment. That is, until I finished reading. Because the rest of the group included Matt, and then as if getting paired with Eva's boyfriend wasn't enough, I read the final name. Bianca Aguilar. The softball player. Who seemed to have a thing for B-Dash.

Feeling sick, I raised my hand, ready to start fighting against the group assignments. But before Ms. Tilfry saw me, I brought my arm down into my lap. Hadn't I just had this conversation with Tarable? As much as I wanted to switch groups, I knew I had to stick it out. Changing groups to get away from Bianca would be a serious red flag. Though all of a sudden Ms. Tilfry's little film festival was sounding like a lot of work and a lot less fun.

As I thought over the situation again that night, I couldn't help but twirl my hair in frustration, unsure of how to approach my group when class met again on Monday. I'd been lucky Sammy's film festival questions had pushed back our kickoff meetings until after the weekend – thank God for block scheduling – though I feared that all the extra time in the world wouldn't help me figure out what to say to Bianca. Or Matt. I could only hope Jake would take control of the assignment and allow me to funnel my contributions through him.

Still unsure of my next step, I picked up the phone, desperate for Tarable's advice. But before I could bring up her number, it began to vibrate in my hand. My cheeks burned as the name B-Dash flashed across the screen. We hadn't talked since I'd run out the other night, except to say 'hi' in the hall. He'd asked if anything was wrong and of course I'd denied everything, claiming only that Eva was getting on my nerves. Which was true, and not a surprise at all. What was a surprise was the phone call. Given my hasty exit and less-than-enthusiastic response to his advances, I'd all but assumed any spark of a relationship was dead. If Brandon was calling, it meant the embers were still hot. But whether they burned with the desire to get to know me or add me to his list of conquests, I had no idea. Especially since B-Dash still maintained that he'd never conquered anyone, despite a whole phone book of girls who claimed differently.

"Hey, what's up," I said, trying not to sound surprised or too enthusiastic.

"I need to talk to you," Brandon said, sounding tense.

"Sure, what's up?"

"Bianca cornered me in the hall today after our team meeting."

"What did she want?"

"First to talk about our throwing contest," he said. "But then she asked me for a ride to Christian's on Friday."

I frowned, thinking back to Sammy's early invitation to this week's party. Apparently Christian had wanted to thank everyone for voting him in by throwing a Friday shindig. Part of the conditions were that Sammy announce it in advance so he could talk about it when he ran into members. The request seemed innocent enough, so Sammy had granted a one-time exception on her never-announcing-party-locales rule.

Only now just hours after the announcement, we'd already hit a snag. B-Dash had been cornered by Bianca. Though I couldn't help but wonder why Brandon thought I'd care.

"Oh, okay," I said.

Silence filled the air as I waited for his response.

"I thought you'd be pissed."

"Well she's your friend, right?"

"Yeah, but not the kind of friend I drive around."

"All right then, so just tell her you can't."

"Already did," he said, his voice sounding playful.

"And? Problem is?"

"Problem is I told her I couldn't take her because I was driving you."

"Oh, okay," I said for the second time in the conversation. Leave it to me to lose all sense of originality and wit under pressure. "That's cool then...you know, if you really do want to pick me up."

Brandon breathed into the phone. "I was hoping you'd feel that way. Because I've been thinking a lot about the other night. I really wish you'd been able to stay, but I get that you and Eva have that girl drama thing going on."

I looked down and bit my lip, wondering what Brandon wished had happened last weekend. And if we'd still be having this conversation if he'd heard me tell him "no." Something told me agreeing to go to Christian's with him was another dangerous move. But given his conversation with Bianca – and the fact that I'd have to talk with her tomorrow in English class – my options were limited.

So instead I forced myself to look into the mirror and smile. Count to ten. Then say, "Yeah, Eva has really been annoying lately. But tomorrow night sounds great."

"Cool, I'll pick you up around 6:00 then. Oh and try not to worry too much about Eva. I don't think she'll be bothering you much longer. After the way she carried on last Saturday, I told Matt either he dumps her or I'm nominating them both for termination."

"Whoa," I said. "But isn't Matt a good friend?"

And one of my new group members? The thought made my hands shake.

"Yeah, but Eva was not his best choice. After you left, she popped open a bottle of wine without asking and proceeded to get so drunk that she walked right into my mom's favorite lamp. Now she's refusing to fork over the two hundred bucks I had to scrounge up to replace it before my parents got home. And Matt hasn't exactly offered to help either."

I paused, waiting for him to fill the silence.

"That's awful," I said finally.

"I know. Eva needs to chill out," he said.

"Well, you know I agree completely," I said, my voice wavering. Because I knew I shouldn't be bad-mouthing Eva to Brandon. But after he'd offered to drive me to Christian's, told me he wanted to see me, and said he'd missed me the other night, did I really have a choice?

"So does that mean you'd second the vote if I nominate them?" he asked.

My esophagus burned as Brandon's breath grew heavy on the phone. I didn't think I'd have to take a stand this soon.

"Um, well, isn't Eva's approval rating already hovering at like a 60?"

"Yeah, but it's been there for weeks. I doubt it will dip below 50% on its own."

I nodded to myself, letting the line go silent.

"So are you with me?"

"Well, I guess if you need me..."

"Cool, well I'll see you tomorrow then. Have a good night."

The strands of hair hanging in front of my face were drenched in sweat by the time the conversation ended. But before they could dry, I brought the phone up to my ear again.

"Hey, what's up?" asked Tara.

"We need to talk. In person. Now," I said.

"Whoa, slow down, what's wrong?"

"I, I 'm not sure. But I think I said something I shouldn't have to B-Dash."

Tara sucked in a breath, then exhaled. "All right, hang on. I'll be there in ten minutes," she said before clicking off the line.

populatti.com

<u>lululivi : 85%</u>

Approved Members: 24
Pending Applications: 3
Access Denied: 45

POP REPORT: And the 24-hour countdown begins… get ready popsters, invitations will be comin' tomorrow at 5!!! ~ Crys

COMMENTS:

EvaBeautiful *posted at 6:23 p.m. ET May 15:* hey val, u drivin tomorrow or u want me 2?

ValieGal *posted at 5:58 p.m. ET May 15:* yay Christian!

Jake *posted at 1:26 p.m. ET May 15:* congrats, man. Can't wait to get after it manaña

celebSAMmy *posted at 1:00 p.m. ET May 15:* so does this mean I can finally see the pics you took in art class last week?

BiancaA *posted at 12:00 p.m. ET May 15:* welcome chrisstian! Thanks for the ride home today

BrandonTheGreat *posted at 8:45 a.m. May 15:* good to see another guy in this joint – welcome!

CHAPTER SIX

Tara peered over the Populatti homepage and sighed.

"What's going on?" I asked. "Are people talking about me? Or Eva? Has Brandon said anything?"

"No, nothing's happened," Tara said. "No one's posted anything in hours. You've got to calm down. Brandon obviously hasn't said anything about your conversation. There's still time to fix this, we just need to act fast."

"Okay well, what about my approval rating? Is that still ok?"

Tara breathed through her teeth as she searched the page. "Yeah, it's holding strong at 85%. Same as earlier today. Like I said, nothing's changed."

"Right. Before Eva's attacks my numbers were never that low. I screwed up, didn't I?" I said, burying my face into my bright pink and purple comforter.

Tara, never one to sugar-coat, nodded. "You're not responsible for all of Eva's comments, but you have given her some pretty good ammo. Lucky for you no one knows about the latest yet. But once they do, it won't be good. Eva and Matt are the very two people I told you to leave alone."

"I know, I know. I panicked. Brandon really didn't give me much choice."

"Oh God. Brandon who didn't call you all week. How weak are you, falling for that excuse about Bianca?"

"What? You think he was lying that she asked him for a ride?"

"Honestly, I don't know. But I do think it was a convenient reason to talk you into making trouble with Matt and Eva."

"But why would Brandon use me? What's he got to gain by bringing them up for termination?"

Tara sighed. "I don't know but my guess is something's going on with him and Matt. We'll have to see if Crystal can get Jake to investigate."

"Ugh. I feel sick," I said, bringing my knees to my stomach.

"Me too, but who knows, maybe this will still blow over. You did say Brandon was just thinking about it, and so far it doesn't look like he's said anything about his plan. So maybe he won't go ahead with the termination after all."

"Yeah, it's a possibility," I said. "He told me it was a threat."

"Okay then, this whole thing might be nothing. All you have to do is call back Brandon. Tell him you've reconsidered. You're out on the termination."

"I can't call back now," I said, my voice breaking. "I'd look like a freak!"

"But this can get messy fast, especially with B-Dash driving it," said Tara. "You're already worried about people posting comments and your conversation just happened. Just imagine what will happen if Brandon does start talking."

"I know, I know."

"Well then, what would you rather? One teeny awkward conversation with B-Dash or a massive fight with half of Populatti?"

"How about neither. Come on, Tarable. There has to be another way."

"I can't think of one."

"Well, maybe people won't react as badly as I'm thinking. I mean, almost everyone agrees that Eva is abrasive. And what have I done besides a little kissing with Brandon? That's like nothing. Especially since I've been friends with most of these people for years. And helped a lot of them out during honor council."

"Yeah, but there's still those rumors about you hurting Bianca. And you've burned quite a few peeps in honor council too. Calling Brandon is our best bet."

I frowned, knowing she was right. But of course calling Brandon was also the last thing I wanted to do, especially now that he was picking me up for Coop's party. I didn't want to do anything to risk losing another car ride with him. Because even if I was unsure of his motives, he was still B-Dash, the most popular and gorgeous and charming guy to ever show interest in me. Years of crushing did not evaporate overnight.

"He won't care if he's really into you," said Tara, reading my mind. "He's got to understand that with all those rumors flying around the site, you're not the best person to take sides."

"I know, but I really don't want to risk it. I already ran out on him the other night. What if I just talk to him tomorrow night on the way to Christian's? If he hasn't said anything yet, he probably won't until the party. I can't imagine him having the opportunity to get into it at school, especially since Matt sits with us at lunch. And it won't seem like such a big deal if I do it in person."

Tara waited to answer. "I guess that could work. But you need to do it early before you get to the party and he has the chance to say something dumb."

"Oh, thank God." I jumped off the bed and

trapped Tara in a hug, grateful to have been spared for a few extra hours.

"You're welcome, but now I really gotta go. I have a test in AP Chem tomorrow and I've already lost an hour of studying." With a weak wave, she left me to my spinning head and woozy stomach.

My appetite didn't return to normal until the next day at lunch. As I walked toward the cafeteria, I found myself reconsidering whether I needed to talk to Brandon at all. Sure, he'd been angry last night, but wasn't everyone allowed to vent? He'd probably forgotten all about terminating Matt and Eva anyway. Matt was his good friend from baseball. Maybe not as close as Jake, but they were still tight. I couldn't see a drunk girlfriend or broken lamp getting between them, and Jake had confirmed that he didn't know about anything else going on between them.

At least that's what I was thinking until Sammy found me on the way to lunch and shoved me into the girls' bathroom.

Not having spoken to her since the day before, I didn't know what she'd heard, but I knew that if she was keeping me from eating my turkey sandwich on whole-grain bread with Lona's special Dijon mustard, it had to be important.

As the bathroom door swung shut, Sammy released her grip and brought her left hand to her lips. The sound of her teeth chomping down on her pinky nail echoed across the tiled walls.

"Good, nobody's in here," she said after inspecting each stall. "Now you need to spill. Right now."

"Spill? About what?" I asked, even though I had a sinking feeling that I knew the answer.

"About Tara."

A wave of relief flooded my stomach just in time for a new fear to take over. "Huh? What's going on with Tara?"

"You tell me. I just spent an hour with her in History and she was catatonic. She wouldn't talk at all for the whole class, even though we had a substitute. All she would tell me was that she went to your house last night, and that she wasn't going to Christian's party anymore."

"Wait what? She's not going to the party? That's crazy! I thought she liked Christian."

"Me too. She's been talking about the party all week. I was supposed to go over there after school to help her pick out an outfit, but she called it off. Said she didn't want to see me and then she stormed out of class and headed to the library, even though it was lunchtime."

"That makes no sense. All we talked about last night was me. I was having some issues with B-Dash."

"Oh yeah, the whole Bianca thing? I heard her in gym class telling her friends that he was taking you to the party tonight. Sounds like she wasn't too happy."

"Well neither am I, but because of Eva, not

Bianca. Seems she's annoyed B-Dash so much that now he wants my help terminating her and Matt."

"You've got to be kidding me."

I shook my head, then spit out all that had happened since Saturday in a long stream of garbled sentences, sparing no detail – except of course for Brandon's unauthorized exploration on the couch. That information was remaining classified until I finished analyzing it myself.

"Whoa," Sammy said as I came up for air. "That is messed up. But congrats. If Brandon turned down Bianca to go with you, that's actually awesome news. Who knows, maybe Chloe did change him. This sounds more like boyfriend behavior than anything else."

I threw my backpack down in the one corner not infested with cigarette ashes or muddy water.

"Yeah, I know," I said, grateful I hadn't told Sammy about the real reason I'd bailed early on Brandon last Saturday. "But the whole Matt and Eva thing is a mess. I know Tara was pretty worked up about it."

Sammy nodded. "Supporting any termination is always dangerous, but if Brandon initiates it, then it's more on him than you. And knowing Dash as I do, I think it's safe to say this blows over without him doing a thing. That boy loves to be liked. I can't see him rocking the boat."

"That's what I thought."

Sammy paced back and forth and shook her

head, her mind still preoccupied. "But is that really all you talked about with Tara last night?" she asked.

"Uh-huh. She said she had to get home early to study for an AP Chem test. You think maybe she's mad 'cause she bombed it?"

"No, I talked to Crys earlier since they're in the same class. The test was easy. And Tara was still in an okay mood then. Maybe a little distant, but talking."

"This is so weird."

Sammy picked up my backpack and headed for the door.

The library was buzzing with juniors for some special college day presentation, making it even easier than usual to slip into the crowd. After scanning a few outdated work stations in the center of the room, we found Tara slumped over a faded wooden table far off in the reference section. She had a large encyclopedia propped open with an arugula and hummus pita hidden inside. Her AP Chem book lay closed nearby, preventing a slew of crumpled papers from falling on the floor. Sammy and I grabbed two empty chairs and sat down.

Tara reached for her sandwich. "I told you I wanted privacy," she said.

"You tell us what's up, and we're gone," Sammy said.

"I don't want to talk about it."

"What about for a homemade 100% organic

chocolate chip cookie?" I asked, reaching into my lunch bag.

"Well I am out of your sugar cookies."

"Good. It's yours. Made by Lona with free range cocoa and wild oats."

"I think you mean free trade," Tara said.

"You know what I mean."

"Yeah, I do," Tara said. She took a bite of the cookie before looking up at Sammy. Tara seemed sad, but not angry – at least with me. Either that, or Lona's cookie had worked a miracle.

"You sure you don't want to talk about it, sweetie," I asked once Tara was done chewing. Lunch was winding down and if she didn't spit it out soon, we wouldn't get another chance to talk until last period, which was still a couple of hours away.

Tara sighed. "Why don't you just ask Sammy what's going on."

"Me? How am I supposed to know? You won't even talk to me," said Sammy.

Tara lowered her eyes. I pulled my melon lip gloss out of my pocket and offered it around, hoping to break the tension.

"Drop the act, Sammy," Tara said after pausing for a minute. "I know you're the one who's been handing out Christian's phone number to every girl who asks for it."

Sammy's jaw dropped. "What are you talking about?"

"You know exactly what I'm talking about. Val was bragging about it after the Chem test today."

Sammy sighed. "That's ridiculous. I only gave Val his number because she told me she was bringing her cousin to tonight's party. He has a serious nut allergy and she needed to discuss it with Christian."

"Since when are members allowed to bring guests?"

"Come on, Tara, it was family. You know there are no rules forbidding that, and Val's always been friendly. Why would I say no? Not to mention she didn't have to go through me for his number. I'm sure lots of people have it."

"But she did, and you're supposed to be one of my best friends."

Sammy shook her head, her face turning red as she tried to keep her cool, which, knowing Sammy, wasn't easy for her.

"Come on, Tarable," I said, bringing my hand to her back. "It can't be as awful as it seems. How do you know they're going out?"

"They're going to some softball party together."

"That doesn't mean anything," I said. "People go to things like that as friends all the time."

"Maybe, but it sure hurts my chances."

"God, you're being ridiculous, Tara," said Sammy.

Tara threw her pita sandwich into her book bag and stood up. "Sorry if I don't feel like hanging out with a backstabbing, so-called best friend."

Sammy jumped up and followed her toward the exit. "Tara, get back here. Let's talk about this."

"There's nothing to talk about," Tara said, as the door swung shut.

Sammy pushed it open and ran after her. But a minute later, she was back, her face splotchy.

"I lost her. Though I have no clue why she's so worked up. Val had a legitimate party concern, that's all," Sammy said, her mascara now creating a black stream down her face.

"I believe you," I said, grabbing her arm. "And Tara will too."

"Where are we going?" asked Sammy.

"To the gender neutral bathroom. Tara's sanctuary."

"She still hangs out there? I thought she stopped after those girls broke the smoke detector and fouled it up with cigarettes."

"The janitors cleaned it last week. Its health grade is back to A-plus," I said, quoting Tara.

"She better be there," said Sammy as lunch's ending bell rang.

I nodded as we reached the bathroom door. We had four minutes before class to repair the teary damage. Judging by the growing smudges under Sammy's eyes, we were going to need ten. Sammy and I entered the one-stall gender neutral lounge, where Tara laid sprawled out on the gender neutral gray couch.

An old teacher's lounge that had been converted to a bathroom after some equal rights protests a few years back, the bathroom was as large as it was clean, featuring a couch, wall of sinks with mirrors, and a single stall with a locking door. Given its luxurious furnishings, I had always wondered why more people didn't frequent it, especially for makeup touchups or hair emergencies. But given its location across from the lobby and principal's office, it had remained deserted, except for last month's incident with those girls who had tried to use it as a smoking club.

I pushed Tara's legs to the ground and pointed to Sammy to sit down.

"All right, I have to book it to class, but you two need to figure things out."

"I'm still not talking to her," said Tara.

"Then use sign language."

Sammy's eyes followed me to the door. I felt bad bailing on my duties as mediator, but having racked up 13 tardies in French class, I couldn't be late.

"I'll see you in study hall later," I said to Tara, then let the door shut behind me.

When I reached the library for the second time that day, the college booths had been dismantled and the librarians were back to patrolling their books in full force. Relieved not to be sneaking in this time, I walked up to the front desk and signed the study hall attendance sheet, before retreating to the table where Tara and I always met. A few seconds later, Tara walked in looking much better than she had an hour earlier. Her hair glowed a pinky gold under the dim lights, and her cheeks looked flushed, but healthy with just enough color to make her freckles shine like flecks of cinnamon showing off her flawless skin.

"Hey, thanks for earlier," she said as she collapsed into the chair next to me. She threw her backpack over one of the empty chairs and placed her black cardigan over the other. "You don't mind if we sit alone today, do you?"

I shook my head and let her rest. A few other popsters shared study hall with us, but none of them was a close friend, making it acceptable for us to take a day off from more gossiping. So as our usual group walked in, I waved, then grabbed a different table on the other side of the stacks. Even though it was Tara who'd asked if we could sit alone, after learning that peeps were still talking about Eva's comments, it felt nice not to get trapped in another probing conversation.

"So are you still going to the party tonight?" I asked.

"Yeah, I'm going. I'm still pretty pissed at Sammy, but I can't hold her responsible forever. I don't think she knew what she was doing."

It was good to hear that even when she was the center of the drama, Tarable was still the voice of reason. Though it didn't surprise me that it had been a short fight. Tara and Sammy had been best friends since way before I moved to town. They'd seen each other through bad hair years, lost crushes, Sammy's parents' divorce, and more. In fact, even though I considered Tarable my best friend, for years I'd always felt like the third wheel Sammy and she had adopted in seventh grade just for the extra Fruit-by-the-Foots Lona used to throw in my lunch pack. Not that I could complain. They'd been there for me when I was the new kid and the other girls shut me out. Though adding Crys to the group had been a good idea. Since the very first day we met her wandering like a lost puppy in search of the Physics lab, Crystal had brought balance to the group. She eased the bond between Tara and Sammy, and her sense of humor had become such a part of our lives that I wondered how we'd ever gotten along without her.

"I talked to Coop in History by the way," Tara said.

I shook my head, wondering why she hadn't spilled sooner. "And?"

"He didn't say much, but he did tell me about Val asking him to that softball party. He wanted to know if there was a nice way to bail and say he had other plans."

My lips curved into a smile. "And you're just telling me now?"

"I thought you'd want to know about me and Sammy first."

I let out a laugh under my breath. "Well then, what did you tell our boy Christian?"

"That if he said yes, he shouldn't break an engagement unless something serious really did come up."

"Wait. Why'd you say that? That was your chance to squash this whole thing."

Tara shook her head. "Yeah but that's not me. Knowing he doesn't like her is enough. This way I can just focus on being myself and see what happens. No pressure, you know."

I nodded, not surprised to hear that Tara had already taken control of the situation. If there was one thing Tara was good at, it was strategy.

"So did you see that Avery is considering dropping out of Populatti?" asked Tara, changing the subject.

"What? Really?" I leaned in, excited to be back to our regularly scheduled gossip sesh.

"Yeah, she told Crystal today that she just didn't think she had enough time for it. That she thought the parties were getting lame."

"Interesting," I said, not too surprised to hear about her complaints.

While we did have a few seniors in Populatti, the club was primarily filled with sophomores like us. Most of the senior girls avoided us because they didn't like taking orders from Crystal, who was quite a bit younger. They also didn't like knowing younger kids could vote them out. But that was what made Populatti so great. The rules were the same for everyone. Apply, get someone to okay your application, attend a few events, and then wait for the community to vote. It was crowd sourcing at its best, which was why even some cute senior guys had been denied membership after mistreating a few too many female members. And it explained why Avery was considering stepping down. With so few seniors in the group, it was only natural she'd want to move onto other things.

After discussing Avery and the dwindling-senior phenomenon, Tara waited for the librarian to circle, then sent a quick text to Sammy telling her their after-school fashion consult was back on. I felt my jaw relax as peace was restored among my crew.

With gossip topics running low, I snuck into the computer lab and pulled up the Populatti homepage to check on the latest comments. Even though all was right with Tara and Sammy, I still felt uneasy about my conversation with B-Dash the night before. When nothing noteworthy loaded, the knots in my stomach relaxed a little more. And I found myself wishing I still had Lona's chocolate chip cookie.

That is, until Tara reappeared and plopped down in the seat beside me.

"So have you given any more thought to what you're going to tell Brandon tonight?" she asked.

Her serious tone brought the knots right back. Tonight would be way more complicated than trying to help Tara make a good impression on Coop. I still had to deal with Brandon. And his reaction.

After inspecting the edges of my cuticles for a minute, I looked up at Tara. "Who knows, I'll work something into the conversation."

"You do have to talk to him, you know," she said, her voice growing sharper.

I logged off Populatti and pulled up the school intranet in its place. "Don't worry. I said I'll take care of it."

"Good," Tara said, oblivious to my forced smile. "Then I will work on snagging Christian and you will do damage control with Brandon. Should be a fun night."

"Yeah, sounds good," I said, removing my sweaty hand from the mouse. Friday nights were usually the highlight of my week. But I had a funny feeling that this Friday was going to be anything but a fun night.

populatti.com

lululivi : 84%

Approved Members: 24
Pending Applications: 3
Access Denied: 46

POP REPORT: it's after 6:00 and time to paartaay!!! 1.5 hrs to go before it's on!! ~ Crys

COMMENTS:

BiancaA *posted at 6:03 p.m. ET May 16*: yikes, tonite's party is a hike. Anyone wanna carpool?

Tarable *posted at 5:47 p.m. ET May 16*: speaking of exclamations, val don't u seem excited...

ValieGal *posted at 5:30 p.m. ET May 16*: so excited to c u tonite co-op!!!!!

celebSAMmy *posted at 4:15 p.m. ET May 16*: eww jake, you are so not fun ;)

Jake *posted at 4:05 p.m. ET May 16*: crys, baby, luv the updates but maybe u should hold some of the exclamations next time...

CHAPTER SEVEN

The sand drifted like snow in the cool spring air as I stared out at the boarded up lifeguard station down at Golden Sands. Even though the weather app on my phone had listed the day's high at 72, now that it was 4:00, the sun felt much weaker. But with most of my best thinking occurring at the beach, I didn't care about the falling temperature or gritty wind that was whipping my cheeks red. I'd convinced Sammy to drop me off after school before she headed over to Tara's, and had been pondering the whole B-Dash-Eva situation ever since.

Now just a few minutes were left before the afternoon bus would pull into the little glass lean-to across the way, next to the Starbucks where I'd spent most of the afternoon, safely tucked between a strip of eclectic shops and cozy restaurants.

The small row of businesses, nestled in close to a thicket of beach houses and across from Golden Hill's only real public beach, had become my favorite place in town during the first week we moved to the area, when I'd been looking for somewhere to replace Boston Harbor. In Boston, I had been obsessed with walking down by the water and watching the tourists mill about. And staring at the boats, always changing. There was something magical about watching the boats – from tiny dinghies to huge yachts and mammoth ships – that helped my mind wander, as I thought about what life would be like on each one that passed by. A sleek sailboat could get me thinking about racing in America's Cup, while huge luxury yachts made me wonder about embarking on a cruise to Bermuda or Florida or somewhere even farther. And fleets of lobstermen and salt-stained fishing boats got me thinking about a life spent working on the sea.

Losing that bustling harbor had been a huge blow, as was losing the whole city, really. It was funny. Despite all the open space, Golden Hill often felt claustrophobic. It was only at the beach that I felt completely free, looking out at the miles of water separating our shores from those of Long Island. Not to mention that the shopping down there was great. It was the place to go for one-of-a-kind finds, something that had made me an area regular ever since Crystal started Populatti.

Buses weren't common in Golden Hill, so I'd been lucky to discover that one ran from the Starbucks across from the beach to the grocery store just a block from my house. It was supposed to help the hoards of senior citizens living country-club style in the development across the way, but really it had become my lifeline for days when I needed to clear my head and wanted some privacy from the realm of Pop. Even the bus ride had become cathartic, as older riders befriended me – apparently it was rare to meet a rider under sixty, let alone eighteen – and doled out the inside scoop on shops, restaurants, and other tidbits about the town. Speaking with Golden Hill's senior set was both informative and relaxing as I could be myself, free from the eyes of my friends. Which was why I planned to continue my bus rides long after procuring my driver's license.

I hugged myself tight and trekked back to the glass lean-to as the squeaking brakes of my ride grew closer. It had been good to spend a couple hours off the grid – especially when the alternative was sitting home alone and stressing out about the night's party – but today not even the lapping waves, shades darker than their usual blue, knew how to completely erase the anxiety clouding my mind. Because I still couldn't think of a good solution to the whole Eva-Brandon situation. Or maybe

I just couldn't figure out what I wanted with Brandon, or what he wanted with me. And that's what made the thought of bailing on Eva's termination so terrifying. Withdrawing support would appease my friends and help my approval rating, but jeopardize our emerging relationship. Though considering Brandon's advances the other night, what kind of relationship was really at stake? And was it worth saving?

As the bus bounced over the ever growing constellation of still unfixed potholes marking our winter storm ravaged roads, I turned each piece of the puzzle around in my head like a three-dimensional logic problem, exploring different scenarios and trying to figure out a way I could have it all. But truth was, no matter how I framed the problem, the same solution kept popping up. I was going to have to bail Brandon and leave the rest to chance. Ever since my Drumstick days, I'd been hesitant to trust a guy, and Brandon hadn't done much to put my mind at ease. Yet the situation left me with no choice. I had to trust he'd understand why I couldn't support Eva's termination vote. And I had to trust that Eva would start to dial back her attacks while my approval rating was still in the eighties. Because as much as I liked Brandon, I needed Populatti.

I didn't just need Pop for the social events or the built-in votes for honor council or even the respect younger girls showed me in the halls. No, I needed Populatti because for the first time in recent history, I had real friends. The types of girls I couldn't risk losing, especially since they would most definitely drop me – not on purpose, of course, but due to a lack of interaction and common ground – if our afternoons and weekends were spent apart. With summer break only a month away, I feared this process would be accelerated, especially with me scheduled to spend my days volunteering at the hospital instead of working in one of the local restaurants or clothing stores where most of our friends hung out. Once again, thoughts of Rachel Herval floated through my head as I envisioned a whole summer of parties – and a whole group of friends – gone. The thought was too much to bear. No matter what happened with Eva or anyone else, I had to do everything possible to preserve my friendships.

A few more bumps and a short walk later and I was home, staring at a note from Dad saying he and the twins were at the batting cages and Mom was working late. With Lona also MIA, I popped open a can of Campbell's tomato soup and fried up a grilled cheese for dinner, enjoying the silence that could only happen with the twins gone. Then I climbed the stairs to my bedroom. Given the importance of the night, I should have been in the shower getting ready hours ago, but the day had left me too tired for any serious primping. Despite my exhaustion, I turned up my music and tried to get excited. Sammy had said tonight's theme was speakeasy chic. Ever since we'd read *The Great Gatsby* in English a couple months back, Sammy had been obsessed with the roaring twenties, having compiled quite the collection of sequined dresses and feather hair accessories in the process. Tonight she was determined to show them off. In fact, we all were, as Crys, Tara and I had each borrowed one of Sammy's signature headbands, complete with feathers and flower appliqués. Mine was bright fuchsia since most of my wardrobe centered on different shades of pink. Only before popping into Starbucks, I'd scored a purple ostrich feather skirt at the resort wear shop that some of the adventurous old ladies on the bus had told me about a few months before. Mrs. Ambly, the velvet-clad lady who ran the shop, had befriended me on my first visit, and now always kept a few prime pieces waiting in her back room. So when I'd walked in earlier, two lattés in hand, she'd thanked me for the coffee, then led me past the displays of bedazzled slippers and flowery shawls to the feathery masterpiece hanging in back with a clearance tag for $10.

The skirt was a little longer than my usual style, but the good thing about feathers was that I could cut them – which I did after slipping it on, stopping when the ends of the feathers skimmed my thighs about two inches above my knees. Wanting to incorporate some pink into my outfit, I paired my favorite black tank with a long pink beaded necklace that fell down to my waist. Next I wrapped my hair around my straightening iron until I had created a mane of loose curls. Then I shoved Sammy's headpiece into my bag and ran down to wait for Brandon. He pulled up at 7:00 on the dot in his father's BMW. B-Dash might not have had his own car, but he always arrived in style.

"Whoa, I didn't know tonight's theme was chickens," he said as I opened the door.

I bit down on my lip, worried he'd somehow heard of Drumstick.

"Is that what they wore in the twenties?"

My eyes drifted to Brandon, then my outfit. The skirt. Of course.

I laughed. "Feathers were huge. Don't you remember watching *The Great Gatsby* in class?"

Brandon shook his head. "I think I slept through it."

"How do you sleep through Leonardo DiCaprio?"

He shrugged. "I'm a guy?"

The ride to Coop's was fast and uneventful. Even though I knew I should bring up the termination topic, every time I opened my mouth, nothing came out. So, sick of spending so much time worrying, I decided to put the conversation off until I had a more natural opening. Instead, I tried to get excited for the night's party.

Christian's family had just moved into one of

the newer developments in the north of town, away from the beach and closer to the big country clubs with the rolling hills that had helped give the Golden Hill Paugussett Native Americans – and our town – their name. His house was a two-story colonial typical for the area with lots of land and a three-car garage, making it plenty big for a Pop party.

Brandon pulled into the driveway, then turned the car around and parked on the street just as Tara, Sammy, Crystal, and Jake pulled up in the Beast. It was unusual to see Sammy driving on a Friday on account of her being the most likely to partake in a sip or two of actual "cocktail," but I figured tonight she must have decided to be responsible. Chances were she was up to one of her cleanses or health kicks again. Unless she was being a little more careful with her own approval rating after seeing mine dip so low.

"OhmiGod Livs, that skirt is insane," said Sammy as we met up in Coop's front lawn, teetering on our heels as they sunk into the ground.

"You gotta see it without my coat," I said, taking a twirl.

"I don't remember that one. Where'd you get it?" asked Tara.

I shrugged, not in the mood to give up my shopping secret.

"Hey ladies, let's bring this party inside," said Brandon, draping one arm on me and the other on Sammy.

"Agreed," said Jake, his arm already around Crystal.

Tara rang the bell, her face ghost white when Coop answered the door.

I fought the urge to laugh.

"You're early," Coop said.

"No, we're right on time," said Sammy, pushing Tara almost off the stoop. "I told you the party planners always come early." Sammy hoisted an overflowing reusable Whole Foods bag of supplies into the foyer. "We've got another bag in the car if you want to go grab it."

"We'll get it," said Jake as he and Brandon ran back to Sammy's car.

"You guys sure do travel in packs," Christian said, leading the way into a game room off the kitchen.

Sammy threw the bag over her shoulders and began following Coop. I took a step forward and nudged Tara. Her cheeks had gone from pale to red in ten seconds flat, and her body seemed stiffer than a popped polo collar.

"You good?" I asked.

"Yeah, I'm fine. But God, I wasn't expecting him to look so hot tonight," she said, looking around to make sure no one could hear.

I shrugged and kept walking toward the back. Christian was attractive, with chiseled arms that were thicker than most guys' and these sexy oval-shaped, but lately the more I talked to him, the more I questioned how I felt about him. Even in his light blue V-neck sweater, which was by far his best piece of clothing, something about him just didn't look right. His hair was long and unruly, and he had this weird habit of squinting his eyes whenever someone said something he didn't agree with. Which was often. I got the sense that Christian wasn't so sure of Golden Hill or Populatti. And even though he claimed to have come from Greenwich, he didn't seem to know anything about Golden Hill or Connecticut in general, saying he always spent his free time in "the city," as in New York City. I knew we were supposed to be impressed by his apparent worldliness, but having come from Boston, I didn't find his familiarity with New York all that impressive. Christian Cooper may have been the new kid, but he was no Brandon Dash, and not even as cute as Jake. Which was strange, since Tarable usually had impeccable taste. But even so, I smiled and nodded as Tara's eyes fluttered between blinks. I wanted Tara happy. If Coop would do it, then I'd do everything possible to help her snag his attention.

At the end of the hall, Christian opened a large barn-style door and marched us into the game room.

"So here you go, ladies. Your party venue," he said, moving over so we could step inside.

"Huh," said Sammy, looking around. "It's a little sparse."

Coop nodded. "Yeah, last room to get unpacked. But I figured the more open space, the better for cramming in bodies."

Sammy nodded, but I could tell she was not convinced.

The room was empty except for a few boxes overflowing in one of the corners, a small end table piled with cups, and a pair of wooden chairs it looked like Coop had carried in from the kitchen. A flat screen TV was propped against an entertainment center, where its wires hung to the ground, uninstalled. A pile of black-and-white photos wrapped in bubble wrap were stacked next to a dismantled foosball table.

"At least there's room to dance," I said, kicking my foot through a heap of dust that had settled on top of the mess.

"You have any folding tables or chairs or something?" asked Sammy, looking at her watch. A half hour was barely enough time to set up the decorations, and now we had a whole room to stage. Christian's house may have had potential, but just like him, it wasn't all there yet.

"The garage is full of stuff. The movers were supposed to have set up this room days ago, but they never got around to it. I'm sure no one will care if we move some things ourselves."

"Good. Then grab the guys," said Sammy.

For the next 20 minutes, Sammy barked orders and we followed them. Coop, Jake, and Brandon heaved couches, tables, and speakers into the empty space. Crystal and Tara synched their iPods to the wireless speakers and tested out their playlists. I covered a table with a red plastic tablecloth and began arranging the fancy sodas and plastic martini cups Sammy had bought, taking time to slice a few lemons and arrange them on a plate with cherries. As a final touch, we strung strands of white Christmas lights from the walls up to the chandelier hanging in the center of the room, reminding me of a thousand small candles flickering in the wind. We pushed a black leather couch along the side wall between two large picture windows, and threw up an eclectic collection of black-and-white photos using the nails stuck in the walls from the previous owner. Then Crystal plugged in the TV and threw in *The Great Gatsby* DVD on mute, for ambiance. Sammy hid the remnants of the foosball table into a closet – there wasn't enough time to set it up, and it didn't fit the night's theme – and then dimmed the overhead lights. With minutes to spare, she cranked up the music.

The room had gone from pitiful to magical in under thirty minutes. The playlist was chock full of dance music, with no B-Dash oldies. And the decorations were classy, even romantic, making my ostrich feathers the perfect choice, especially next to Sammy's beaded sheath and six strands of pearls that she'd tied into a big knot at the end.

Breathing in deep, I pulled out my fuchsia

headband and placed it my hair, using my reflection in the photo frames for guidance.

"You look hot," said Crys.

"So do you. That green is smoking. Had I seen the potential I would've grabbed that one," I said, pointing to Crys's emerald headband and matching belt she'd put together with sequin fabric she'd bought at Target.

"Crys, you are ridiculous. Fashion diva and computer genius," said Tara, joining our group.

I smiled as Tara leaned in. "So did you and Dash have your little chat?"

I hesitated, then frowned.

"No? Seriously?" said Tara.

"I wanted it to come up organically."

"Livs, what are the odds of getting him alone again? Eva is going to be here. What if he gets pissed and starts talking to people?"

I sighed. "Crys, what do you think? Don't you think I should wait until it comes up naturally? Instead of coming out of nowhere with it?"

Crys shook her head. "You know I love you, Livs, but I gotta say I agree with Tara on this one. Just spit it out now so you can enjoy the party. Just like ripping off a Band-Aid."

"Yeah, one that could ruin my social life."

"Stop being a drama queen and just talk to him," said Tara.

"Look, I told you I would do it and I will. Just stop pressuring me."

I broke away from the circle and headed toward the drinks. Plastic martini glass in hand, I eyed the open bottle of Ocean Spray that I usually filled with Sprite. Next to it was a flask of God-knows-what. I wasn't sure where it had come from or what was in it, but knew this wasn't its first appearance at a Pop party. I reached out and grabbed it, feeling the weight of stainless steel and leather in my hands. But then, thinking of my parents and honor council and my future as a law abiding prosecutor, I put it back. Talking to Brandon wasn't going to be easy, but alcohol would just complicate things further.

As I finished mixing my cranberry and Sprite, Populatti's finest stampeded into the house. It was time to party. I walked over to Christian, wanting to make sure everything was under control, as a group of lacrosse players sauntered into the room.

"Sweet room, man," said one of the shorter ones whose name I could never remember.

"Glad you guys could make it," said Coop, extending his hand into a half fist-pump, half secret handshake that was supposed to look impressive, but really just looked like a spastic attempt to swat a bee. "I figured only the best for Populatti, right?"

I shook my head in disbelief as Coop accepted multiple compliments for the setup. As more popsters rolled in, I waited for him to throw some credit our way, but none came.

"Hey cutie, where have you been hiding?" asked Brandon, emerging from the crowd. "I need to grab a drink, wanna come?"

I nodded and took his hand, no longer interested in chatting up Christian.

At the drink table I grabbed a second plastic martini cup and reached for the Sprite.

"Shaken or stirred?" I asked, even though Populatti had yet to invest in a martini shaker.

"How about on the rocks," he said, reaching for some ice. He plopped three ice cubes into the Sprite, then reached for the flask.

"Aren't you driving me home?" I asked.

He laughed. "Of course. Sorry, you know, old habits."

But I didn't know about old habits, or at least not about Brandon's, and the revelation that he'd been known to sample the forbidden flask made the hairs on my neck tingle. Here I'd known B-Dash for five years and been friends with him for two, yet at times I still felt I knew nothing about him at all.

"So I was talking to some peeps, you know, off the record," he said, directing me to the leather couch.

"About?"

"You know."

I sat down on the couch and brought my knees to my chest like they taught me to do in Sammy's yoga class to relieve stress. This was it. There was no denying he was talking about Matt and Eva. Meaning I couldn't postpone the conversation any longer. Though the fact that he was bringing it up had me on high alert. Tonight was supposed to be fun, not time to discuss group dynamics. Unless he'd already started talking to others. A metallic taste made my mouth water.

"So, have you told anyone your, um, plans?" I asked, praying the answer was no.

Brandon hesitated, then nodded.

I swallowed a gulp of tinny saliva. "Who'd you talk to?"

"Just Jake and some peeps at lunch."

I frowned. "Lunch? Where was Matt?"

Brandon shrugged. "Off somewhere I guess."

Of course. Matt decided not to show on the one day I was playing referee in the library with Tara and Sammy.

"Sounds like a lot of people," I said, thinking of our table for ten in the cafeteria.

"I guess. I wasn't keeping count," he said. "Maybe I should have. We need what, 12 votes to terminate?"

"With Coop now it's 13. You need more than half," I said. "That or an approval rating below 50%."

"I think we'll get 'em on votes. Most people seemed receptive."

"Really?" I said, taking my first breath in minutes.

"Yeah. No one likes Eva, and they agree Matt is acting like an idiot."

"But did you actually ask them about a termination vote?" I asked, my knees shaking.

"Not yet but I told them I was pissed at Eva's drama and the way the two of them trashed my house. I said if they didn't fix the situation soon, we were gonna be forced to do something."

I brought my hand to his cheek as he shot me one of his signature smiles, but after a few seconds, I pulled back.

"You didn't mention anything about having my support, did you?" I asked, remembering the speech I'd practiced earlier in the mirror.

Brandon shrugged. "Why? I thought you were cool with it."

"I was, I mean I am, I just was thinking that with my approval rating and all, that maybe it wouldn't be the best time to..."

Brandon cut me off, bringing his hand to my lips. "Calm down. Everything's cool. Most people are on our side. And your approval rating's fine. You just have to chill. You're like Populatti's honorary prom queen. And besides, with that honor council thing no one would even think of voting you out. Believe me, it's in no one's best interest to be on your bad side."

I leaned my head back into the soft cushions of the couch as Brandon's lips crept closer and closer to my mouth.

"I hope you're right." I said, wondering if honor council could really work in my favor. Tara was right. I'd helped plenty of members, but had voted to discipline a bunch too.

Luckily, Brandon didn't seem so concerned.

"On this, I know I'm right," he said, leaning closer.

"Is that so?" I asked, his breath tickling my eyelashes.

"Uh-huh."

"Well then, I guess I should relax."

"That's what I've been telling you," he said, bringing his lips down to mine.

I closed my eyes as he kissed me to the beat of the music, his lips rising and falling with the changing tempo of the song. I hugged him tight as we sat there on the couch and I tried to forget all about Eva and Matt and approval ratings and my botched conversation with Brandon that didn't really didn't go as planned at all.

But it was on that last thought that a lump began to swell in my throat, making it hard to breathe, let alone kiss Brandon back. Because even if he was sure that my Populatti standing was secure, I knew the girls would feel differently. And the last thing I wanted to tell them was that I'd buried myself deeper in Brandon's termination plot.

Feeling dizzy, I pushed off Brandon's shoulders, in need of air. He brought his hands to my cheeks and smiled, his eyes all soft and hazy like he'd just woken from a dream.

"You all right?"

"Yeah," I said. And catching a glimpse of his

calm smile, I decided I meant it. I was all right. At least, I was going to be for now. Whatever happened when I filled in the girls, well that would happen later. So I did my best to ignore the butterflies in my stomach as I brought my hand to Brandon's neck.

He chuckled, leaning in again for a kiss as I scooted closer to his lap.

Before I could reach it, I froze as Eva's shrill voice cut through the crowd.

"And what is this?" she asked, loud enough for half the party to hear. She was standing over Brandon and me, one hand on her hip, the other pointed at my face.

"What are you doing?" Brandon asked, pulling back.

"Stopping this party from becoming indecent," she said.

Brandon jumped off the couch. "Eva, what is wrong with you? Livs and I are doing nothing wrong."

"Oh, so public makeout sessions are acceptable Pop behavior now. Just like talking behind your friends' backs, huh?" Eva asked.

"Eva, we haven't talked to anybody all night," I said, my voice faltering.

"Good thing you talked to them today then, huh? The way I heard it, you and your little boy toy over there have been talking a big game about termination. That's big talk for someone who's usually all about playing fair."

I felt the blood drain from my face.

"Who told you that?" Brandon screamed.

"Dude, relax. Leave the girl alone," said Matt, running to Eva's side.

"If you controlled your woman, I wouldn't have to," Brandon said.

"Are you kidding?" said Matt. "Dash, you are way out of line here."

"Yeah, well so were you and Eva when you stole my parents' booze and smashed up their lamp."

"I told you I'd get you the money," said Matt. "It's just gonna take awhile."

"Yeah, three months. But I had to shell it out now," said Brandon.

"Well I'm sorry we're not all rich. Some of us don't have allowances. We have jobs."

Matt took a step closer to Brandon.

Brandon took a step closer to Matt.

Matt raised his hand, curling it into a fist, then dropped it back to his side.

Brandon's eyes widened. "That's it. I'm through. You wanna fight, then let's fight," he said.

Matt laughed, then took a step back. "Oh come on, man, I'm just fooling. No one wants a fight."

"You sure about that?" said Brandon, not backing down.

Matt's face turned white as Brandon stepped even closer.

My heart racing, I scanned the crowd for Crys

or Tara or Sammy. Someone. Anyone who could save me. But all I saw was a jumble of faces, mouths open, eyes black in the dim lighting of Co-op's game room. The energy of the party had shifted as everyone gathered around the couch, just waiting to see what would happen next.

If Brandon would throw the first punch.

Knowing a fight would even further complicate matters, I decided I needed to step in. Breathing in deep, I left the couch and jogged over to the shrinking space between Matt and Brandon.

"Hey, I agree with Matt," I said, touching Brandon's shoulder. "Let's not fight over this."

Eva smirked, mimicking my words under her breath.

"Shut up, Eva. This doesn't concern you," Brandon said.

"Like hell it doesn't," she said.

"Oh, so you want to fill in for Matt? Think you can throw a punch?" asked Brandon.

"Sorry, I'm not barbaric," said Eva. "Though I am sick of your act. You think you can badmouth Matt and vote us out of the group? Well I have news for you. You aren't the only one who can play this game."

Eva pushed Brandon aside and stepped onto the back of the couch.

"Wait, Eva, what are you doing? I told you, I don't want to fight," I said, reaching for her purse as she breezed by me.

"Sorry, Livs, but I'm afraid this is overdue."

My nose scrunched as I tried to think back to why Eva hated me in the first place. But as always, I seemed to be missing that critical piece of information.

"Please Eva, isn't there anything I can do?" I asked.

She shook her head, then straightened her back, ready to address the crowd.

"To all of Populatti," she said. "I, Eva Mallot, hereby nominate Brandon Dash and Olivia Stanley for termination."

I choked back tears as a chill ran down my spine. I looked to Brandon, hoping for some assurance that this couldn't be happening, but his eyes were fixed on Matt and Eva. Turning to my right, I spotted Crystal in the crowd, but she was silent, her eyes glued to the ground as Eva scanned the group for supporters. Tara and Sammy were still missing in action.

"On what grounds do you propose termination?" asked someone in the crowd.

"Where do I start?" said Eva. "Brandon and Livi are guilty of disgusting PDA, backstabbing other Popsters, and as you have seen here tonight, they have a complete disregard for civilized behavior. So, does anyone second the motion?"

"This is insane," I said, staring up into Eva's fiery eyes. "A vote doesn't even count unless it's online. I thought you'd know the rules, but then you've been in the group for what? Two weeks?"

"Three. And don't worry, we'll make it official. So do I have a second?"

My eyes darted to Matt, daring him to speak. He dropped his face to the floor, but kept his mouth shut. Brandon grabbed my hand and clasped it tight. Eva continued to taunt us from her perch.

"Don't worry, she'll never get the votes," he said, giving my hand an extra squeeze.

I nodded and squeezed back, even though I didn't share his confidence. Guys were more forgiving than girls. In the female kingdom, grudges were common. And judging by the number of popsters I'd dealt with in council for sneaking off campus, forging hall passes and skipping class, there were probably plenty of them that would be happy to see me gone. I held my breath as I realized the gravity of the situation. Even though I was Crys's best friend, even though I was an honor council rep, even though I tried my best to play by all the rules, I was still vulnerable. Deep down, no different than Drumstick. Open to ridicule. Open to termination.

"Anyone? A second? Matt, a little help here," said Eva.

Silence enveloped the crowd.

I let out my breath as Matt walked to the door.

Maybe I was going to be okay after all.

Matt may have been pissed, but he would never turn on B-Dash – a good friend and teammate – in public. And without his support, this whole thing could die. Eva was out of control. Anyone who didn't know that already knew that now. No one would listen to her. And no girl would support terminating the gorgeous, all-popular B-Dash, especially without support from any guys. Why risk tainting the remaining dating pool?

"Sorry Eva, looks like the only one they want to get rid of is you," I said under my breath.

"Yeah, everyone just relax. Fight's over," Brandon said. "Eva, why don't we talk later, okay?"

Eva's shoulders slumped as she crawled down off the couch. Glancing back at Crystal, I held up my hand, buying myself a minute. But before I could utter another word to B-Dash, a sharp voice made my blood run cold.

"Wait a second," it said. "Eva, I'm with you. I'll second the vote."

populatti.com

<u>lululivi : 72%</u>

Approved Members: 24
Pending Applications: 3
Access Denied: 45

POP REPORT: sorry guys, I'm speechless ☹ ~ Crys

COMMENTS:

celebSAMmy *posted at 2:45 p.m. ET May 17*: THIS IS RIDICULOUS!! THERE IS NO POPULATTI WITHOUT LIVI OR BRANDON!!

Tony45 *posted at 1:30 p.m. ET May 17*: can we vote for matt and not eva or does it have to be a package deal?

Tarable *posted at 1:03 p.m. ET May 17*: Brandon and Livi I luvvvv you!!!

ValieGal *posted at 12:45 p.m. ET May 17*: sorry livs, but uve been WAY outta line lately….

JessisBest *posted at 11:01 a.m. ET May 17*: eva, do u think u really can get 13 votes?

Jake *posted at 12:54 a.m. ET May 17*: sorry matt, gotta go with dash on this one…

CHAPTER EIGHT

I pulled my comforter over my head as Dad barged into my room without knocking.

"Olly honey, you ready for driving?" he asked.

I rolled over and moaned. "Not today. I think I've got the flu or something."

He frowned, then drew closer and placed his hand on my forehead. "Well, no fever. But if you're not up to driving, this must be serious. Let me know if your throat starts to hurt and I can do a strep test. There's been a lot of it going around the hospital."

"Thanks Dad. It feels fine now, but I'll let you know."

He turned off the overhead light and closed my

door on his way out. As soon as the door clicked shut, I peeled off the blankets and crawled down under my bed, flicking off the heating pad that was supposed to have produced a fever. With two parents as doctors it was almost impossible to pull off a fake sickness, but it never stopped me from trying my best.

With the heating pad turned off, I returned to Populatti. Everything looked just as it had ten minutes earlier, except for a new comment from some freshman asking which side to take. Ugh, as if she needed to ask. I still couldn't believe anyone thought Eva deserved to be in Populatti at all. And terminating Brandon and me? What were these people thinking? Didn't they know that we'd done nothing wrong? Eva and Matt had been the ones to steal booze and break a lamp. All we'd done was steal a few kisses. Oh and discipline Eva for cheating on her Physics test. As if that could justify this kind of reaction.

I brought my hands to my temples just as my phone lit up with an incoming call. The caller ID was restricted, but I picked up anyway, forcing my voice to sound friendly. Right now was no time for call screening. I needed as many friends as I could get.

"I just tried the house but your dad said you're sick. What's going on?" Tara asked.

"What's up with the restricted number?"

"I dropped my phone in the sink this morning

so I'm using my mom's. She scrambles it for work."

"Eww, that sucks. When you gonna get a new one?"

"I'm on my way to Verizon now."

"Want company?"

"Think you can escape quarantine?"

I peeked out my window just in time to see my dad loading the twins into the car along with two bags of bats and balls. "Depends. How long will it take?"

"I don't know. An hour?"

"Pick me up in ten. My dad's taking out the twins. That'll buy us at least two."

"Okay, hang tight. I'm three blocks away," she said before clicking off.

Deciding I'd better look sick in case I was caught in public, I slid off my pajamas and replaced them with a tank top, yoga pants, and hoodie. After fastening my hair in a ponytail, I slid down the staircase with a magazine in hand, almost colliding with Dad on the last step.

"Hey Olly, I was just gonna come talk to you. I'm taking the boys to the Sports Zone to hit some balls. You think you'll be okay here for a few hours on your own?" he asked.

"Yeah sure, I'm just gonna lie down on the couch for a while, maybe throw on a movie," I said.

"All right. You can get me on my phone if anything comes up and Mom should be home by 3:00 if you need her."

"Thanks Dad," I said, leaning in to kiss his cheek. After a tight hug, he gave a wave and disappeared out the door. I waited until the car had exited the driveway before lacing up my sneakers and turning on the TV. By the time Tara arrived, the scene had been set. I'd placed a Gatorade bottle on the coffee table along with two tabloid magazines. My favorite fleece blanket was crumpled over the couch cushions and the TV was tuned to MTV. Since it was Lona's day off, I knew the room should be undisturbed until my return. If anyone did pop in early, I'd say Tara picked me up to grab something to eat. No one could argue with a sick girl, as long as the ruse was convincing.

"Oh God, not the pink hoodie. You look terrible," Tara said, entering without a knock.

"Unfortunately, it's not life-threatening."

"You're not really sick, are you?"

"Nah, just wasn't in the mood for driving lessons. I needed some time alone."

"This is all going to blow over, you know. I talked to Bianca this morning. She was apologetic."

I slid into Tara's Prius without a word.

"It's not her fault Val seconded the nomination," Tara said.

"Then why did Val bring up the toe incident? How many times do I have to tell people I didn't smash Bianca's toe on purpose?"

"I don't know, Livs, really I don't. I'm floored too. I always thought Val liked us. But I guess when you and Dash started making out at Coop's, Bianca got upset and ran to Val. I guess she thought she had to stand up for her teammate."

I banged my hand into the passenger window, scuffing the tops of my knuckles.

"So this is all because Bianca likes Brandon?" I asked.

"Potentially."

I looked out the window at the swaying trees and clusters of blooming hydrangeas and lilacs and azaleas. Tara turned left then right down another winding side road. Usually, looking at the changing landscape was one of my favorite activities. Especially when I could stare out at people's gardens. Mom had hooked me on flowers back in Boston where she was known for her flower boxes, always overflowing with brilliant blooms. It was one of the few activities she'd always made time for, and even now we usually spent a few hours each spring planting snapdragons and begonias and petunias in the garden lining our front walkway.

But today, despite my best efforts to stare at the passing flowers and focus on the present, the past never left my mind. Every time I blinked I was taken back to the night before, to the scene following Val's declaration when Brandon had run after Matt and screamed at him for being a thief and having bad taste in women. All true, but none of it helpful for Brandon's approval rating, which like mine, had dipped into the seventies overnight. Apparently even the females were turning on B-Dash.

"So as of now there are two votes against you," Tara said as she navigated the Prius into a brick-covered strip mall.

"They need 13, right?" I asked, even though I had the number memorized.

"Uh-huh. So far we've got ten on our side voting to keep you both in. There's the four of us girls, Brandon, Jake, Christian, my friend Jess from Chem class, Sammy's friend Ella, and Tony."

"So we need three more. We should be able to get that by this afternoon, right?"

"That's the idea."

"And to think, I left the house looking like a recluse for nothing."

Twenty minutes later, we were back in the car and on our way to my house with Crys and Sammy set to meet us there. I'd called the house and Dad was still out, making it the perfect time for a quick powwow to catch up on the latest developments. Sammy and Crystal were in the driveway when we pulled in. Tara parked under a plume of gray smoke spewing out of the Beast's exhaust pipe, shaking her head as she threw the car into park.

"It's bad enough she has to drive that thing, but to leave it running in a parking lot? Does she want to deep fry the planet?" Tara asked.

"She does like French fries. And besides, it's cold outside. You can't expect them to go without heat. They could get sick."

Tara made a face before bursting into laughter. "At least someone's feeling better."

"That's all thanks to you. Ten votes. Amazing."

But Crystal and Sammy did not seem so enthused. After leaping out of the Beast, they walked to the front door, their mouths sealed until we entered the family room. Neither one would look me in the eye. Or crack a smile.

"Is Brandon coming?" Sammy asked after an awkward silence.

"Jake's bringing him. They should be here in a half-hour," Crystal said.

"Good. Let's get started then."

"Guys? What's going on? Tara said we had 10 peeps ready to vote for me. Isn't that a slam dunk?" I asked.

"When's the last time you checked Populatti?" Crystal asked.

"I dunno, right before Tarable picked me up. Around 1:30 or so?"

"Yeah, something like that," Tara said.

"I stopped checking once Tara told me things looked okay."

"Well then we better sit down," Sammy said.

"Why? What happened? Did someone post something?" I asked.

"Livi. It's awful. I don't know how else to say it, but they're beyond commenting. People started voting, and not how they told us they would." Crystal whispered the words, as if she was handing down a death sentence.

Before I could even process what she was saying, my tongue got heavy in my mouth and my arms broke out in goose bumps. I grabbed the sleeves of my sweatshirt and hid my hands inside, searching for warmth I knew was no longer there. Then I collapsed down next to Crystal and brought my knees up to my chin.

"What, what's my approval rating?" I asked.

"65%" said Sammy.

I cringed, then nodded. "So I'm still safe there."

"For the time being, yes," said Crystal. "But the approval rating seems to be matching the breakdown of votes. And not everyone has voted yet."

I looked down, clasped and unclasped my hands, then looked into Crystal's eyes.

"What's the tally?"

"As of right now, they've got 11."

"Eleven! How on earth did they get 11?"

I jumped up off the couch, surprising myself with my newfound energy. The pile of magazines and half-full Gatorade I'd laid out earlier went flying onto Mom's braided rug as the coffee table toppled over. Crystal ran toward the kitchen for a rag as the purple sugar water seeped into the rug's swirling pattern, forming an amoeba-shaped stain.

"Calm down, hon. They're still two votes short," said Tara, reaching for my arm. But for once even the voice of reason didn't look reassured. Her face was ashen. Her honey pink hair looked white.

"Yeah, and we're gonna work hard to keep it that way. Crys and I have been rounding the troops all morning and so far we've gotten six votes. Once Brandon gets here we can go online and enter your two votes so that we have eight," said Sammy.

"So what happened to our 10?" I asked.

Sammy turned to Crystal. When she nodded, Sammy continued. "We lost my friend Jess today, and Christian is still unsure. I guess Bianca made them change their minds."

"But you told me that Bianca was apologetic! That she didn't want any trouble!"

"That's what she said when I talked to her after breakfast, but then something must have happened. I don't know what Val said to her, but it sounds like she's been trying to steal votes all day."

"This is a nightmare," I said, as my nose began to run.

"I know," said Crystal. "And that's not even the worst of it."

"What could be worse?"

Sammy coaxed me back onto the couch. "Remember how we entered Matt and Eva in together, so that you had to vote both of them out at the same time?"

"Yeah, of course. It made sense that way since Eva is only a member because she's dating Matt."

"Right. But Eva entered it differently. She brought you and Brandon up in different posts. So people could choose who to vote for," Sammy said.

"Why would she do that? Doesn't that just mean that people have to vote twice?"

"I think that's the point. You've got 11 votes, but Brandon's only got four. They're using this to get rid of you and keep Brandon."

"What? What the hell!" I was crying now. Hysterical. Not making sense. The room was spinning like the swirling carpet underneath my feet, moving faster and faster until all the colors and faces and furniture melted together. I closed my eyes and let the tears flow out of the creases, without making any effort to stop them.

"What's gonna happen if I get kicked out? Why would they do this to me?" I stuttered, realizing no one could make out what I was saying through my sobs.

"Calm down," said Crystal. "They're still two votes short and we're gonna keep it that way. Brandon and Jake are gonna be here soon to help us brainstorm. There are a few members who are still undecided. If the guys work their magic, I'm sure we can sway them."

"I hope so."

"I know so," said Sammy. "Now Tara, you're closest with Coop so why don't you give him a call, and Crystal, can you help get Livi cleaned up? You don't want B-Dash seeing you a mess, do you?"

I shook my head.

"All right then, let's get to work. Livs, I promise everything is going to be okay," said Sammy.

"If you say so."

"I do. Now where's your laptop? I'm entering Tara and your votes now before it's too late."

My teeth clenched as Sammy's voice faded into the distance. *Before it's too late.* I played the words over in my head as Crystal steered me toward the bathroom, knowing full well that what she meant was, we had to get our numbers up before they hit 13. Because once Eva had 13 votes, anything we did was useless. In the bathroom, I collapsed onto the rim of the bathtub and let Crystal drench my face until it was cool to the touch. As the red faded, she brushed out my hair and pinned it back in a neat bun.

"Crys, is there anything you can do? You know, from the backend?" I asked, staring down. "Like, at least to save my approval rating?"

Crys nodded as she smoothed my flyaways. "I've already manually entered a stop at 60%. I did it a long time ago, actually, for all four of us. They can't get rid of you based on your approval rating."

I turned back, blinking away tears as I looked into Crystal's eyes. "Really? You mean it?"

She smiled. "Yes, but don't tell anyone, especially the girls. The whole group would probably collapse into chaos if they knew I wasn't playing fair."

"But it's your site. You should be able to do what you want."

"Yeah, but the site works because everyone's

supposed to be treated the same. Which is why I have to let this vote happen or else risk having the site implode. And you know how much this site means to my college application. It's only impressive if I can send them a live link, you know, to show that people actually use it."

Once again, I looked away from Crystal, letting her rearrange my bun. I knew it was selfish to want her to choose helping me over MIT and a lifetime of parental disappointment. Especially after she'd already rigged my approval rating.

Back when Crys started the site, she always said she wanted everyone to like her for her personality, not just for her ability to rule Golden Hill's social life. That seemed important. Like how I always played fair in honor council because I didn't want friends who thought they could get away with bending the rules. I wanted to be in Populatti because people wanted me there, not because of Crystal. Because what fun would it be to belong to a group where everyone just had nasty things to say behind my back?

Crystal finished scrubbing mascara off my face just as Tara burst into the bathroom.

"I've got Coop back," she said, pausing to catch her breath.

"Thank God," I said.

Crystal pulled out her phone. "He just voted. We're up to nine now against Eva and Matt."

"Oh God, we still need four more," I said.

"Coop's going to ask Val to change her vote," Tara said.

"Can she do that? Even though Val seconded the nomination?" I asked.

"There's no rule against it," Crystal said. "And given Val's crush on Coop, he might have a chance convincing her."

"I hope this works," I said as Brandon and Jake barged through the door.

Jake was holding a bag of McDonald's in his left hand and his leather gloves in the other. His shirt was untucked and his expression looked concerned. I figured he was worried less about me than about upsetting Crystal. He knew how close the four of us girls were and something told me the idea of dealing with Crys being down a best friend was not something he wanted to think about. Not to mention that he was still in my English group. I shook my head as my eyes turned to Brandon, still in disbelief that any of this was happening.

Brandon looked like Brandon, well groomed and laid back in a light pink polo and slim cut jeans. I wondered how he could look so relaxed when his own approval rating had dropped to 72%. But then, that was still far from the danger zone. And Brandon only had four votes against him. Meaning he was still cool, calm, and apparently not worrying about what would happen to me. Because except for the squeeze he gave my arm when he walked in, he acted like nothing was wrong.

Brandon sat on the couch next to me and rolled back his shoulders, then ran his hand through my hair. "I am so sorry babe," he said, "I promise I'm gonna make this right. There is no way you're getting kicked out."

His eyes met mine for a second before drifting to the TV, then Jake, and then the kitchen down the hall. They were everywhere but looking into mine. Feeling more alone than ever, I tried to hold back the waterworks.

"They've got 11 votes against me," I said.

"Make that twelve. Bianca's friend Michelle just sided with Eva," said Crystal, waving her phone.

"This is ridiculous," said Sammy. "Isn't there something we can do? Crys, can't you just sign in and change the votes?"

Crystal frowned.

"It's okay guys," I said. "I don't want to win like that. Besides, if Crys changes someone's vote, everyone will know it. The last thing we want is more trouble. All someone needs to do is get angry enough to show the site to a parent or teacher and we're done."

Brandon reached for the Gatorade bottle rolling near my feet. "This sucks," he said, taking a sip. He brought his free hand to mine. Feeling his sweaty palm, my eyes met his. B-Dash may have been putting on a strong face, but he was scared. Relief rushed though my veins. Maybe he cared more about me than I realized.

"Wait guys, I have a thought," said Tara, inching closer to the group. "I agree that Crys should not mess with the votes or anything. But why don't we take the site offline for a bit until this blows over? Claim there's server trouble or something," she said. "That way we're not messing with the results directly, just buying ourselves some more time."

All eyes turned to Crystal as she waved her head from side to side.

"Huh, that might work," she said. "We could say it's down due to increased traffic, and that we'll get it back up tomorrow. That'll buy us a day to get in touch with the undecided."

"OhmiGod, Tara you're a genius," I said, running into her arms.

She laughed before hugging me back. "I am not a genius, Livs. I just don't know what any of us would do without you in Populatti."

"Dismantle the site?" I said without thinking.

Crystal scooted Sammy away from the laptop and signed into her account. "If I didn't need this baby up and running for my MIT application, that's exactly what we'd do," she said.

"Girl, you know you don't need some website to get into school. You're like the freaking valedictorian," said Sammy.

"Maybe so, but I have to get into their new computer science program. And this site is the ticket. Who knows, if they like it enough maybe they could even get me hooked up with investors, help me launch it to the world. At the very least, getting into the program would definitely help chill out my mom, for the first semester anyway," Crystal said.

"And that is why we are not going to let you get voted out of Populatti," said Tara. "This way Crys keeps her site, we keep our Livi, and everyone except Eva is happy."

The air felt warmer as everyone crowded around Crystal and her magical phone. After a few swipes in her custom app, she let out a breath, then reached for my laptop. She pulled up the internet, then typed a string of numbers and letters into the browser without looking up. Five sets of eyes stared in awe as she clicked furiously, ignoring the chatter of the group.

Feeling dizzy, I leaned into Brandon and buried my head. "Is the site down yet?"

"Just one more sec," Crystal said. "I just have to redirect the site here. Place the files into the folder... Okay. Sammy, test it on your phone. It should be down."

Sammy hunched over her screen as I held my breath. "It's temporarily unavailable," Sammy said. "You are amazing!"

"I know, I know," Crystal said, taking a bow.

My muscles relaxed as I pulled my weight off Brandon.

"Now let me just check one more thing on my phone. I wanna make sure I'm signed out everywhere." Crystal reached into her purse and pulled out her phone. After unlocking her keyboard, she pursed her lips. "Uh-oh," she mumbled, throwing it onto the counter.

"What is it now?" asked Sammy.

"I got an update while I was taking down the site. I think... it looks like Christian changed his vote. Livi, that gives them 13."

populatti.com

This Site is Temporarily Unavailable. Please check back later.

CHAPTER NINE

"Hey honey, feeling any better?" asked Mom as she hung her coat in the closet. Only two hours had passed since everyone had scattered, but it felt like an eternity. Even with the site down, knowing I'd been voted out of Populatti had made me sick for real this time. And wishing that the girls could have stayed longer.

"Yeah, I'm all right." I lied as I tried to ignore the rumbling in my stomach. I was on the couch now cuddled under a heap of blankets with a sappy romantic comedy on the TV.

"Dad said it isn't strep, so that's promising. Probably just a virus," Mom said.

I sighed, thinking about how hard I'd had to work to appear sick that morning. And how easy it came to me now.

"Yeah, I guess," I said, my voice wavering.

"I'm going up to shower. You need anything first?"

"Nah, but I did just talk to Tara. She was going to come pick me up to watch a movie at her house. I thought it could be good for me to do something."

Mom walked over, pulled a thermometer out of her back pocket, placed a sterile plastic sleeve over the metal indicator, and shoved it into my mouth before I could say another word. I gagged as the cold plastic caught under my tongue. I tried to look away and concentrate on my breathing, but before I could regain control, my stomach was pushing out not only the thermometer, but the handful of fries I'd stolen earlier from Jake. Lucky for me, my ever-prepared mother grabbed the trash can just in time.

"You all right, sweetheart?" she asked.

My lungs burned. "Yeah, I'm okay."

"Looks like you should lie down. You can see Tara tomorrow if you're feeling better."

My head began to throb as she shot down my plans. "But Mom, I'm fine. The thermometer just made me gag like it always does."

"Livi, your color is bad, you're sweating through your clothes, and you've been on this couch all day. I'd say you're sick, and you need to rest or you won't get better."

"This is important though," I said, my mind searching for a reason why that didn't mention Populatti.

"Tara's been freaking out because of this guy she likes who was going to ask her out until this other girl interfered, making a big old mess. She really needs advice, Mom."

As expected, Mom didn't buy it. "If you need to talk about this tonight, I am sure you can use the phone. Otherwise, you'll be much more of a help tomorrow once your head clears. Now let's get you back in bed. I'll bring up some dinner in a little while."

I nodded and followed her lead, knowing it was better not to argue. It was just a matter of time before another woman went into labor or something happened in the ER that summoned both my parents back to work. And then I'd be free to do whatever I wanted without having to fight. Dealing with Populatti was crisis enough. I didn't have the energy to wage another battle with my parents.

And sure enough, Mom wasn't home for an hour before her beeper was vibrating, and she was running toward the phone, then door, keys and coat in hand. One of her patients pregnant with twins had gone into labor a month early, meaning it was going to be a late night.

"Pray for us," Mom said as she rushed out the door, repeating the familiar phrase she said every time one of her patients was in trouble.

"Good luck honey," Dad said as his phone started ringing. His call was nothing serious, though, and he was back at the Monopoly board with the twins after ten minutes. Around 8:00 after hearing two breakdowns from Charlie pelting plastic hotels at Chris, I gave up on the idea of sneaking out and called Tara.

"What's the latest?" I asked as soon as I heard her pick up.

"One sec, I'm on the other line with Crystal," she said.

I crinkled my toes underneath the blanket and braced myself for the worst. Last we'd left it, Tara was going to invite Coop over to try to talk some sense into him. Because while we all knew he'd changed his vote, no one else did. As long as we could change his mind before Monday, I was still in Populatti. But hours had passed since Tara's supposed meeting and I still hadn't heard a thing.

"Hey, sorry about that," said Tara. "I was just talking to Crys about getting people to change their votes while the site's down. Coop said he'd consider it."

"OhmiGod, really?"

"Don't get too excited. I didn't get the best vibe. He seemed hesitant, like he was worried about what everyone would think."

"Everyone? Who would know?"

"I guess Val, and he doesn't want to upset her.

Apparently in addition to the Bianca incident, Val's pissed because Eva told her you've been badmouthing her to guys for years and that's why she's never had a boyfriend."

"What? That's insane! I like Val. I've never said anything about her in my life." My voice was starting to crack.

"I know, that's what I told Coop."

"Did he believe you?"

"I'm not sure."

"Has everyone lost their minds? Lemme call Val, I'm sure we can work this out ourselves," I said, as I thought back to our past conversations. What had I ever said? Nothing came to mind but mindless chatter about parties, classes, and congratulatory comments after her softball games. Sure, it was common knowledge that Val didn't date, but I'd always thought it was because she didn't want a boyfriend. That she would rather be one of the guys than lose that intimate camaraderie that comes with being just friends. Kind of like how Sammy loved to be a flirt, but couldn't imagine being tied down.

But what if her laissez-faire attitude was all a ploy to get a guy? I brought my hand to my mouth as I realized I might be on the right track. Maybe she would believe Eva, and think someone like me was sabotaging her. But why was Eva working so hard to destroy my social life? For the millionth time, I tried to think of a reason but came up short.

"You know, maybe you shouldn't call," said Tara. "Last thing we need is for you to say something that gives Val more ammunition."

"You sure that's smart? I mean, I really think Val has the wrong idea about what's going on."

Tara paused. "Yeah, let's leave Val out of it," she said. "We don't want her any angrier."

"All right. If you think that's best," I said, still unconvinced.

"I really do."

"So my fate still hinges on Coop."

"Yeah, and oh Livs, that's him calling now. I'll call you back in a second," she said before clicking off the line.

I spent the next thirty minutes going through my closet, trying to make myself feel better. Ms. Tilfry had gotten the film festival idea approved by the principal and the event had been growing more lavish by the day, thanks to Sammy's involvement. Meaning I was going to need a dress for the occasion. Even though the premier was still weeks away, I figured it was safe to at least scope out my dress collection in case I needed to buy something new. The film festival was the one event that wasn't dependent on Populatti. Even if Eva did succeed in getting me offline, she couldn't kick me out of school.

After trying on two dresses I'd bought last fall and still hadn't worn, my phone began vibrating on my bed. I ran over and grabbed it. A message from

Tara flooded the screen. All it said was 'b there soon.'

Tara showed up with Crystal and Sammy around 9:00 just as Dad and the twins went up to bed. I waited for the hall lights to go off before ushering the girls into the sunroom located in the back of the house. With no second floor above it, the sunroom was the quietest, and coldest, room of the house. It also had a sliding back door that provided the perfect escape route should anyone hear us. So after spreading out a heap of blankets, I plopped onto one of the wicker chairs in the corner and waited for the girls to speak. Just like earlier, Sammy was the spokesperson.

"Christian's leaving his vote as is," she said in a monotone. "He talked to Eva earlier and I guess she threatened to destroy his reputation if he didn't go along. Since he's still pretty new here, he didn't want to take the chance."

Surprising myself, I didn't scream, or curse, or cry. I just sat there, unable to even blink.

"You okay Livs?" asked Tara. "We've already talked about it. We're gonna take turns. One of us will skip the Pop parties and hang out with you each weekend, and then after a couple weeks, we should be able to vote you in again."

"Can you take a few weeks off from throwing parties?" I asked, my voice a whisper.

Sammy frowned. "Next Saturday Eva's parents are going out of town for Memorial Day. It's the big party I've been planning with Matt for weeks. If we cancel now, Eva could bring the rest of us up for termination as well."

"And we can't get you back in if we're not members," Tara said.

"Nor can the site survive," said Crystal.

Listening to their excuses, a wave of anger replaced the shock.

"This is so not fair. I'm out of Populatti and Brandon escapes unscathed, even though he's the one that started everything with Matt."

"Yeah, I'd ask him to resign if I were you," Crystal said.

"Really? You're my best friends and you won't even cancel a party. And you're the one who made the site, Crystal! You could pull the plug at any time!" I was yelling now, even though I knew if I didn't shut up, I'd wake up Dad.

"Livi, I'm sorry, but I need the site for college. I've been working on it for years now!"

"I know. MIT is more important than my friendship."

"I didn't say that. But you do know what my parents will do to me if I don't get in. And like I said, we'll have you back in as soon as possible. Like two weeks, tops. I promise."

"But what if you still don't have the votes in two weeks? Can't you just work on something else? A new site?"

"Not by September. First I'd need a new idea,

and then I'd have to somehow find the time to build it, get it running, and spread the word. Between SAT prep and that summer math camp I'm going to, that's pretty much impossible."

"But Crystal, I need this."

"Look, I'm applying to MIT early action next fall. If this means that much to you, then as soon as I hear back, I'll disband the site."

"But that's not 'til December. By then I'll have missed the entire summer and fall. And how will I see you guys this summer if I'm not able to go to any parties? Everyone will forget about me!"

"You know that's not true," said Crystal. "And I'm sorry, but that's the best I can do. Though you really need to calm down. In a couple weeks this whole thing will be over and we'll have you back in the group, long before summer break."

"Easy for you to say. You can do whatever you want and no one can bring you up for termination. But here your best friend, the one that freaking introduced you to Jake and everyone else important, gets into trouble and your hands are tied. It's insane!"

Crystal made a face as Sammy cut in. "Livs, it's gonna be okay. Tara will chill with you next weekend, and after Eva's party we'll reevaluate. Who knows, maybe Matt will break up with her right after the party like he's been saying. If that happens, she'll lose her membership and getting you in will be a cakewalk."

"Yeah, exactly," said Tara. "But one thing. Sammy, I thought you were skipping Eva's next weekend. I told Coop I'd be there. We need to win him back as an ally."

Sammy nodded, then started thinking out loud. "Hmm, as social chair I really should monitor this one with it being Eva and all, but I'm sure we can figure something out. Maybe Crys can stay?"

Crystal smiled, then shook her head when she thought I wasn't looking.

I picked up a pillow and folded it in half as my head throbbed. Then I walked over to the sliding door, unlatched the deadbolt, and swung it open.

"Maybe it would be best if you all just leave," I said. "And don't worry about who has to give up their precious Saturday night to deal with poor LuLuLivi because I don't want to see any of you, got it?"

"Livi, stop it, you don't mean that," said Tara, reaching for the pillow. I flung it at her face just as her fingertips reached my arm.

"Oww, that hurt," she said.

"Get out," I repeated louder.

Crystal grabbed her purse and marched out the door. Tara shook her head, then followed.

Sammy stood up out of her chair and walked right up to my face. "I'll call you tomorrow, Livs, but you need to calm down. We're your only chance at getting back into Populatti. I suggest you don't forget it."

That night sleep did not come easily. Even after a tearful call with Brandon where he promised to skip Eva's party and only stay in Populatti to help get me back in, I couldn't shake the feeling that my friends didn't care about me enough to sacrifice one iota of their happiness. It didn't help that every time I closed my eyes, all I could see was Crystal's forced grin as she claimed there was nothing she could do to help. And every time I rolled over, I heard Tara, pretending that she was the one person in all of Populatti who was close enough to Christian to sway his vote, as if her crush made her an expert on a guy none of us knew two months earlier.

The site went back up the next morning, and the results of the vote confirmed what I'd already been told. I was kicked out, Eva and Matt were still in. In the end they had received seven votes against them too – and B-Dash was the safest of all, having received just four, despite igniting the spark that caused the whole incident. And while my friends all posted about how Populatti had lost its greatest member, I knew deep down it was just for show. Not one of them called me all day. Not that I cared since the nighttime powwow in the unheated sunroom had given me a real cold I couldn't talk myself out of.

Though things started to look up when Mom took pity on me that afternoon and said Brandon could come over for a quick visit. Only ten minutes before his scheduled arrival, he canceled with a text, saying something had come up with his parents. Leaving me to prepare for Monday morning alone. Without my friends. Without Brandon. And without Populatti. All of a sudden, my days flying under the radar as Drumstick didn't look so bad. At least then I hadn't known what it felt like to be included. I'd always just been the odd one out.

populatti.com

Please Sign In!

Username: LuluLivi

Password: ********

I'm sorry but the password and username provided do not match. Please reenter and try again.

CHAPTER TEN

"No!" I said as I tried entering my password and username into the Populatti site for the fifteenth time. When the same message appeared, I sunk my head onto the clunky school keyboard and cried.

"You okay?" asked the girl sitting next to me.

I lifted my head and forced a smile. "Yeah, I'm fine, thanks. It's just not my day."

The girl nodded before turning back to her screen.

With only fourteen minutes left on the clock before English class, I'd been desperate to sneak a peek at Populatti so that I could at least have some inkling of what was going on before having to face

Jake, Matt, and Bianca – not to mention Sammy, Crys, and Tara, who were also in the class. But with Crys changing my password sometime in the past eight hours, learning anything new seemed unlikely. She'd even gone so far as to change her own passwords, as if she knew I would be snooping. And as if letting me snoop could somehow harm her precious site.

Having no intel to work with, the thought of meeting with my group seemed overwhelming, especially since, to the best of my knowledge, not one of us had talked to another about solidifying a topic for our video. We were supposed to be handing in a one-page summary on our topic, explaining why we selected it. Knowing I could type a page in five minutes flat, I debated putting something together right then so we wouldn't arrive empty-handed. Chances were I wouldn't pick the best topic, but it could win me points with Bianca and Matt. Only problem was that when I tried to think of what to write, not a single topic came to mind. Except maybe describing the injustices of Populatti, which I knew would never fly.

So off I went dreaming of Plan B, which included a trip to the nurse's office and an early dismissal. While my fever had broken early the night before, I looked weak enough that I knew I could convince the nurse, and my parents, that I was sick. The thought was tempting, tantalizing actually, except that I knew even if I played sick today, I would have to face school again tomorrow, not to mention English class on Wednesday. And as much as I wished it would, that group project wasn't going away. So I settled on Plan C. Go to class, avoid the girls, and accept that for the first time in my history as a student, I was going to class unprepared.

Tension filled the air as I entered the stuffy classroom. Ms. Tilfry had arranged the desks into clusters of four, allowing for easy interaction with group members. And eliminating any possibility of ignoring the fact that we had to work together. Eying my pod across the room, I shuffled over, head low, and tried to pretend that no one was looking at me. Though given the stares I'd been fielding all day, I assumed about eighty percent of the eyes in the room were on me.

The twenty percent not looking included Jake, Matt, and Bianca, who seemed even more enthralled by the floor than I was as I slid into the empty seat next to Jake. Under normal circumstances I would have been relieved to have a desk length of distance from Matt and Bianca, but given that Crys and I still weren't talking, Jake also wasn't exactly my biggest fan.

"All right class, welcome," said Ms. Tilfry, saving me from a classroom of awkward glances.

"As you can see, today and for the next few weeks, this will not be English class, but Film 101. You will sit with your groups and use these sessions to work on your scripts and summary assignments, and later to go out in the field or around the school to film your short videos. Any filming you need to do off school grounds will have to be arranged for after school hours. Once a week we will also conduct check-in sessions, where we'll run through the rubric and checklist I handed out last week to ensure each group is on pace to complete their video ahead of premier night."

Ms. Tilfry's voice rose as she discussed the film festival, thanking her insightful students for such a wonderful idea. The event was indeed approved, would take place on a Friday night in the auditorium, and would include the entire sophomore class. Freshmen would be invited as well to help them learn what would be expected next year, as this was to be an annual project. All in all, it was shaping up to be the biggest event of the spring. I could only imagine the after party Sammy was probably already planning.

After wrapping up her speech, Ms. Tilfry told us to get to work and that she would visit each group to collect our topic summaries and discuss the issues we had chosen. My hands shook as Ms. Tilfry turned to me, a smile plastered on her face. Her enthusiasm made me feel even worse about having failed to throw something together in study hall. English had always been one of my best classes, and Ms. Tilfry with her zany projects and less than orthodox reading list was by far my favorite teacher of sophomore year. Yet here I was smiling back at her as I sat on my shaky palms, knowing full well that I'd let her down.

Still hopeful that maybe Jake or Bianca or Matt had felt the inclination to step up and write something, I turned to them, half expecting them to fill me in on a missed group meeting, or at least a casual conversation. But their heads were still staring into the fake wood grain Formica desks, analyzing each crack and pencil marking as if somehow they would deliver us a topic.

Turning to Jake, I sighed. Ms. Tilfry was talking to the group next to us. We didn't have much time. "So, uh, have any of you given this some thought?" I said.

Bianca shook her head. Matt pretended not to hear me.

"I did, but came up with nothing. Guess there's not a lot of issues out there that bother me," said Jake, not sounding the least bit angry at me.

I resisted the urge to hug him.

"Okay, well, I know we need something, so I was thinking..."

Ms. Tilfry cut me off with another thousand-watt smile. "So Livi, what were you thinking? After the alternate ending you wrote for *The Scarlett Letter* last unit, I have to say, I have high hopes for this group. I am so impressed with your creativity."

The shaking spread from my palms to my wrists and elbows as Ms. Tilfry looked down at me.

My eyes darted from side to side, out the window and into the parking lot, then back in around the classroom, then up to the tiled ceiling, still water-stained in the center from the pipe bursting the year before. And that's when it came to me. *Of course*, I thought, breathing deeper. *The pipes. The mold. The overcrowding.*

My confidence building, I looked up at Ms. Tilfry and smiled. "Now I was thinking, that, even though our topic is pretty narrow, that it is actually quite important."

Bianca and Matt perked up as I began talking with my steadying hands.

Ms. Tilfry nodded, waiting for me to move on. "You know, sometimes the narrowest problems are the best to tackle. Take on too much and it can become difficult to make your point, especially in ten minutes."

"Exactly," I said, "Which is why we decided that our video is going to focus on Golden Hill High. And not on the school in general, but on the building, and all the problems it's had. Just in the two years I've been here there's been the water main break, the mold, and the overcrowding that seems to get worse each month. These are big problems that really affect the way students here learn. We talk a lot about the school environment in terms of people and teachers and stuff, but not a lot is said about the actual building. And the building has really been failing."

"Interesting," said Ms. Tilfry. "Though a lot of the problems you mention have been fixed. How will you address that?"

I paused, unsure how to answer.

"Through interviews," said Jake, "with students and faculty members like yourself. We will have them talk about the lost productivity from these incidents. And then at the end, we'll have an estimate of lost hours. And the message will be that we shouldn't skimp on quality when it comes to this kind of thing, because even if it saves money, it ultimately leads to lost learning time. We're hoping this helps prevent situations like this in the future."

Now Ms. Tilfry smiled. I turned to Jake and mouthed a thank you under my breath.

"Well I was expecting creativity and it looks like once again you've all delivered. Nice work, team," she said. "I look forward to reading your summary."

"Oh about that," said Bianca, looking up. She'd had her head bowed down to her thighs throughout the entire conversation, not paying attention at all. And now she was going to undo all the goodwill we'd just banked.

Cringing, I looked away as she kept talking.

"It was actually my responsibility to print it," she said, "and I think I left it on the printer in the library. Mind if I go pick it up?"

Ms. Tilfry shook her head. "Of course not, just take a hall pass on your way out."

Bianca thanked her, then slid her phone into

her pocket once Ms. Tilfry was out of view. During our conversation, she'd been typing fast enough to create an entire one-page document. Apparently her speed wasn't just limited to softballs.

"That was, uh, pretty impressive, Livi," said Matt as Bianca slipped out of the room.

"Yeah, great topic too," said Jake. "I can get into that."

"Thanks for backing me up," I said. "And Bianca, I can't believe she typed it up so fast. And that Ms. Tilfry didn't catch on!"

"Yeah, I know, right," said Matt. "Lucky Ms. Tilfry was all up in your face. She didn't glance over here the whole time."

"I guess she liked our idea," I said, "which is good because I feel like it is actually pretty important. Who knows, maybe our video could help get things changed around here. Even make the school better."

"Sounds good to me," said Jake. "Think we can talk our way into some air conditioning?"

"It's worth a shot," I said, as Bianca returned with our summary.

"Here it is. Nice work, Livi," she said between breaths.

"You're the one who saved our grade," I said.

"It was a team effort," she said with a smile.

I nodded just as she leaned in, lowering her voice to a whisper.

"By the way, I never meant for Val to vote

against you. The whole thing was a misunderstanding. Really, I didn't mean to get involved."

"Well I'm sure it will get straightened out soon."

"In the meantime, you really should talk to Tara. Guess she was pretty shaken up over your whole falling out the other night."

"Tara? When did you talk to her?" I asked, turning toward the red-haired ponytail parked on the opposite side of the room. Tara and I might not have talked since Saturday, but there was no way enough time had passed for her and Bianca to become friends.

"Oh, I didn't," she said. "Val just mentioned it when we talked earlier. Guess she heard it from Eva."

"Eva?"

Bianca shrugged. "I think that's who she said."

Shaking my head, I turned back to the front of the class, just as Ms. Tilfry began her wrap-up speech. Bianca must have been wrong. Maybe Tara had talked to someone about our fight, but there was no way it was Eva. Certain Bianca must have jumbled her facts, I listened to Ms. Tilfry, then jumped back into filming and script discussions with the group.

By the time the bell rang a few minutes later, our team was excited and talking, which did wonders for unraveling the large knot that had been living inside my stomach. Of course there was still the whole fight with my friends to deal with and then the larger issue of my Populatti membership, but at least as I stepped out into the hall – moving fast enough to avoid contact with Tara and the girls – I had one situation under control. And seeing as it involved making ins with Matt and Bianca, I had the feeling the goodwill could help with my other problems as well.

As I rounded the hall corner leading to my locker, Brandon popped up from behind, slinging his arm around my neck, just as he had done after almost every class of the day. The only silver lining of the whole Populatti fiasco was that Brandon seemed to feel guilty about the part he'd played in my termination, and for canceling our Sunday afternoon plans. Meaning he was being extra attentive.

Close enough to smell his cologne, I breathed in deep. B-Dash might have still been in Populatti, but he was showing the world that he didn't care about hanging out with a nonmember. His fawning was welcoming, even calming, though I couldn't help thinking that if he hadn't been such an idiot in the first place with his accusations against Matt and Eva, then maybe we could have just continued on a normal progression toward a relationship, instead of jumping into such turbulent, uncharted waters.

We walked to his locker, then mine, as he sung some old classic rock tune under his breath.

"You have practice today?" I asked, already knowing the answer. Baseball practiced every day, even some weekends too.

He nodded, his eyes already drifting toward the locker room. "You have council, right?"

I shook my head. "That's tomorrow. We're going over some new cases. Looks like some more minor offenses. No popsters this time. Don't know if that's good or bad."

Brandon shrugged. "Means you can't lose or win any votes. I'd say neutral."

His breezy tone made me laugh.

"Anyway, I should go," he said, slamming his locker. "I'll call you later. Oh, and think about what you want to do Friday. Maybe pizza again?"

"Uh, yeah, that'd be great," I said, already excited to fill him in later on my win in English. "But are you sure you want to miss the party?"

He laughed. "Of course I'm sure. Last thing I want to do is step into Eva's house. And I see the guys at practice enough. All those parties were ever good for was seeing you."

My face flushed as Brandon's gaze met my eyes. "Well good thing I'm free then."

He smiled. "Populatti isn't everything."

"Guess not."

"Well I better go change."

"Yeah, and I need to catch the bus. That's one thing I do miss."

"What? Having a ride?"

"Sure beats an hour bouncing over potholes."

"I'm pretty sure Sammy or Tara would still drive

you. You don't have to be in some stupid group to be friends with them."

I sighed, thinking of how I'd avoided them all day, even resorting to eating lunch in French class to work on an extra credit assignment.

"They owe me an apology."

Brandon shook his head. "You should just call them. At least so you can hitch a ride."

"Yeah, maybe," I said, then shuffled down the hall toward the bus.

The hour long ride felt like two as the bus barreled down over half the side streets of Golden Hill. Even as a freshman, I'd only taken the bus a few times since Tara's mom used to insist on driving her to school – she was never one to trust bus safety – before Tara got her license this past fall. So by the time I threw open the front door, my nerves were fried. The manicure I'd attempted was runny and chipped and in serious need of a touchup. And the magazine I still hadn't read was covered with so much nail polish that half the articles were incomprehensible.

If ever there was time for a bubble bath, and a reconciliation with the girls, it was now. Still not ready to confront the latter, I headed toward the stairs. The twins were at school, my parents working, and judging from the humming of the vacuum, Lona was working hard somewhere downstairs. Meaning the next forty-five minutes were between me and my tub.

Relieved to be alone, I pushed open the door to my room and threw my backpack under my desk. Then I rubbed my eyes, stretched out my arms and turned toward the bed. But as I opened my eyes and prepared to jump onto my cushy mound of covers, I shrieked. Sammy was sitting on my bed, hands and legs crossed like a Buddhist monk. I brought my hand to my mouth to muffle my scream.

"What are you doing here?" I said.

"I was wondering when you'd get home," she said.

"What are you talking about? Who let you in?"

"Lona. Oh, and she gave me a plate of cookies for us to share. Oatmeal chocolate chip. They're just the right amount of moist and crispy." Sammy unfolded her legs and stretched out her back in a yoga pose as if nothing was wrong.

"Okay," I said, grabbing a cookie, "but that still doesn't tell me what you're doing here."

Sammy dropped the pose and fell onto her back. "Making sure you're okay? We missed you at lunch. And you ignored us in English."

"Well I'm fine, so can you go?" I said. While part of me was happy to see Sammy, the other part couldn't help but feel annoyed that she thought I couldn't handle myself.

"Nope."

"God, you are so annoying."

"Look who's talking, girl. Now Tara dropped me

off and she isn't picking me up for an hour. So, you can either choose to talk, otherwise I'm gonna just keep on doing my yoga right here on your bed."

"Fine. Knock yourself out," I said, eying my robe. "As long as you stay out of the bathroom."

"Why? Whatcha doing in there?" said Sammy, smiling from a lopsided shoulder stand.

"None of your business."

"I'm a born social chair. Everything's my business."

I inhaled through my nose and relaxed. It was hard to stay mad at Sammy when she laid on the charm. "Fine. If you must know I'm all wound up like a freaking yo-yo and I need to calm my nerves. So if you will excuse me, I have a date with a bubble bath."

"Aw, come over here. You know I give the best shoulder massages," said Sammy. "At the very least, it'll prime you for the tub."

Clutching my robe, I took a step toward the bathroom, then stepped back toward my room. Sammy was right. Her shoulder massages were great.

"All right," I said. "But only because you offered."

"Does this mean I'm forgiven?"

"I dunno. Maybe."

"Maybe?"

"Yeah, sure. I guess."

"Thank God." Sammy wrapped her arms

around my neck until I couldn't breathe. "I know we've only been incommunicado for like 48 hours, but let me tell you it's been rough."

I couldn't resist hugging her back as she held me in her killer grip. "I've missed you too. Probably more."

Sammy sighed. "I know. And don't worry. I promise we are going to sort everything out."

I frowned. There was something about the certainty in Sammy's voice that sounded too dismissive, too unconcerned about my future. So even though I knew I should steer clear of any hot topics, I found myself zeroing in on the one that had been haunting my dreams all week.

"So everyone excited for the big party with Eva?" I asked, plopping back down on my bed.

Right away, her smile dulled. "No one knows it's at Eva's yet except the inner circle, but it seems like the usual amount of excitement."

"That's good," I said, trying to sound like I didn't care. "Just make sure you lock up your valuables. Rumor is she's a bit of a thief and a vandal."

Sammy walked to her purse and fished out her phone. "Come on, girl. We all know Eva's not your favorite person right now. Though I've hung out with her quite a bit this week for party prep, and she's not as bad as you'd think. Maybe if you eased up on her a bit, she'd cut you some slack. She's insecure, that's all."

I whipped my head around as Sammy pulled up

Tara's number, ready for her ride home.

"Cut her some slack? What did I do to her? And what does Crystal think about this? Is she just magically ready now to forgive that cheating incident? Eva's done nothing but sabotage us for months! How can you say that?"

"Sorry, I'm not defending her. I just meant it would be in the best interest of getting you back into Populatti if you two could at least pretend to get along a little. I told Crys the same thing."

"So now my reinstatement in Populatti requires me to suck up to the girl who tried to ruin me?"

I bit my lip and focused on my breathing. I knew that on some level, Sammy was right. Holding a grudge wasn't going to help me win back votes. But even so, I couldn't shake the feeling that my best friends were trying too hard to keep Eva happy.

"Oh Livs, we're doing everything we can," Sammy said. "But we've gotta be nice to Eva a little longer and it would be helpful if you played along. Plus, she's got the inside scoop on Coop and Tara's dying to get it out of her."

My stomach churned as Sammy hit 'Send' on her phone. Eva had the inside scoop on Christian? Tara was talking to Eva? All of a sudden Bianca's comments from earlier didn't seem so unbelievable.

"I'm actually not feeling that good all of a sudden. Maybe we better put off that massage for another day."

"You sure? It could help."

"Not right now. I think I need to lie down. But I'll see ya tomorrow."

Sammy nodded. "I'll wait for Tara downstairs. Oh and Livs, you know you don't have to hide during lunch forever. There are some rules we can bend."

I forced a smile. "I've got a lot of council stuff to catch up on, but thanks. I'm sure I'll be back soon."

"Well hurry it up. Because if I have to stare at Dash's celebrity pout instead of eating my lunch for much longer, I might starve to death."

"He's been pouting?"

"Looked like it today."

"So maybe he does like me."

"Honey, B-Dash is way beyond just 'like.' It's a miracle every girl in Golden Hill doesn't hate you."

"Most of them do."

"But not all," she said before giving a wave and walking out the door.

As soon as I heard her feet on the stairs, I reached for my book bag and pulled out the purse I kept stashed inside. After sifting through a mound of old cough drop wrappers and waxy receipts from the nail salon three blocks from school, I found the scrap of paper Bianca had handed me earlier that day. I juggled the paper from hand to hand as if it were a hot coal as I contemplated whether to dial the number. Things were back on track with Sammy, meaning as far as our crew went, I was forgiven. But there was still something about the way Sammy brought up Eva that made me uncomfortable. All of a sudden it seemed possible that Tara was talking to Eva. And maybe had been talking to her all along. And while there was no way I could confront Eva, I was pretty sure Bianca felt badly enough about her role in my termination that she'd be willing to help me out. So I flipped open my phone and punched in her number.

Bianca picked up on the third ring, sounding hesitant. Programming my number must not have been a priority.

"Hey, it's Livi," I said. "I'm just working on our English project."

"Oh hey, what's up?" she said, sounding nervous.

"Not much, just was throwing around some ideas for the script. Was gonna write them down, but thought it could be helpful to go over them before wasting too much time."

"Oh yeah, good idea. You wanna discuss in person?" asked Bianca. "I was on my way to Starbucks for a frappuccino. Want me to pick you up?"

My sweaty fingers tightened their grip on my phone as I fought the urge to say "no."

"Sure, sounds great," I said.

"I'll see you in ten then. And thanks for calling, Livi. I'm so glad working together isn't weird."

"Me too," I said, thinking it already was.

populatti.com

BrandontheGreat: 86%

Approved Members: 23
Pending Applications: 1
Access Denied: 48

POP REPORT: get ready popsters, invites go out in an hour. sammy promises tonite will impress!! ~ Crys

COMMENTS:

EvaBeautiful posted at 5:32 p.m. ET May 23: word on the street is pretty in pink! ;)

Tarable posted at 5:16 p.m. ET May 23: anything gorgeous val my dear :)

ValieGal posted at 5:02 p.m. ET May 23: Bianca, fraid so tho think it's just gonna b a lil rain. anyone know tonite's theme or what to wear?

Coop007 posted at 4:09 p.m. ET May 23: lax starts on tues if that helps...

BiancaA posted at 12:09 p.m. ET May 23: val, does practice really start on Monday? I heard it's supposed to be a MONSOON?!?

Jake posted at 11:23 a.m. ET May 23: anyone up for pizza before tonight's party? Crys, babe, what u think?

CHAPTER ELEVEN

"Eww, Pretty in Pink, that's disgusting," I said as I gagged on a sip of coffee.

Brandon patted my back until it made its way down my throat. "I told you it was bad."

"There's not even a single comment about me anywhere on the site. Doesn't anyone miss me?"

It was Friday night and Brandon and I were doing our best to settle our pizza-heavy stomachs and forget about Eva's party by hanging out at my favorite Starbucks by the beach. It was the same one I'd been in days earlier with Bianca, who for all her helpful insight on the school's mold problem, hadn't done much to shed light on the whole Eva-Tara alliance. But then, given that Bianca and I were not exactly best friends, I also hadn't done much to push her on the topic. That I had saved for Sammy, who despite following through on her promise to let me rejoin the lunch crew, still had little to say on anything important.

With Eva's party happening as we spoke, somehow it seemed necessary to know if Eva and Tara were now friends. But even reading Populatti did little to confirm my suspicions. All it did was leave me feeling hurt. I knew the group was moving on without me. But in my head, Populatti was suspended in time, locked away to all members as it was to me, its last posts still frozen somewhere around noon last Sunday. Scrolling through an updated screen of comments I'd never seen brought me back to reality. And made Eva's party feel all the more threatening. Eva had already stolen my membership. It seemed now she was after my friends too.

"Don't worry, babe," said Brandon, catching my pursed lips. "There were tons of comments about the whole termination thing right after it happened, but a few days ago Crys deleted them. I'm sure she's just trying to cool everyone off so when we nominate you again, no one remembers why they voted against you in the first place."

"Yeah maybe," I said, wondering if Crys was still on my side. After talking with Sammy, I'd chatted with Crys and Tara a bit, and all four of us had shared a tearful reunion a day earlier at lunch.

Which meant technically things were okay. Yet still Tara seemed pretty distant. And while Crys seemed as sincere as ever – she wasn't one to hold a grudge or tell a lie – seeing myself wiped clean from the site left me feeling uneasy.

I sighed, leaning into Brandon as he reclined further into the burgundy couch, his vanilla frappuccino wedged between the cushions. He was being more hands-off than usual, his eyes fluttering all about the room instead of focusing on me. I wondered if I'd done something to turn him off. It was hard not to worry, especially since I hadn't been too open to his advances, choosing to spend the night at a coffee shop instead of his place. But I just hadn't found the right way to tell him that I wasn't ready to round the bases, no matter who the guy. Avoiding the situation was easier. Yet now I wondered if my logic was wrong, if having an awkward talk could have cleared up a lot of confusion.

Though there was the possibility that whatever was bothering Brandon had nothing to do with our alone time. Like maybe I'd been calling too much. Or asking him too many questions about Populatti. Had my exile from the site made me too needy? Perhaps. I bit down on my lip as my thoughts continued to swirl around the party happening just blocks away. As thrilled as I was to have Brandon with me instead of mingling with the popster girls, I couldn't help but wonder if I should have forced him to go without me.

"So I saw Bianca in the weight room today. I'm glad you two are getting along," said Brandon, interrupting my thoughts.

"Yeah, she's been a big help with our English project."

"That's what Jake said. Though I have to ask. Back on your birthday. You didn't really smash that girl's foot on purpose?"

"What?" I asked.

"Bianca. Her foot. You know that's the reason Val gave for voting you out."

I sighed. "Yeah. I know. And no, it was not on purpose. I mean, maybe I was a little annoyed at her for getting all in your face, but honestly, the toe part was an accident."

"Good," he said. "I didn't think you were that kind of crazy."

I brought my knees up to my chest and smiled. "No, I might be crazy but I'm not sadistic."

He laughed. "Glad to hear it. Bianca's really nice when you get to know her. She's also a ridiculous athlete. Watching her pitch is insane."

"I can see that," I said. "She really seemed upset that Val used her story to vote me out. Though honestly it doesn't even seem she's super into the site."

Brandon nodded. "She probably isn't. Her friends come from softball. All Populatti brings to the table are parties."

"But you play sports and you seem into it."

"Ah, well I'm in it for the girls."

"The girls?"

"One in particular."

"Anyone I know?"

"Maybe," he said. "Blonde hair, blue eyes. A tendency to say just enough to get her in trouble."

I smiled as my eyes met his. "Oh yeah, I hear she hasn't been around much."

"Not online, but I promise that's gonna change. Because it's not a party unless you're there with me," he said, bringing his hand to my cheek.

My skin burned as his fingers grazed my face. "Yeah, about all that," I said. "I kind of don't want Tara and the girls to know that I've been talking with Bianca about anything but school stuff. We're still on the rocks and I don't want to do anything to make things worse with them."

"Don't worry, I've got your back," he said, then downed the rest of his coffee. "Though there is a baseball/softball party tomorrow if you're interested in hanging with some other people. I was gonna skip it, but if we go together it could be all right."

I nodded, thinking back to when Val had asked Coop to that softball party. This must have been what she'd been talking about.

"So what do you think?"

"Can I let you know tomorrow?" I asked. "I think I need to know how Eva's party goes first."

Brandon laughed. "Sure, whatever you want. Though without us there, I can't imagine you're going to hear about anything that would help you make up your mind."

I sighed. "Okay, okay, you're right. So let's just say I'll go then."

"Really?"

"Yeah. But let's not go telling anyone who could tell Tara or the girls about this one yet either. I'm still not sure how they'll take it."

Before heading home for the night – 11:00 always crept up on us too quickly – I made Brandon give me one last glance at Populatti. The first comments from Eva's party were coming in, and despite Brandon's insistence that Eva's would be dull without us, from the sound of it there had been some kind of issue involving Val. I wondered what had happened to laid-back ValieGal. She'd always seemed above the Pop drama, yet here she was hanging in the eye of the storm two weekends in a row. The pieces didn't seem to fit. But then these days, not many of them did.

Either way, I was starting to question the sanity of my decision to crash the baseball/softball party when my phone rang. Having just entered my pitch-black room, I answered the call without looking at the number, hoping the noise wouldn't wake my parents. I figured it was Sammy or Tara calling to check on my date with Brandon or tell me how oh-so-wonderful their night at Eva's had been. Thankful that my first night in exile had gone off without a hitch, I waltzed into my closet, ready for my super-cozy fleece pajamas with matching fleecy socks. But as soon as I started changing, Tara's voice pierced my ears.

"She's awful, Livs, just awful," Tara said. Her voice sounded blurry, as if she'd been crying or maybe sipped from the forbidden flask. Knowing this was Tara, I figured it must have been the former. The only thing she'd ever taken shots of was wheatgrass and last I'd heard, that didn't do anything except turn your pee green.

"So what did Val do this time?" I asked, pulling on my socks.

"Get this," said Tara. "She accused me of trying to steal Coop from her. She said she heard that I was fishing for information about his schedule and flirting with him at lunch!"

"Were you?"

"Of course not! I would never try to sabotage Val in public. And besides, I was waiting to make my move until after her stupid softball party was over."

"Yeah, I remember the plan."

"So anyway, I figured since Val ruined your life, you would understand. She is a total jerk! I can't believe we used to be nice to her!"

"I don't think she's a jerk," I said. "This sounds more like a misunderstanding. Who do you think is behind the rumors? Eva?"

"Oh, I don't know. I can't imagine Eva would be causing more trouble, not after just surviving a termination vote."

"Really? Don't forget, she's a cheat. And she convinced everyone to vote me out. Who knows, maybe she's after you now. Maybe she has a crush on Coop and wants to steal him from both of you," I said, baiting her to spill more about Eva.

"I don't think she's after me. We just threw a very successful party for her, and we got along fine through all the planning. It's gotta be someone else."

"I'm still betting on Eva."

"Just because you and Eva can't get along doesn't mean she's out to get everyone."

"Can't get along? What did I ever do besides help her when she got into trouble? You do know she hates me for no reason."

"Ah, and let me guess. Stomping on Bianca's toes and carrying on with Brandon were nothing, right?"

"Eva hated me way before that." I couldn't believe Tara was still defending her.

"Look Livi, just stop it. I know it wasn't Eva sabotaging me," Tara said abruptly. She sounded sick of rehashing my termination.

"And how do you know that?"

"Because I think Eva's angry with you for stealing Nick from her last year. I don't think she's after anyone else."

"What?" I gasped as the phone dropped out of my hand. I fell to my knees and crawled toward my closet, taking refuge under a row of dresses.

Finally. Here it was. The big lie spreading behind my back.

I thought back to Eva's comments about me stealing boyfriends, and how I'd assumed she'd been referring to Bianca. It was hard to believe how wrong I'd been. Or to imagine where Eva had gotten such a crazy idea.

"Nick asked me out," I said once the phone was back up at my ear. "I didn't steal him from anyone. And we only dated for like ten minutes. Who did she hear this from?"

"I don't think anyone," said Tara. "She just said that her and Nick were hanging out last fall and then you flitted in wearing some hot outfit, and the next day he wouldn't even talk to her."

"That's insane!" I shouted, forgetting all my efforts at sound-proofing. "I never flirted with Nick and it's not my fault he decided to ask me out. You can't possibly think Eva's right here."

Silence.

"Right?" I said.

"Of course not. And I told her that," said Tara.

"Did she understand that she's delusional?"

"Who knows? I thought I'd convinced her, but that was before the termination. Looks to me like she held a grudge."

"Wait, you talked to Eva before she nominated me? And all this time you've been telling me she's just insecure? Why didn't you tell me the truth?"

I was definitely shouting now, shocked that my parents hadn't burst into my room, but I couldn't stop myself. With my outcast status growing with each passing day, I knew better than to get Tara upset, but the idea of her withholding critical information about Eva was baffling. Not what I'd expect from a best friend.

After a long pause, Tara cleared her throat. "I'm sorry, but I didn't think telling you would be helpful." Her voice sounded cool and logical. Typical Tara.

"Don't you think it might've been helpful if I could've explained myself?"

"At the time, I didn't even think of Nick. It was just a passing comment she made months ago when we had Spanish together. When I told her she was mistaken, she seemed to listen. I thought she was happy with Matt. It was old news. It wasn't until later that I put it all together."

"And you did nothing to help."

"That's not true. I did everything I could, not that you made it easy, refusing to talk to B-Dash about the termination thing until so late in the game. But right now, the problem is Val. Not Eva."

My blood boiled as Tara went on the attack, as if she were the real victim.

"Oh, okay Tarable, that's right. Bring it back to Val," I said, trying my hardest not to scream into the phone. "How dare she have a crush on the same guy and get mad when you try to steal him away.

Just sounds to me like you're finally living up to your name."

"What's that supposed to mean?"

"Nothing. And by the way, my first night exiled from Populatti went fine, thanks so much for asking."

I ended the call, then turned off my ringer, and fell into a deep sleep.

The next morning I awoke with nothing on my social calendar except the softball party that night. So I spent eight hours going back and forth between helping the twins with their science project – they were building a diorama of their favorite ecosystem, the estuary, which happened to be my favorite as well– and signing into Populatti as Brandon.

Knowing it was unhealthy, I tried to stay away from the site, but found myself unable to stop rereading the messages that had been posted since my termination. For the most part the messages were what I expected. There were multiple entries about Eva's party, about whether jeggings were a fashion do or don't, and whether the next pop party should have a summer-related theme. Interspersed were a few comments about the English film festival and sports victories – our volleyball team had just clinched the conference title – and other informal Pop events that came up on the weekdays. As expected, there was nothing about me or Brandon.

After analyzing so many comments, my head

began to throb, clouding my vision and making it difficult to think. Two Advils did little to kill the pain. All the drama was seriously affecting my health.

Turning back to the computer, I frowned. Here I'd signed onto Pop hoping to find some simple allies and all I'd gotten was bombarded by comments about dress codes and party themes. Nothing helpful. Meaning that when I reapplied for membership, I was going to need Tara, Crys, and Sammy's votes, even though their efforts to help me appeared non-existent. They weren't even inviting me to hang out away from Populatti. Well, Sammy was. She'd asked me a couple of times to accompany her to yoga class, and to hit up the gym after school. But besides her, all I got were a handful of calls venting about Val or Eva or the English project. No invites. And no questions about how I was holding up.

Their indifference made me wonder why I wanted to be in a club built around hanging out with them in the first place. Were friends that dropped you when you were no longer convenient really friends? And were all the missing invitations deliberate? Or were the girls just so wrapped up in their own worlds that they'd forgotten I was no longer in their orbit? Despite my doubts, I figured I had to assume the best. That our friendships were strong enough to recover. And that if I could rejoin Populatti, the drama would blow over.

If only rejoining were easy. My only hope was

that I'd be able to convince Val and some of the other softball girls that they were wrong about me. Or that Eva would screw up big at another party, so everyone would realize they'd kicked the wrong girl out. Yet part of me was starting to wonder if that would really help. Or if Eva was even the problem. Maybe she was just a pawn in someone else's game.

About an hour before B-Dash was supposed to pick me up, Tara called apologizing for her earlier phone call and inviting me to the movies. It was the first invite she'd extended since I'd been voted out of Populatti, and judging by her bubbly voice and mindless banter about the new organic cherry banana perfume she bought, she was trying to be nice. Even so, I enjoyed telling her I had plans.

"Sorry Hon, I'm going out with Brandon," I'd said, making it sound as exciting and important as any Populatti party.

"Didn't you guys hang out last night?" she'd asked.

It had been hard not to laugh, to tell her that indeed we had hung out the night before and that yes, we'd had such a good time that we'd decided to break bread with Tara's biggest enemy. But somehow I'd held in the laughter tickling the back of my throat and proceeded to thank her for the invitation. There was nothing to be gained by telling her, or any of the other girls, that Brandon and I would be going to the very softball party that Val was attending with Coop. Especially since I planned to spend the night apologizing to Val profusely for my sins. It was the only way to win her back, and figure out exactly what had happened with Tara.

populatti.com

BrandontheGreat: 87%

Approved Members: 23
Pending Applications: 1
Access Denied: 48

POP REPORT: killa partaay peeps. Thanx 2 all u popsters for makin eva's special!! ~ Crys

COMMENTS:

Jake posted at 5:33 p.m. ET May 24: anyone else struggling w this video editing thing? if u can help, please holla

EvaBeautiful posted at 4:32 p.m. ET May 24: who knows – at least im not in it ☺

Coop007 posted at 3:09 p.m. ET May 24: whats up w all the drama popsters?

Tarable posted at 2:13 p.m. ET May 24: thanx eva, too bad some pple don't know the first thing about common courtesy. Im sooo not impressed

celebSAMmy posted at 12:02 p.m. ET May 24: though next time we def need more cherries...

BiancaA posted at 11:00 a.m. ET May 24: thanks for the party eva – awesome time!

CHAPTER TWELVE

"So where's this party again?" I asked as I turned up the air conditioning in Brandon's car.

"Ryan's house. One of the captains," Brandon said.

"He's not in Populatti," I said, the words coming out as a statement. I knew every guy on the site by heart, even if I was still rusty on a bunch of the girls. Ryan must have been a senior, super quiet, or both. But then I remembered I also wasn't in Populatti. Meaning it was probably time to stop making assumptions.

"He never applied for membership," Brandon said. "He was dating this girl Marina when the site first came out, so he never saw the need."

"Wait, Marina Bentley?" I asked, slapping my hands on the dashboard.

"Yup. I take it you know the story."

"Who doesn't?" I said, laughing.

Marina Bentley was a Golden Hill legend. A couple years back she'd released over 200 lab rats before an experiment in AP Bio, telling them to 'run wild and free.' Rumor was the fugitive rats had fled through the cracks between the ceiling tiles and had infested the entire school – it was actually a topic we'd discussed adding to our English video – though every time someone asked the janitors about the rats they'd just shake their heads and claim it was all a myth. Something I still wasn't sure I believed given the strange smell that plagued the science wing on hot days.

"Are they still dating?" I asked, wondering if I'd get a glimpse of the legendary Marina.

"No, they broke up when she started college last year."

"But Ryan still hasn't joined Populatti?"

"Livs, he dated Marina for two years. You know as well as I do he'd never get in."

"True. She is responsible for stinking up the school."

Brandon crossed the Post Road and slowed the car. We were nearing the beach, but before we reached the small maze of side streets that weaved between crowded beach houses and brackish estuaries, Brandon made a sharp left turn into the empty driveway of a small clapboard cape. I fumbled with my seatbelt as Brandon opened his door and jumped out of the car.

"You okay?" he asked.

"Do you think we should maybe go around the block or something? There aren't any cars here."

Brandon laughed. "Always one to make an entrance, huh? Well you don't have to worry. The Jetta on the street is Val's. A lot of the other kids are younger. They usually get dropped off."

"Oh," I said, again questioning the sanity of my decision. I could be sitting in the plush stadium seating of the Regal Cinema downtown, pretending to be 100 percent okay with Tarable and the rest of the gals and at least looking the part. Instead I was gearing up to chill with the very girls who had run me out of Populatti.

The uneasy feeling crowding my stomach grew when the front door opened up to an older woman in jeans and a sweatshirt. Pop parties with parents home were rare. Make that nonexistent. Yet Brandon didn't seem the least bit disturbed as he greeted Mrs. Hood and dove right into a lengthy discussion about the baseball season, how they were doing better than expected given that they had so few seniors, but how they were already out of contention for States.

"We're not in Populatti anymore," I said as Brandon led me to the wooden basement staircase located off the tiled kitchen. As we descended, I lowered my eyes, adjusting them to the dim light coming from the bottom of the stairs. Given the number of spider webs I could make out in the dark, I decided to avoid the railing. Instead, I crossed my arms and picked up the pace, as I tried to block out the images of the black widows I was sure were lurking in the shadows.

"Hey, you're the one that said you wanted to come," Brandon teased, flicking my stiff shoulders.

"You didn't tell me about the spiders."

"That's because they don't bite."

"But what if they do?" I asked, my palms growing sweaty. "And what if tonight doesn't work? What's the code word if I wanna leave?" I was starting to panic. It was all too much, the idea of being in a foreign basement, filled with spiders that might bite and girls that most definitely bit harder.

"How about you just grab my shoulder? It'll be less obvious," Brandon said, sensing my anxiety.

I reached for his shoulder and dug my nails into his polo. "Like this?"

"Not so hard," he said, scrunching his shoulders, just as Val's voice rose above the buzz of the crowd.

"Ready, set, go!" she said. As I entered the basement, I saw two groups of unfamiliar faces screaming and waving their hands as a guy and girl flailed around in the center of the room.

"Ry, you look like a fish," Brandon said, pointing to the guy.

Ryan turned around and grinned. "Dash, my man. Didn't think you'd make it."

The crowd quieted as Ryan and the girl next to him stopped dancing around the room.

"You caught us in the middle of charades. You wanna play?"

"Big balls versus small," said a stocky girl in the crowd.

I looked up.

"Softballs are bigger than baseballs," said Brandon.

I clutched Brandon's shoulder, hoping he'd fake illness and let us leave. Coming was a mistake. Not only did almost everyone know each other – except for the few dates that had tagged along like me and Coop – but even the party setup was unfamiliar. Where was the finely tuned playlist? And the decorations? And little umbrellas for my cranberry Sprite drinks? Was there even cranberry juice present? And what about dancing? Did parties exist without it?

Brandon grabbed my fingers, then brushed my arm down to his side. "Go and mingle. Remember, you need votes," he said into my ear.

And then he was off, walking toward Coop and Jake and Ry and whatever other baseball players were in attendance.

As the game of charades disbanded, I scanned the crowd until I caught sight of Bianca's frizzy ponytail. She was talking with Val and a couple other girls, teammates most likely. I wondered if they were in Populatti.

I tugged at my sheer ivory top, rearranging the fuchsia tank that sat underneath, wishing I hadn't chosen to wear a color brighter than a stop light. Bianca and her friends had definitely dressed for a different occasion. They sported light denim flares and graphic tees covered in sports puns I couldn't figure out. Even Val was dressed down despite Co-op's presence, though at least she'd thrown on some makeup. Besides for her, there wasn't an eyeshadowed lid in the crowd.

My head spun as I contemplated whether to walk over to Bianca. Having been befriended by Sammy and Tara soon after moving to Golden Hill, it had been years since I'd actually had to break into a conversation. Usually people wanted to talk to me. It was hard being thrust back into the role of outsider, and harder still not to let memories of nights spent without any party invites come creeping back.

Once again, I told myself to forget my middle school past and focus on the present. As far as these girls knew, I was still Livi Stanley, best friend of Tara, Sammy, and Crys. Not to mention that I was currently hanging out with B-Dash. And even though it wasn't anything official, it seemed to be heading in that direction. Which meant I was far from an outsider, even if I did currently lack a

Populatti log-in. With a renewed sense of confidence, I raised my head and started walking toward the group, reveling in the clicking of my gold stiletto sandals.

"Hey Livi," she said as I grew closer. "I didn't know you were coming. Or Brandon. Last I talked to him he couldn't make it."

I shrugged. "Yeah, something with his parents fell through."

She nodded. "I'm glad it did. This is our first party to include dates, but not too many people followed through."

"So you're saying I'm a hot commodity."

"Obviously," she said, laughing.

I felt my heart regain its normal rhythm as the conversation moved on. Talking to Bianca was easy, easier than I envisioned, and as she introduced me to her friends and teammates I found myself forgetting about the vote count and actually enjoying the party.

An hour later, Val left Christian to join our group. Her face was flushed and her eyes brighter than usual. Things with Coop must have been going well.

Even so, I dropped my hands to my sides and looked down. Having seconded my termination vote, Val was an enemy. Or at least an unknown. Much like Eva, I wasn't sure if she was angry with something I'd done, or part of some larger scheme.

Though if Val was still angry, she didn't let on.

At least that's what I thought until two classic rock songs later when she invited me to the cooler to grab a soda.

Too scared to say no, I excused myself from the pack and followed Val to the back corner of the room. My palms grew sweaty as we inched further from the crowd.

"Wasn't expecting to see you here," she said once we were alone.

"Sorry about that," I said, staring at the plastic white and red cooler.

"No worries, you're Dash's girl now, so I guess I'm not surprised."

"I'm not his girl. We're just hanging out, but he invited me and I didn't want to be rude. I don't want any trouble."

Val looked me up and down, then nodded. "And I assume then that your talking to Bianca has nothing to do with winning her vote for Populatti?"

I gagged on a mouthful of soda.

"That's what I thought," she said before I could answer.

I swallowed hard and wiped a slick of sweat from my forehead. "Obviously I'd like to rejoin the group," I said, "but that's not why I was talking with Bianca. We're in the same film group for English. We've been talking because of the project."

"Well I just hope this time you don't fall on her arm."

I frowned. "Look. I know you think I stomped

on Bianca's toe last month on purpose, but I assure you I didn't. And I know you're probably still pissed at me for whatever Eva's been saying, but you have to believe me that whatever you've heard, it isn't true."

"I know," Val said.

"Huh? Know what?"

"That what Eva's saying isn't true."

"Then why the nomination?"

Val sighed. "I found out too late. Yesterday actually. And I have to say, I was pretty shocked. I never would've seconded your nomination had I known, and I apologize. But that still doesn't mean I'm ready to trust you after the way you treated Bianca. Even if you didn't purposely break her toe, you were pretty rude about her crush on Brandon."

I looked down, knowing she was right. "I'm sorry," I said, "though what was I supposed to do? Brandon and I were already talking."

"Then you shouldn't have worried about Bianca."

I nodded, again knowing she was right "So, uh, how'd you find out Eva was lying?"

"You haven't heard?"

I shook my head.

"Wow, you really are out of it now."

I stared ahead, waiting for her to continue.

"All right then. So I was talking to Eva last night about Tara, who was blatantly flirting with Coop in front of me. Like laying it on super thick even though she knew I'd asked him here tonight. And that's when Eva got all upset and took me aside. She apologized for contributing to the problem by giving Tara information about Coop."

"Why would Eva be talking to Tara?" I asked.

"Apparently they were bartering information. Tara gave Eva gossip to help her fit into Pop and in return Eva told Tara private information about Christian. I guess Tara offered up the gossip since she knew Eva and Coop were close. Seems she sacrificed you to get to him, screwing us both in the process."

I took a few steps back, searching for the wall.

"I, I don't know about any of that," I said. "Tara and I are best friends. I can't imagine her making up lies. We've never even had a fight."

Val frowned. "I'm sorry to be the messenger. I'm afraid I don't know all the details, but from what Eva told me, Tara started this whole mess a few months back by telling her you pursued Nick, even though you knew Eva was obsessed with him."

I gasped, then rolled back my shoulders, trying to loosen the knot forming in the middle of my back. When that didn't work, I stepped forward, leaning into the wall.

Only as I straightened my legs for balance, my right stiletto lodged itself in a crack. I flapped my arms back and forth, trying to regain my balance, but it was too late. My knee crumbled under the weight of my body, sending me crashing down to the concrete floor.

"Oww!" I said, bringing my knees into my chest. With memories of the cake fall at Club Dash still fresh in my mind, I tried to scramble to my feet, but the pain in my foot was too great for me to stand.

"OhmiGod, are you okay?" said Val.

I shook my head, trying to blink away the tears.

"Hang on, let me grab Brandon. Dash, we need you, right now. Ryan, you too. Bianca, can you kill the music?"

I tried to lift my head off the floor as Val continued to bark orders, but before I could get my neck to cooperate, Brandon was by my side.

"What happened?" he asked.

"I fell. Again," I said, blinking my eyes.

"Where does it hurt?"

"My ankle."

"What about your head?"

"It's fine."

"Okay, then Ry and I are gonna carry you upstairs. You ready?"

"I guess."

Brandon slid his arm under my shoulders while Ryan lifted my legs. A second later, I was in Brandon's arms, on my way up the stairs.

"Livi, you sure you're okay? Do you want me to get you some water or something?" asked Val once I was settled on the living room couch.

"No, I'm fine," I said, as Mrs. Hood brought me a bag of ice. I thanked her, then tried to channel some of Sammy's toughness. "I actually feel a little better. I think it's just a twist."

Brandon stroked my back. "Yeah, unfortunately for Miss Klutz over here, this isn't her first time on the floor."

"Oh right. I heard about the cake incident," said Val.

"I hope you're not holding that against me too."

Val sighed. "I'm sorry. Honestly, I'm not evil. And I admit that kicking you out was a pretty hasty decision based on some less than stellar intelligence."

"Thanks. I'm sorry too. I didn't mean to insult Bianca. Or start such a mess."

"I know," she said.

I rubbed my ankle and tried not to think about the pain pulsing up my leg.

"I should get you home before your ankle blows up," said Brandon. "You'll need more ice when you get there."

I laughed, thinking about my parents' over-stocked first aid closet. "I think I can manage that."

"Then let's get you up," he said, reaching for my arms.

I slid my feet off the sofa as Brandon handed me my coat and purse.

"Thanks guys, and sorry for leaving so early," I said, my eyes lingering on Val's.

"No problem," she said. "And Livi, I'll give you a call tomorrow. We have a lot to catch up on."

After saying goodbye to Ryan and Mrs. Hood, Brandon carried me to the car. The party had not gone exactly as planned, but it hadn't been a total disaster either. Even if I hadn't scored any Populatti votes or gotten to finish my conversation with Val, speaking with Bianca and her friends had gone well. Sure, it had been different than a Populatti party, but right then it felt like just the type of different I needed. Kind of like Ryan's house. It might not have been Club Dash, but as I looked back at the front door, I saw that it also wasn't as scary as the spider webs made it seem. In fact, with the stars shining overhead, it almost looked charming. Like the type of place where real friends gathered to talk, not plot.

"So I guess that couldn't have gone any worse," Brandon said, pulling into my driveway.

"At least for my ankle," I said, waving my foot.

"Still glad we went?"

"Yeah," I said, finding that even I was surprised at my answer. "It was good. I learned a lot."

Brandon smiled. "Glad to hear it. Now you should get some rest. I'll call you in the morning."

"You better."

"I guarantee it."

He brought his lips up to mine and kissed me deeply, leaving me breathless.

"Oh, and I was thinking," he said, "that since we've been hanging out so much that we should, uh, you know. Make this official."

I looked at him, the corner of my mouth rising into a crooked smile. "Like boyfriend-girlfriend?"

He laughed. "I guess that would be it."

"Even though I'm not in Populatti?"

This time, he laughed harder. "I don't think that would change the terms."

"No. I mean, I know. I just thought that, since I'm not a member and all, that maybe you wouldn't want to hang out like that."

He smiled. "Come on, Livs, I told you before. The last thing I care about is Populatti. But I do care about you."

"Well in that case, I would love to be your girl-friend," I said, unable to hide my smile.

Then B-Dash lowered his eyes and kissed me again before leaving me at the front door. I ran my hands through my hair and tried to stop them from shaking as I listened to his engine speed away.

Back in my room, I downed two Advil for my ankle, then debated texting Sammy or Crys or even Tara with the news. Learning about Tarable's potential crimes had done little except fuel my need to know more about what had really happened between her and Eva. Yet right then, even that didn't matter.

Being B-Dash's girlfriend was a big deal. Given that our relationship started when I was a pop member, I knew I wouldn't get automatic membership back to the site, but still. Populatti had always been about seeing B-Dash. Now that I had him, I was beginning to see his point. Did the site even matter? As my eyelids grew heavy, I crawled into bed, massaging my swollen ankle before drifting to sleep.

I didn't stir again until my phone buzzed at 9:00 a.m. It was two hours before I was even considering getting up, but thinking it could be Brandon calling to check on my ankle, I grabbed the phone in a hurry. Turning onto my side, my body ached. When the caller ID told me it was Crystal, I moaned. After a few rings, I decided to answer anyway. Crys and I had barely talked since the outburst in the sunroom last weekend. If I wanted our friendship to continue, I couldn't avoid her much longer.

"Missed you last night at the movies," she said.

"Missed you too," I said, playing along.

"B-Dash still treating you well?"

"Yup, hung out with him last night," I said, matching her tone. "Decided to make it official now too."

"Really? That's awesome," she said, not sounding too surprised. "Tara mentioned you were with him last night. Anyway, my SAT tutor canceled for this morning and I was thinking of getting out of the house for a while. You wanna grab some coffee?"

"Sure," I said, my stomach growling. "Mind if we throw in some breakfast?"

"Only if you promise me not to smother your

pancakes in syrup. You know the smell makes me sick."

"It's a deal," I said, stumbling out of bed.

One thirty-minute shower later, I was seated at the Olympia Diner with Crystal in a booth, struggling to sit still. Since I had no plans to tell her what I'd learned from Val at last night's party, there was no way I could complain about the Antarctica shaped bruise running down my back. Or the fact that I wanted to cry every time I put too much weight on my ankle. Yet Crystal seemed too distracted to notice anyway. After we placed our order for two bagels with cream cheese on the side – the only diner food I could eat without piling on the syrup – she dove right into the conversation, her eyes darting from side to side as she talked.

"We missed you Friday night at the party. Sammy put together an impressive fiesta, but without you it was pretty lame. A lot of people thought so," she said.

"Really?" I said, suspicious anyone could really miss one person in a big crowd.

"Of course," she said. "You're the one who always starts the dancing. And insists on everyone using those stupid drink umbrellas. Without you, something's just lost."

I smiled, surprised by her words. "Well in that case, did anyone mention supporting my reinstatement?"

"No, but people are coming around. I'm sure it

won't be long."

"Thank God."

"Anyway, I'm sure you heard that Tara and Val went at it towards the end of the night," she said.

"Yeah, Tara called me afterwards. She was pretty fired up."

"Tell me about it. She was screaming and swearing like I've never seen. But the thing is, for the first time, I wasn't so sure I was on her side."

"Really?"

"Yeah. Now, we all know she's obsessed with Christian, even though Val's made it clear she's into him too."

"Well, nothing wrong with some healthy competition," I said, playing dumb.

"Obviously," said Crys. "Except that Tara's been hatching plans to make Val look bad."

I took a large gulp of orange juice that stung on the way down.

"I thought Tara told Coop to go on that date with Val. And that she just wanted to be herself and see what happened."

"Well let me tell you, on Friday Tara was all over him. And I overheard Tara telling Sammy she wanted to create some rumors about Val that would turn off Christian. Not exactly playing fair," said Crys.

I sighed. "So what do you want me to do about it?"

Crys frowned. "Talk some sense into her. You

know, give her a call, get her talking about Coop, and tell her it's a bad idea to trash Val. I know she'll never listen to me."

"Then why not go to Sammy?" I asked. "I'm not supposed to know about any of this. I wasn't at the party, remember?"

Crystal's face turned red. "Well, I just thought since you and Tara were closer…"

"Sounds to me like Sammy and Tarable have cut you out of the loop."

"No, I just missed the conversation," she said, looking away. "But speaking of them, they don't know I'm here. No offense, but I think we should keep it that way."

"Wait, is there a popster rule against talking to nonmembers?"

"No, I just don't want them asking why I didn't invite them. The three of you have been like sisters to me and I don't want Tara thinking I'm going behind her back."

"But isn't that what you're doing?"

"Only because I don't want to see another friend booted out."

"So you want me to save Tara's membership even though none of you did the same for me?"

"Hey, we did tell you to cool it with B-Dash. But honestly, we didn't take it too seriously because we never thought you'd get voted out. We underestimated Eva."

The waitress arrived with two bagels and refills

of orange juice. We thanked her, then got smearing with the cream cheese.

"I'm afraid it's hard to want to help Tara when she hasn't exactly been bending over backwards to help me."

"Which is why you need to talk to her," said Crys.

"Correction. It's why you need to talk to her. Lately every time I talk to her we just fight. Especially since she's been defending Eva."

Crystal dropped a bite of bagel to her plate. "Wait, what has she been saying?"

"Just that Eva really isn't that bad and I need to be nicer to her. Sammy was saying the same thing too."

"Seriously? What are they thinking? After what she did to me and you? I know we have to be civil, but nice? That's news to me."

"Told ya you were out of the loop."

Crys continued eating her bagel. "I'm not out of anything. I've just been busy with school, as always."

"Sure you have. And I wish I could help you, but in case you've forgotten, I've been booted off the island."

"I know. But I promise that as soon as we have the votes, we *will* get you back in. We just need a few more weeks."

"A few more weeks?" The timeline had just shifted. "Last week you said you'd get me back in two."

"Look, you've already made it one, so what if you wait a few more? Better to wait until things blow over than to get rejected again, right?"

"If peeps already miss me, then why would I get rejected again?"

"I dunno, you might not. Things are just crazy right now. The timing doesn't feel right."

My phone buzzed in my purse as Crystal wiped away the sweat running down her forehead. I pulled it from my purse and walked away from the table.

"Hey Crys, it's my mom, I gotta take this," I said.

"Yeah sure, I'll be here."

I nodded then walked out the door, picking up on the last ring before voicemail.

"Hey Val," I said. "I'm so happy you called."

populatti.com

<u>BrandontheGreat: 87%</u>

Approved Members: 23
Pending Applications: 1
Access Denied: 48

POP REPORT: countdown to golden hill's first film festival begins…time 4 dress shopping w the gurrls!!~ Crys

COMMENTS:

Tarable *posted at 3:01 p.m. ET May 24*: okay dress procured. along w awesome accessories!!

Matt *posted at 2:13 p.m. ET May 24*: jake, i've got the editing thing down. let me handle it, you just worry bout bringing the camera to class

BiancaA *posted at 2:13 p.m. ET May 24*: yes, val, much more productive

ValieGal *posted at 11:00 a.m. ET May 24*: forget dress shopping, it's softball time ;)

Jake *posted at 11:00 a.m. ET May 24*: trying again for video editing help? anyone?? wanna figure this out before we film...

CHAPTER THIRTEEN

"Dress shopping for the film festival. Huh. Funny I wasn't invited," I said as I read over Crystal's status update. Yet another thing she didn't tell me when we were together just that morning. Keeping her shopping trip secret was as ridiculous as hiding our breakfast from Tara and Sammy. For someone who didn't like sports, Crystal was sure good at playing games. But before I could concentrate any more on Crystal, the doorbell rang.

Downstairs, Mom was talking to Val.

"Ready to go?" Val asked.

I nodded, then threw on my coat.

"Nice to meet you," Mom said.

We bolted out the door before Mom could begin

prying. Mom may not have known my friends well, but she at least knew who they were. Pretty much no one but Sammy, Crystal, or Tara had been over to the house in years. So while I wasn't surprised at Mom's sideways glance at Val, I didn't have time to get into it. Right then I was in crisis mode and needed to escape.

"So the beach sound good?" Val asked once we were buckled into her car. "It's supposed to reach 70 degrees today so it could be a good place to talk."

"Sure," I said, hoping I could finagle my way into a Starbucks stop along the way.

Luckily, Val had similar intentions.

After a ten-minute coffee detour, we were on the boardwalk, plastic cups in hand. The beach looked just as pristine in May as in July. The sand was raked and piles of black seaweed waited for removal in a large heap at the edge of the beach, next to the white picket fence separating the public bathing area from the private residences dotting the crescent-shaped coastline. The boardwalk was almost empty today, and except for a few energetic dog owners and oversized sea gulls that had spent too much time in the McDonald's parking lot, Val and I were alone. We walked in silence for the first ten minutes, shuffling down the wooden stairs of the boardwalk and onto the long stretch of faded decking that meandered down the sandy strip for almost a full mile before ending just as the cliffs of Watcher's Point began.

"So Bianca told me you're filming your English video this week. Sounds exciting," Val said between sips of her iced vanilla latté.

"Yeah, should go well," I said, relieved to talk about something other than Populatti. "We've got five different interviews scheduled with students and teachers, and I think we're gonna get some solid information. If we make a strong enough case I was even thinking of submitting it to the Board of Ed. You know, so that they maybe look into some of the problems like the overcrowding."

"You are so lucky you have such an awesome topic," Val said. "I think the entire student body will be forever grateful if you get the air quality fixed,"

I laughed. "I don't know if we'll get that far."

"But at least you're trying," she said. "We finished filming our video last week, but it's nowhere near as exciting. We're doing it on fast food, and I just feel like it's overdone. Your topic is so much more relevant."

"Fast food sounds good," I said. "I think Brandon's group's is doing something similar. Not fast food but whether calorie postings are accurate?"

Val shoved her hands into her pocket as a puff of wind glided over the sand. "Yeah, I was talking about it with him the other day after practice. Neither of our groups is too original."

"Well I like our topic, but I really wish I could've done it on Populatti."

Val laughed. "Oh God, tell me about it. That would be classic. Talk about a social commentary."

"Yeah, can you imagine the look on Crystal's face if we did that? Do you know she invited me to breakfast today, but then failed to mention she was going shopping for a dress to wear to the film festival? Ugh. Sorry, I shouldn't vent," I said, shaking my head. Usually I wasn't one to complain about Crys or the girls to others, but lately my defenses were weakened.

Lucky for me, Val just nodded. She seemed to understand my predicament better than expected, maybe because she'd helped cause it.

"So what exactly happened Friday night anyway?" I said.

"Oh the usual. Tara and Coop were talking a lot, though of course stupid me thought nothing of it. I know they're close because they have that photography class together, and obviously it's not like Coop and I are dating. Just talking, you know?"

"Uh-huh," I said, letting her continue.

"But then I was getting myself a drink and Eva came up to me acting real upset. That's when she told me I had to watch out because Tara wanted Christian and was going to start rumors about me, kind of like what she did to you."

I swallowed, knowing that Crystal had told me the same thing at breakfast. Meaning that whatever Eva told Val was true. Eva and Tara had been talking after all.

Val seemed to understand the implications.

"Eva and I have never been super close, but I know she's a decent person. We've hung out off and on for years and the one thing she's always done is tell the truth. Which is why I believed her when she told me you were a jerk about Nick," she said.

"But then when I was talking to Crystal the other day, she made it clear that you never even liked Nick that much and that he pursued you. That made me start reevaluating everything. I mean, what Crystal said made sense, given that you and Nick barely dated."

A gust of wind whipped across my face. "I swear, I never had a clue that Eva had a crush on Nick."

"I believe you."

"Then what does this have to do with Friday's fight?"

Val sighed. "Well, initially when Eva told me to watch out for Tara, I got angry. I'd never known Eva to be a liar, but it just seemed too convenient, you know? Like another rumor she was starting to eliminate you and your friends. And too similar to what happened with Nick."

"OhmiGod, did you tell her that?"

"Pretty much."

"And what did she say?"

"First she got real quiet. Then she started to cry. So I brought her into another room and calmed her down. That's when she spilled about Tara. She claimed Tara approached her three months ago asking for intel on Coop."

My stomach churned as the story shifted to Tara. "I know you said that last night too. But I don't get it. Why would Eva know anything special about Coop?"

"Because he moved into her neighborhood and they carpool together every morning. Been doing it since October. I guess Tara promised to get Eva into Populatti if she could give her info on Coop."

"Okay," I said, amazed at how much Tara had kept hidden. "But then how do I fit in? I had nothing to do with any of this."

Val turned to look out at the crashing waves. "No, but once Tara got Eva into Populatti, I guess Tara got annoyed that Coop still wasn't interested in her and figured she needed to learn more about him. Somewhere around then, she told Eva that she was going to help her out and give her some secret intel that would ensure her membership would last, even if she broke up with Matt. Eva was so grateful that of course she continued to spill about Christian. And so the perfect storm was made."

I tried not to cry as my face grew hot. "Then why didn't anyone else get voted out too?"

"Whatever she said about them must not have been as bad."

"But why did Tara pick me?"

Val shrugged.

I followed Val's gaze to the foamy water as I bit

down on my lip, willing it to stop shaking. Tara had gone behind our backs to learn more about Christian, getting Eva into Populatti by setting her up with Matt and then helping her open up more by gossiping. The always rational Tara had sold out her friends for a guy.

"I know it's a lot to take in," said Val. "But I think Tara really just got in over her head. She was pissed that Coop didn't like her and she thought Eva had info that could help. So she made up a story that kept Eva talking."

"I can't believe Tara let it go so far."

My eyes welled over as I thought back to all the times I'd listened to Tara go on about Coop, all the cookies I'd baked for her, and all the outfits I'd let her borrow – some of which she still hadn't returned. Not to mention all the sleepovers, dance parties, karaoke contests, group projects and lazy summer days that had shaped our friendship over the last five years. Tara was than just a friend. She was my closest, very best friend. Even closer than Sammy and Crys. She'd been there for me when no one else was. When I thought of myself as nothing more than Drumstick. And now there was no question. My very best friend had betrayed me.

Val looked away.

"I don't think Tara wanted to hurt you. I think she just got stuck," she said. "Once Eva started talking termination, Tara couldn't tell Eva she'd made up the story, or tell anyone else about what she'd done without jeopardizing her own membership."

"That doesn't make it right."

"Of course not. And I'm not telling you to forgive her either. I just want to make sure you understand the situation."

I nodded, my face hot. "So Eva's comments never had anything to do with the whole cheating-suspension thing."

Val shook her head. "Not at all. I don't think Eva was ever angry about that. More mad at herself for cheating. Especially since it ruined her friendship with Crystal."

I sighed, relieved. "Then do you think she'd at least consider voting me back into Populatti?"

"That depends," said Val. "Are you willing to give up Tara?"

"Uh, how so?" I asked.

"Well, as you can imagine, Tara isn't our favorite person right now. She's been lying to Eva for months and openly plotting to destroy me next. We want her out of Populatti."

I nodded. "Um, well what if I try to help lower her approval rating?"

Val shook her head. "We'll never get her rating low enough. We need to vote her out."

"I, I don't know if I can do that," I said, feeling dizzy. Even if Tara had betrayed me, we had a history. For the second time in ten minutes, I thought about all our friendship had weathered. Even with the facts laid out before me, giving up on Tara seemed too harsh. Not to mention dangerous. Because turning on Tara would most certainly mean risking my friendships with Crys and Sammy, no matter what the truth turned out to be.

Val seemed to expect my response. "Just think about it. She tried to ruin you too, remember?"

I nodded, feeling sick. Tara might have betrayed me, but risking my remaining relationships with Crys and Sammy was more than I could bear. Without them, not only would I be votes short of getting back into Populatti, but I'd be out of friends as well.

I spent the rest of the week focusing on everything except Populatti and Tara. On Monday, my parents took advantage of a rare day off to take the twins and me to the local Memorial Day Parade, then christened the grill for the season, making hotdogs and hamburgers with chili, my favorite.

The rest of the days passed in a blur. Not only were we filming our video, but with the end of school only a month away, it seemed every class had an upcoming test or paper or project, keeping me plenty busy during the afternoons. During the nights, having Brandon's Populatti password softened the isolation. Even though I couldn't post comments or talk about Pop in conversations, by knowing what was going on, there was little difference in my everyday life. I sat with the popsters at lunch, rode to school with Sammy in the Beast, and still acted like I was everybody's best friend. B-Dash called every night and he seemed content to miss most of the planned popster events, though he warned me that this Friday would be different. It was Jake's birthday party and he couldn't miss it.

Even Val seemed cool with the arrangement, though she did stop me on Thursday to see if I'd decided to vote against Tara. With the film festival just over a week away, I told her I was too busy working on our project to give it any thought. Which was true enough. Even though we'd finished filming our interviews, we'd been spending more time than expected hovering over Jake's Mac editing the footage, giving me little time for much else. While I was able to push Val off with a promise that I'd get back to her after the weekend, the conversation brought up bad memories of our stroll down the beach. I was living in the eye of the hurricane. No matter which direction I headed, the storm was sure to hit.

My next step didn't become clear until that Friday around 10:00 p.m. I was at home with the twins – trying, and failing, to forget about the night's Populatti party – when Brandon appeared on my doorstep. He'd been with the popsters celebrating Jake's birthday and was supposed to be calling to say goodnight, not standing outside my house. So there I was with no makeup, wearing my bright pink puffy slippers with my matching flannel pjs that were anything but flattering, with B-Dash

standing there in his party best. The only thing going for me was that Mom and Dad were out, but
given that the twins were very much awake, even
this was a very small positive.

"Where's your phone? Do you have any messages?" Brandon asked as I opened the door. He
flew into the living room where my phone balanced
atop a pile of empty Chinese takeout containers.

"Slow down. No one's called since you did an
hour ago," I said.

"No texts or videos?" he asked as he flipped
through my saved messages.

"Nope, nothing at all. Me and the boys were just
watching a movie," I said, pointing to the TV. "Now
what are you doing here? Aren't you supposed to be
home by now? Don't you have that big tournament
tomorrow morning?"

Last I'd heard he was stopping by Jake's then
heading home early to rest for his morning start on
the mound.

"I know, I was gonna leave early but Jake
wasn't thrilled with the idea and since he's on the
team too it was hard to argue…"

"Shhhh," whispered one of the twins. Both
Charlie and Chris were sitting there wide-eyed, fists
tense. We were watching the latest disaster movie,
which I'd agreed to rent thanks to the cute actor
who was supposed to be saving the world from killer slime.

"Oh, hey, sorry to interrupt," he said, noticing

the boys.

Charlie let out a squeal as another car chase filled the screen.

"Livi, we can't hear the movie," Chris moaned as the music intensified.

Knowing we couldn't go to my room even if my parents were out – heaven forbid the twins found out and told them that a male teenager had seen my bedroom – I led Brandon to the kitchen, which I figured was the safest place. Though our game room was technically an option, right then I wasn't sure I wanted to be so isolated. If there was one thing Brandon and I still hadn't discussed, it was my feelings on how far I was willing to go. Now that I was his girlfriend, I didn't want him getting the wrong idea. So instead I pointed Brandon to the kitchen table and threw a bag of popcorn into the microwave. As the kernels of corn began exploding, I wandered back to the table.

"Hey, you smell funny," I said, running my hand through his hair.

Brandon looked down at the counter. "Matt got us some beers to celebrate the occasion."

"Wait? You guys were drinking? Before a base-ball game?"

He closed his eyes and nodded. "I know, I know. We messed up. But it was only a couple beers."

"And you drove?" I asked, trying hard to keep my voice level.

"No, I walked."

"Isn't it kinda cold out?"

He sighed. "Not if you run. The party was less than a mile away. And this was an emergency."

"Is everything all right then? Did someone get hurt?" I pulled out the popcorn and held it away from my face as a plume of steam shot out of the bag.

"Nobody's hurt."

"Then what is it? OhmiGod did Val say something to Tara? Did they nominate her for termination?" I asked, my voice growing manic. What if someone mentioned that I'd been talking to Val? That I'd considered turning on my best friend? I shoveled a handful of popcorn into my mouth and tried to relax.

But as I looked over at Brandon, I couldn't help but worry.

Without a word, he leaned over, took my hand and stared right into my now spastic eyes. Then he shook his head and broke the gaze.

"They didn't nominate Tara. This has to do with me."

My arms broke out into goose bumps. "Please tell me they didn't try to kick you out again."

"This has nothing to do with Populatti."

"Then what happened?"

"Livs, I am so sorry. But I was talking to Sammy about trying to get you back into Populatti and all of a sudden she leaned in and kissed me. On the lips."

populatti.com

BrandontheGreat: 73%

Approved Members: 23
Pending Applications: 0
Access Denied: 49

POP REPORT: happy birthday Jakey. I looovvveee u!!!!! c ya all soon!! ~Crys

COMMENTS:

Matt *posted at 10:49 p.m. ET May 30*: matt has shared a video. Click here to view

EvaBeautiful *posted at 10:36 p.m. ET May 30*: OMG!! DID THAT JUS HAPPN???

BiancaA *posted at 6:09 p.m. ET May 30*: happy bday jake! time to paarttty!

Jake *posted at 5:03 p.m. ET May 30*: thnx 4 all the bday shout outs!

ValieGal *posted at 4:07 p.m. ET May 30*: happy birthday jake!

celebSAMmy *posted at 3:02 p.m. ET May 30*: yaaay jake!! Happy birthday gorgeous!

BrandontheGreat *posted at 2:24 p.m. ET May 30*: hbd man

CHAPTER FOURTEEN

"She kissed you? Without warning?" We were in my room now, breaking house rules, hovered over my laptop. Not that it mattered. I was pretty sure that when a video was circulating of one of your best friends kissing your boyfriend, all rules were off.

"Livs, I'm telling ya, I didn't see it coming at all. And as soon as I figured out what she was doing, I pushed her away. I didn't kiss her back."

I blinked my eyes and looked away as the tears started streaming down my face.

"I am so sorry. I care about you so much, I'd never do anything to hurt you..."

"God, Brandon. Sammy? How do you just let

that happen?"

"I'm sorry. I don't know what else to say."

"How about nothing. I really don't think I can talk about this right now."

"Well I'm afraid we have to."

"Why?" I asked, my arms shaking.

"Because of the video."

"Are you sure there even is one?" I asked.

He nodded. "It was a birthday video for Jake. Matt and some of the other guys were making it, just capturing crazy messages and stuff. When they noticed Sammy was drunk, they started following her around."

"Drunk? Sammy doesn't get drunk!"

"She did tonight. I dunno what she and Tara were up to, but both of them were acting insane. Even Crystal didn't seem herself."

"And this all happened at Jake's?"

"The party was at Crystal's."

"It was?"

"I thought you knew."

"Oh right. Because I'm so tight with the popsters right now. Even you didn't tell me."

"Sorry. I forgot you don't get the invitations."

"That's not the only thing I don't get."

"I didn't try to kiss her. Honest."

"Well that means Sammy tried to kiss you. Either way, someone I care about tried to hurt me."

"Aw Livs, she was wasted. I don't think she knew what was going on."

"Sorry, I don't buy it. And I don't get it. What was Sammy doing drinking? And what were you doing? I thought you were just going to make an appearance, not stay all night!"

As Brandon opened his mouth to respond, we heard a pounding coming from the front door.

"If that's Sammy, I'm gonna kill her." I said.

The knocking intensified as we ran down the stairs.

"Why doesn't someone answer the door?" I yelled to the twins.

"Thought we weren't supposed to open the door for strangers," Charlie said.

"Ugh, what are you? Like ten?"

"Actually we're eleven," Chris called back.

I ignored the response and opened the door. It was Crystal.

"What are you doing here? From what I hear, you probably shouldn't be driving," I said.

"Neither should your boy Dash."

"He walked."

"And I got a ride. Seeing as I just left over 20 popsters at my parents' house to talk to you, I don't appreciate the attitude."

"Hey, I'm not the one that did anything wrong."

"Take a good look at that boyfriend of yours. He's not that innocent."

Crystal pulled up her phone and started playing the video. Benign party scenes filled the screen as the picture jumped from side to side, making me dizzy after just a few seconds of watching.

"Can't you fast forward this thing?"

"Hang on. It's coming up in a minute."

A moment later, Sammy was center stage. She was wearing a pink party hat shaped like a cone that reminded me of the ones kids used to hand out in grade school. Only instead of featuring Sponge Bob or the My Little Ponies or some other cartoon character, the hat was covered in silver glitter that spelled out Happy Birthday.

"Good call on the decorations. That's so Jake," I said as we watched Sammy stumble around.

The video was shot from too far away to capture the audio, but even without it, I could tell Sammy was drunk. When the scene started, she was on the dance floor, hips swaying and fists pumping up on some guy I didn't know, but who I was pretty sure played lacrosse. As the music ended and the dancing stopped, she placed her arms around him and whispered something in his ear. He bent his head down to her neck, kissed her, then whispered something back. Whatever he said, Sammy must not have liked it because just as the guy started laughing, Sammy was bringing her arm back like a slingshot and preparing to fire.

"Jesus, what is she doing? And who is that guy?" I asked.

"That's Andy, one of Jake's friends. You guys had Geometry together last year."

"And why did Sammy try to belt him?"

"She asked him to go out next weekend and he said no. She got pissed, even though he had a legitimate excuse. He's going away next weekend with his parents."

"Hey, the video's on Jake now. What happened to Sammy?" I asked as the footage turned back to the dance floor.

"Don't worry, it'll come back in a minute."

"What is Jake wearing across his head?"

"My belt. Don't ask."

A pang of sadness struck as I watched Jake dance around the screen. Everyone seemed to be having so much fun dancing and having a good time, while I was forgotten back at home, watching movies with the twins. But before I could complain, Sammy was back in the video. She was at the drink table now, her hand grabbing the forbidden flask. Brandon appeared in the frame behind her, reaching for a beer just as she turned around.

For the next two minutes, I watched as a conversation between them unfolded. Brandon had told me they were talking about getting me back into Populatti, and judging by his body language, I'd say it was possible. Brandon was leaning up against the table, his hands balled into fists at his side. He did not inch forward, or peer over Sammy's low-cut tank top, or even help her as she struggled to open a bottle of Coke. Instead, he seemed subdued and almost disinterested, like he knew that Sammy wasn't acting herself.

As Sammy poured the Coke, having defeated the cap, Brandon extended his arm to hers and mouthed what looked like "See ya." Then he took a step away from the table and started backing away. But Sammy grabbed onto his arm and leaned in, losing her balance and falling into his chest. Brandon then hugged her with both his arms until her feet were planted on the ground. Sammy smiled back at him, then jumped up onto her toes and kissed his cheek. Brandon dropped his arms from her back and moved his right foot behind his left just as Sammy jumped up again, this time smacking her lips right onto Brandon's.

"OhmiGod, I can't watch!" I said, closing my eyes.

"It's all right, it's over now," said Brandon. "But look at this. See how she was acting afterwards? She's completely insane."

Squinting, I turned back to the screen. The kiss was over and Brandon appeared to be yelling. Sammy was laughing and raising her cup as if preparing to give a toast.

"What is wrong with her?" I said. "Why would she do something like this?"

"Dude, what are you talking about?" Crystal said. "I'm pretty sure Sammy was ambushed. Didn't you see him hug her? The way he didn't pull away after that first kiss? Which was all innocent on the cheek? Brandon totally went in for that second one on his own."

I tried to control my shaking hands as my eyes met Crystal's. Brandon had hugged Sammy, but Sammy had jumped up twice to kiss him, not once. Yet Brandon hadn't gotten out of the way. A mixture of emotions clouded my thoughts as I tried to make sense of the situation.

"What are you talking about?" said Brandon, shouting at Crystal. "It was all Sammy! I didn't try to kiss her at all!"

Crys shook her head. "Yeah, you did. I think you got excited when Sammy gave you that peck on the cheek, thinking maybe she liked you. So, you went for it. Only Sammy was just being polite."

"How is kissing my boyfriend polite?" I said.

"Come on, Livs. Are you really gonna believe B-Dash over your very best friends in the world? When you weren't even there?"

My voice cracked. "Crys, I just watched the whole thing. I'm not saying Brandon's innocent, but Sammy was out of line. Why are you defending her?"

"Because I knew he'd poison your brain," said Crystal, pointing at Brandon. "If you'd just watched this before he got here, I'm sure you'd have seen things differently."

I took a step back, wondering if Crystal was right. Closing my eyes, I pictured the scene again, cringing as Sammy's lips again met Brandon's. And deciding that Brandon's account made sense. Sammy had pursued him. Brandon had been upset by her advances. I could see it in his body language, even if he had stuck around a little too long after that first peck on the cheek.

Knowing full well that I was about to lose the last of my friends, I brought my hands to my hips. "I'm not changing my mind," I said. "Sammy was wrong. She pursued Brandon. And even if Brandon had gone after her, she'd still be at fault. She was laughing afterward! How can you not see that?"

Crystal shook her head. "I don't know what happened, but you've changed, Livi. Now I need to get back to the party. What do you want me to tell Sammy? She'll be devastated when she hears you don't believe her."

"Wait, Sammy sent you here? Why didn't she just come herself?"

"Because she knew how you'd react. Everyone knows that all you care about is B-Dash. You even got kicked out of Populatti because of him."

My mouth dropped as Crystal's tone grew sharp. A lifetime had passed since our breakfast at the diner.

"No, I'm pretty sure I got kicked out because someone was feeding Eva rumors," I said.

"Oh and let me guess. You think that was Sammy too."

"No, but I wouldn't be too sure she didn't know about it..."

Brandon cut me off before I could finish. "Ladies, ladies, come on. You're tired and this is stupid. Crystal, why don't you go home to the party, and I'll stay with Livi. I'm sure Sammy will call in the morning and explain herself."

"But Sammy has nothing to explain."

"We've all seen the video now, so why don't we let people decide for themselves, okay?" said Brandon.

"Crys?" I said, interrupting. "Are you going to walk back or should I call you a cab? I really don't want the twins hearing all this."

"A cab? Don't bother, I'd rather walk." Crystal swung her purse over her shoulder and turned toward the street.

"Text me when you get there, so I know you're safe," I said.

Crys waved her arm in acknowledgement before breaking into a jog.

With my muscles still shaking, I closed the door, then opened the hall closet and pulled out a sweater, throwing it over my head in one motion.

"I'm sorry you had to see that," Brandon said.

"That's all right," I said, my voice wavering. "At least now I know for myself."

"And you believe me?"

I sighed, wondering if part of him did like Sammy. Most guys did. And could I blame them? Sammy was gorgeous, funny, outgoing. Most importantly, she was off limits. Her no-dating policy had made her stock soar. But Brandon had never looked at Sammy, at least not from what I could remember.

"I don't think you wanted it to happen," I said. "But that doesn't mean I'm okay with it."

Brandon bowed his head. "I know. I should have seen it coming, especially the second time. I should have gotten out of there sooner. And not taken those beers from Matt."

I nodded, happy to hear the words, and hoping he really meant them. Brandon had been loyal since my termination, and my trust in him had been growing. It was hard to believe all those trips to my locker and missed pop events had been part of an act.

"I promise I'll make it up to you," he said, his eyes glassy.

"Whatever," I said, not wanting to forgive him, but not wanting to lose him either. "Right now I need to figure out what to do about Crystal. Obviously she's trying to tear us apart."

"Or keep you girls together."

I sighed. "Maybe, though taking Sammy's side was definitely not the way to mend our relationship. But you know, right now I just don't care what she was thinking."

As soon as I said the words, I knew they were true. Tara had betrayed me and now Crys and Sammy were out of line. Brandon, while not perfect, was standing by me. Right then, he was the only one who mattered. Well, and my stomach, all that nervous energy having burned through dinner.

"I'm starving," I said, pacing through the foyer. "We've got a few DiGiorno's in the freezer. Will you eat some if I heat one up? Or no, you need to get going. You still have that tournament tomorrow."

Brandon shrugged. "So do the rest of the guys and they're still at Crystal's. And you know how I feel about pizza," he said.

I nodded, pleased with his answer.

"Should we ask the twins?" he asked.

"Good idea."

As I shuffled off to the kitchen, my phone buzzed. Crys was back safe. Shaking my head, I grabbed a supreme flavored DiGiorno and turned on the oven. I still couldn't believe Crys had come over here to fight with me, but the text was promising. While I wasn't ready to forgive Sammy, maybe my friendship with Crys could be saved.

Twenty-five minutes later, we were gathered around the kitchen table with Chris and Charlie, chowing down on two supreme style pizzas covered in extra mozzarella and parmesan that I'd tossed on about halfway through the baking process. The added layer of warm cheese calmed my nerves, helping to block out the conversation with Crystal and that damning video of Sammy.

Not that I could've dwelled on it even if I wanted to. The twins were so excited about the late-night movie and pizza binge that they couldn't stop talking. At least Brandon didn't seem to mind the distraction. Especially since he'd seen the same movie a few months ago and had his own theories about the mutant slime that was infecting earth. I'd never seen the twins eat pizza so slowly, as they hung on Brandon's every word. The only person that came close to entertaining the twins so well was Sammy and even she lost out to B-Dash, especially when he brought up baseball.

The party broke up around midnight when my parents came home early. They'd been at a benefit for the hospital and I hadn't expected them home until much later. Luckily, they didn't seem to mind that I'd kept the boys up two hours past their bedtime or that B-Dash had shown up without an invitation. Instead they just kept talking about how nice it was that we were all hanging out together, which sounded lame to me, but kept me out of trouble.

The next morning I woke up feeling fat and bloated. All that pizza had made my fingers swell until my rings were almost cutting off the circulation to my knuckles. After chugging a glass of water in the bathroom and forcing the silver and turquoise ring I'd gotten from Sammy for my 15th birthday off my pinky with my teeth, I texted Brandon good luck on his game, then headed downstairs for breakfast. Mom was up early trying to make Dad's famous pancakes, but judging from the smell coming from the kitchen, something had gone wrong. It wasn't that Mom was a bad cook, she just never took the time to learn, and with Lona preparing feasts on the weekdays, there was little incentive for her to whip up a turkey dinner or a batch of fluffy pancakes on a Saturday. But surprisingly, the pancakes weren't horrible, even if they did have a tinge of scorched butter on one side.

"It was nice to see Brandon last night," Mom said as she flipped a stack of pancakes onto a plate. The twins were leaving for baseball practice in ten minutes and needed to eat fast.

"Yeah he stopped by after his party to see how I was feeling," I said.

"That's nice. You know I was talking to Mrs. Hood down at the batting cages last week. Her son Ryan is a couple years ahead."

"Yeah, he's one of Brandon's good friends."

"His mother seemed lovely. She told me there's some big event coming up at the high school next weekend? A film festival or something?"

I chewed my bite of pancake extra long before responding. "Yeah, it's got to do with that English project I told you about. They're gonna show all the videos and then we get to vote. Best one wins some sort of prize."

"Ah, I remember you talking about your video. Sounds like a fun event."

"Yeah," I said, sighing. "I'm excited, I think our film has a real shot at winning. Though I still don't have anything to wear. I can't believe Crystal went dress shopping without me."

As soon as the words slipped out, I regretted

saying them. Confiding in Mom had never been my strong suit. Because Mom wasn't one to just listen. She was a fixer. And she never seemed to realize that most of my problems didn't need fixing, just a sympathetic ear. So I braced myself for her response. And was surprised to hear her gloss over my anger with Crystal.

"Well it's too bad shopping with your friends didn't work out," she said, "but if you need a dress, I have the afternoon off. Maybe we could go shopping and get some lunch."

My phone rang just as Mom finished talking. It was Sammy. I silenced the ringer and threw it into my lap.

"Where would we go?" I asked.

"Wherever you like. How about Westport? There are lots of shops there."

The phone vibrated against my thigh, reminding me of my missed call. Avoiding Sammy for a day of shopping was tempting. There was less than a week until the festival and I did need a dress, especially now that I'd talked to Ms. Tilfry about sending our video to the Board of Ed. She'd loved the idea and decided to take it one step further and invite the Board of Ed members to the festival so they could watch all the films. Knowing our voices would be heard was exciting, yet as the group spokesperson, it made my dress – and my introductory speech, which I had yet to start writing – that much more important.

I contemplated calling Bianca since we were in the same group and could coordinate dress colors, but given that we'd just patched our relationship enough to be acquaintances, I feared shopping together would be too much, too soon.

"Westport sounds good," I said. Twenty miles south on I-95, Westport's shopping district bordered the Saugatuck river, making it the perfect place to spend a warm spring day. And with lots of independent boutiques rather than mall chains, a dress procured there was less likely to surface on one of my peers, adding to the appeal.

Mom's face lit up. "That sounds great. Why don't you get dressed and I'll meet you in an hour after I drop the twins at practice?"

"Sounds good."

"Great. And we should take the Escape too," said Mom, still smiling. "I still haven't seen you drive."

populatti.com

<u>BrandontheGreat: 87%</u>

Approved Members: 23
Pending Applications: 0
Access Denied: 49

POP REPORT: in desperate need of a tan ~Crys

COMMENTS:

BrandontheGreat *posted at 10:51 a.m. ET May 31*: watch the video, tara. The evidence is clearly incriminating...

BiancaA *posted at 10:42 a.m. ET May 31*: uhhhh any1 up 4 shopping?

Tarable *posted at 10:23 a.m. ET May 31*: ITS ALL BRANDON'S FAULT!!

ValieGal *posted at 9:45 a.m. ET May 31*: yea except get totally wasted

celebSAMmy *posted at 3:04 a.m. ET May 31*: stay out of this eva!!!! I DID NOTHING WRONG

Matt *posted at 10:49 p.m. ET May 31*: matt has shared a video. Click here to view

EvaBeautiful *posted at 10:36 p.m. ET May 31*: OMG!! DID THAT JUS HAPPN???

CHAPTER FIFTEEN

"So I'll talk to you later this afternoon, okay? And tell the team good luck," I said as Brandon and I finished discussing the morning's victory.

Despite the heavy partying of some less-than-committed team members, the baseball team had just won the first game of their tournament in extra innings, meaning they still had anywhere from one to three games left. Even with the long day – and long night before – Brandon was in good spirits, having only let in two runs while on the mound. While I was relieved staying out late hadn't hurt his game, it was hard not to be a little annoyed that the beers – and drama with Sammy – hadn't had some negative impact on the team.

"Thanks it should be an exciting afternoon," said Brandon. "And have fun with your mom. Maybe we can grab some pizza tonight if you're free."

"No pizza. I can still taste last night's grease."

"How 'bout a movie then?"

"Sure. Pick one out after the games and text me the time," I said, hanging up the phone.

Breathing in deep, I entered the foyer with a sense of purpose. Now that I had plans for the night with B-Dash, my day was Sammy-proof. My ringer was off and shopping with Mom would take at least four hours, bringing me within an hour or two of my date with Brandon. If all went well, I wouldn't have to speak to or see her until Sunday at the earliest. By then maybe she might be ready to apologize, I thought, thinking back to the voicemail she'd left an hour earlier where she accused me of plotting against her with Brandon. It was funny. I could be accused of all sorts of things even when I stayed home and watched a movie with the twins.

Out in the car, I flipped down my turquoise Wayfarers and adjusted the mirrors like they'd shown us in driver's ed the week before. Mom jumped into the passenger seat with her purse and two Diet Cokes as I finished running through my routine.

"Don't forget to take off the parking brake," she said as I turned the key.

Nodding, I released the large black lever adjacent to my seat and threw the car into reverse. I was about a quarter of the way through my road hours for driver's ed and my confidence was growing with every session. But for some reason having Mom in the car made my palms sweat. She'd never taken me driving before, and I didn't know what to expect. Given the disapproving glances she gave me pretty much every morning for my less-than-stellar housekeeping skills, I had a feeling she'd have plenty to say on my driving style. I decided to play it safe and drive five miles under the speed limit to give her less ammunition.

"Do you think you're up to the highway?" Mom asked.

"Yeah, Dad took me on 95 the other day. He said I did great," I said, leaving out the part that I'd driven about the span of one exit.

"Okay, let's take the Merritt then," she said, referencing the parkway that ran north of town. "And be careful when merging. There's a huge pine tree that hurts your visibility."

I gripped the steering wheel tighter and navigated toward the parkway, focusing on my speed the entire time. The good thing about driving was that it filled my mind completely, not allowing me to dwell on Sammy or Populatti or anything else. When I was driving, I was in control.

A few minutes later, I guided the car to the top of the on-ramp. Just as Mom predicted, an overgrown pine tree was hugging the stop sign, and blocking my view of the road. Remembering my driving lesson on obstructed intersections, I inched out over the white line and smiled, feeling like a pro. But as soon as I had a view of the road, my enthusiasm waned. Cars were flying by at a million miles an hour with no end in sight.

"Just wait it out," Mom said, sensing my nerves.

"Do you think I can go now?" I asked, seeing a break.

"Yes, go," Mom said.

I inched out a little more, then slammed on the brakes as a large SUV switched into the right lane.

A loud honking filled my ears as the driver behind me grew impatient. All of a sudden I was aware of everything that wasn't right with the situation. The seatbelt cutting into my stomach was piercing my flesh right where my t-shirt was supposed to meet my jeans. And speaking of my pants, they seemed tighter than they had just ten minutes earlier, probably from that stupid sip of Diet Coke. Finding a dress that made me look good would be even more difficult than passing next week's Algebra test. And all of this to go to Westport because I didn't have a single friend willing to go shopping. I debated getting out of the car and walking home, or just crawling under the massive pine tree that had ruined my day. But with the cars weaving and honking and the wind swirling all around, even I knew that was a bad idea. So instead I gripped the steering wheel until my knuckles tingled and listened to Mom as she talked me through the merge.

"You're doing great, honey. Don't worry about the cars behind you. Like it or not, they have to wait their turn. Now what you need to do is start accelerating as soon as you see an opening. Do you see that red truck in the distance hugging the right lane?"

"Uh-huh."

"Good. Now, see how you can't make out the car behind it? It's just a little dot, right?"

"I guess."

"Great. That is our opening. After the red truck passes, hit the gas. Once you're in the lane, keep accelerating until we reach 55. Then we can just stay put until our exit."

"If you say so," I said, just as the red truck whizzed by.

"Okay, now! Hit the gas hard!"

I moved my right foot off the brake and felt the car jerk forward as I steered it onto the highway. My body flew into the seat as my purse ricocheted off the center console, exploding onto the floor of the backseat.

"Don't worry about that, we'll get it later," said Mom. "Just focus on the road. And give it a little more gas."

Even though more gas sounded like the last thing I should be doing, I pressed my foot harder on the pedal. The car surprised me as it accelerated smoothly, reaching 55 mph a few seconds later.

"That's it! You got it," Mom said. "Great job! That's one of the most difficult merges in the area and you handled it perfectly."

I loosened my grip on the steering wheel as Mom beamed. Had I done something right? Talk about a weird day, I thought, as I checked the rearview and side mirrors for any impending dangers. After my glances confirmed that everything was in order, I smiled.

"Thanks for your help," I said.

"You did that all on your own."

I nodded and kept driving, not knowing what to say until we arrived in Westport a half hour later. Once out of the car, I stretched out my knuckles and rolled my shoulders. There was something about being in the driver's seat that made my whole body ache. The stiffness seemed to be related to the amount of criticism – or in some cases, near accidents – I collected on each drive. Thankfully, my fingers could bend this time, a good thing given the purse explosion waiting for me in the backseat.

Maybe shopping with Mom wouldn't be so bad, I thought, just as my phone vibrated from somewhere in the back. I fished it out of the seam where the seat back met the bench, and stared down at the screen. There were five missed calls. Two from Sammy and two from Tara. One unknown number. No voicemails. Typing as I walked, I punched out a joint text to the girls that I was busy and would talk to them tomorrow, if I had time. The phone buzzed almost instantly with a message from Tara asking where I was. Not wanting to answer for fear of being hunted down – the girls had been known to show up uninvited to anywhere within a thirty mile radius of Golden Hill including the twins' baseball games – I wrote back asking if we could meet tomorrow for lunch at the diner, knowing that would get them off my back. Then I threw the phone into my purse and accompanied Mom into the first store.

By the time I reached the fitting room with a pile of potential dresses, I'd received a new message from Tara. The four of us were on for lunch at noon, giving me less than 24 hours to prepare for Sammy. But despite the ticking clock, I decided not to dwell on it. There was nothing I could do now but find the perfect dress, which was a necessity regardless of what happened tomorrow.

After striking out at two stores with dresses better suited for school dances than a serious film festival, Mom and I found a trendy shop that was much more me. With rows of sophisticated dresses embellished with ruching, beads, and satin, it was like walking into a candy shop packed with Swedish Fish, gum balls, and Twizzlers. My mouth watered as we thumbed through the rainbow of fabric.

"What do you think of this?" I asked, holding up a purple wrap dress with sequined embellishments.

"Don't you think that's a little too formal?" asked Mom, pointing to the open back.

"Not if I wear a sweater."

"Why don't you try it then?"

"I think I will," I said, disappearing into the fitting room.

Once inside one of three curtained stalls, I slipped the dress over my head and tried to position it on my body. But as much as I loved the color, the top refused to sit right across my chest. Deciding there was little hope for the dress, I hung it up and handed it to the sales woman manning the dressing room.

"No luck?" she asked.

I shook my head. "Guess I'm still looking." As I turned back toward the store, I spotted two familiar faces walking toward me.

"Hey Livi, what's up?" said Val, waving me over to her and Bianca. "We were just talking about you. Actually tried calling you earlier."

Bianca nodded. "Yeah, but it went straight to voicemail."

"Sorry, I was driving," I said, not addressing why I hadn't been in touch since leaving the car.

Luckily, the girls didn't seem to care.

"We just wanted to, uh, discuss last night," said Val.

Seeing Mom a few racks over, I knew I needed to be quick. "Yeah, this isn't really the best time..."

Bianca cut me off before I could finish. "I know," she said, "And you need to know that from our viewpoint, Dash did nothing wrong."

I sighed, a flood of emotions breaking through the dam I'd worked hard to build the night before. "Thanks," I said.

"Don't worry about it," said Val. "But we better go. We're film festival shopping."

"Yeah, me too," I said, forcing a smile. So much for Westport being unique.

"Well I was thinking of wearing green," said Bianca. "In case that helps."

I nodded. "Actually it does. I'll wear something different, so we don't blend together."

"Sounds good," she said, waving as she turned toward the front of the store.

Just as the girls left, Mom popped up behind me.

"Hey honey, I found another dress for you to try," she said, holding up a shapeless black number that I never would have picked out myself.

"Oh, thanks," I said, deciding not to argue.

"I'm sorry I missed your friends," she said, pointing to the backs of Bianca and Val.

"That's okay. I would've introduced you but they were in a hurry. Bianca's in my English group and you met Val the other day. They're nice girls. Both on the softball team."

"Next time then," she said, smiling. "And I re-member Val. Seemed very sweet."

"Yeah, she is," I said. And despite the role she'd played in my termination, I meant it.

"I have to say it's good to see you expanding your horizons. Not that I don't love Crys, Sammy, and Tara, but I'm glad you have other friends too. It can be nice to see the world from different perspectives. That can be a powerful thing."

"Yeah, I know," I said, familiar with the speech.

Before she could continue talking, I retreated to the dressing room, happy to have a reason to end the conversation.

Mom's black dress actually didn't look half bad once it was on, though she agreed that it wasn't quite right. Even if it did flatter my figure, it was still black and plain and not the dress I wanted to wear for the debut of our very important film. I needed something subtle but glamorous. Serious but fun. Still, I was surprised when Mom agreed with my assessment.

Two stores and about sixty castoffs later, Mom and I headed back to the car as I cradled the perfect film festival dress in my arms. The winner was a bright blue dress covered in small iridescent blue beads. It had started as a compromise that Mom had made me try because she liked the color, even though it had little shape or embellishment besides the beads. But it had turned out to be one of those dresses that looked better off the hanger. The back plunged down just low enough to look daring, without feeling too dressy for a school event. And the front dipped down in a matching V that gave the dress a very Hollywood feel. The shiny silk fit close to my body then flitted out just above my knees, reminding me of something a fairy would wear. Even Mom had been impressed, though she did beg me to have the store take down the hem, which I refused. Just because you could see my knees did not mean it was inappropriate, even if I was wearing it for a school project.

Later that night, Brandon seemed to agree with my reasoning after I bored him with a description during the coming attractions. It wasn't that I expected him to offer any insight, but discussing fashion choices was one of my favorite conversation topics and without any girlfriends to talk to, my brain was going into information overload. Another week of no girl talk and I was sure to explode. Lucky for me, Brandon took it in stride as the theater dimmed and another end of the world movie illuminated the screen.

An hour and a half later, my neck was sore but my mood better, as I found myself looking over at Brandon, thankful he was still there. With me. Despite everything that had happened.

So when he invited me to his place afterwards, the first word that popped into my head was 'yes.' Until I remembered that last time we'd ended up alone, I'd done nothing but wrestle with how to tell him 'no.'

"My parents are at some show in New York," he

said, oblivious to my shaking hands. "They're not coming home until late."

"All right then," I said, looking at my watch.

It was 9:00 p.m., giving me two hours until curfew. And that included driving time to and from Club Dash. What could happen in less than two hours? I hoped not much.

Back at Brandon's, he ushered me downstairs to the leather couches we usually moved to the side during parties. He plugged his music into the surround sound system. A burst of yelling and screeching guitars shook the room as he reached for the volume.

"Sorry about that," he said.

"At least it's better than that geriatric music."

"Ah, the one thing we still need to work on is your taste in songs." He chuckled before kissing my forehead. "Though tonight I'll listen to whatever you want. I owe you that at least. You know, for believing me, over Sammy and Crys."

"I only believed you because your story matched the evidence," I said, feeling much more confident in my answer since talking with Bianca and Val. "But I will take you up on your offer."

I walked over to the stereo, found the radio, and tuned into Z-100, my favorite pop station from New York.

Brandon grabbed my arm and led me to the dance floor. I wrapped my arms around his neck as he started swaying, letting him push my hair off my shoulders and kiss my neck until every inch of my body tingled. I sighed. Long. Deep. And wondered why I was so scared. Because being with Brandon felt good. Right. Like what I'd wanted for longer than I could remember.

But then as he lowered me onto the couch, still kissing my neck, and then my chin and lips, something changed. My back stiffened. My head started to spin. Without thinking, I sat up, pushing Brandon away. The room felt hazy and hot and opaque, and I needed air. I needed to breathe.

"You okay Livs?" he asked, his eyes looking sleepy.

"Yeah...I'm fine."

Brandon smiled, then leaned back in for a kiss.

I tried to relax again, letting my muscles melt into the soft leather sofa as Brandon played with my hair. After hanging out almost nonstop for weeks, being together felt natural. Yet somehow I still couldn't shake the feeling that something was wrong. Again, I pulled away.

This time, Brandon sat up too.

"What's wrong?" he asked.

"Nothing. I just don't know if I'm ready to do this," I said, finally finding the words I'd meant to say back when we first started hanging out.

Brandon took in a deep breath and stood up. He blinked his eyes then reached down to the floor and grabbed his soda, taking a swig before placing the can on an end table. He didn't say a word.

And right then I knew it. After losing the girls, I was going to lose Brandon too.

"I'm sorry," I said, not knowing what else to say.

Brandon sat down on the edge of the sofa. "Don't be," he said.

My eyes widened. "You're not angry?"

"Of course not," he said, his voice sounding softer. "I love you, Livs. What we do doesn't matter."

My heart jumped as he said the words aloud. It was the first time any guy had told me he loved me, let alone B-Dash.

"I love you too," I said, as I tried to control my smile.

He grinned. "Well then. We still have an hour until curfew. And I know how you feel about ice cream and hot fudge. I'm pretty sure we've got a stocked fridge if you're up for some dessert. Maybe with a glass of Cherry Coke?"

"Uh, sure," I said, my headache lifting.

After inhaling two scoops of vanilla ice cream and a generous portion of fudge, Brandon and I threw on the TV and watched my final hour of freedom slip away.

"Well, I guess we better get going," he said at 10:30. "I know you need to be in fighting shape for your big powwow tomorrow with Sammy."

My throat tightened at the sound of her name. As perfect as the evening was, I knew it was coming to a close. And that meant there were only hours until my lunch at the diner with the girls. Could there be a worse way to kick off a Sunday? Actually, given recent events, there probably was. But with betrayals now from Tara and Sammy, and my votes for Populatti still up in the air, I was pretty sure this would be about as bad as it got. So as Brandon dropped me off at home and kissed me goodnight, I held onto him extra long, burning the salty smell of his hair and the small creases of his dimples into my mind until the motion sensor lights on the porch flicked off, signaling that it was time to go. Then I ran up to my room and willed myself into a deep sleep. I knew that as angry as I was with Sammy and Crystal and Tara, if I wanted back in Populatti, burning bridges was not an option. But pretending to be nice when I couldn't even look any of them in the eye was going to be impossible. Once again I found myself wishing that Populatti had never existed at all.

populatti.com

<u>BrandontheGreat: 78%</u>

Approved Members: 23
Pending Applications: 0
Access Denied: 49

POP REPORT: and so starts the one week to the film festival diet! Remember, every calorie you don't eat this week'll make u look that much better on the red carpet!!!! ~Crys

COMMENTS:

EvaBeautiful *posted at 10:08 a.m. ET June 1*: whatever, like u can make me go on a diet crystal mmm pizzaaa

Matt *posted at 9:39 a.m. ET June 1*: tara u might wanna watch the video again bc im thinkin dash was right...

Tarable *posted at 9:34 a.m. ET June 1*: bc she didn't do anything wrong, val!! we luvvvv u sammmy baby!!

BiancaA *posted at 3:04 p.m. ET June 1*: umm can we vote in a new social director?

ValieGal *posted at 10:04 a.m. ET June 1*: whoa, jus saw the video... and y is she still a popster???

Coop007 *posted at 8:00 a.m. ET June 1*: uh 4get the diet, what about finishing your film lol

Jake *posted at 1:00 a.m. ET June 1*: thanks guys for the awesome party and bday!

CHAPTER SIXTEEN

I arrived at the Olympia Diner ten minutes early, armed with a pile of dirt from the morning Populatti postings, not that I could ever tell anyone I'd read them. Crystal was the first to join me, looking beat in a pair of faded jeans and a bulky grey sweater that looked way too heavy to be wearing in June. And this is the heartbeat of Populatti, I thought. With dark circles, zero makeup and borderline attire, Crys never would have gotten voted in now. As it was, if she wasn't the founder, chances were people would have been talking.

"So are you ready to listen to reason?" Crystal asked as she slid into the booth opposite me.

"What's that supposed to mean? I'm here, aren't I?"

"If you're gonna be difficult, I'm gone. I just finished a three-hour session with my SAT tutor and I am not in the mood for your complaining."

"And I just finished two hours of driver's ed. We're all busy."

"But I'm not the one who caused the problem."

"Oh yeah, like I asked Sammy to go kiss my boyfriend."

Crystal brought her hands to her forehead and started rubbing.

"I'm sorry. You're right," she said, finally sounding like herself.

I nodded as Tara and Sammy strolled down the aisle.

"Hey ladies," Tara said.

"Hi, gorgeous," Crystal said, waving.

I tried to smile back as my stomach grew more unsettled. It was the first time I'd seen Tara since Val filled me in on her secret relationship with Eva. I thought about maybe throwing my coffee in her face and storming out of the restaurant, but decided that might be classified as making a scene.

"So should we get on with it?" Sammy asked as she moved in next to Tara. All three of them were sitting across from me now, even though the bench seat was a tight squeeze for two.

The waitress appeared before anyone could answer Sammy.

"Are you waiting on someone?" she asked, viewing our seating arrangement.

I shook my head. "No, this is it. You guys ready to order?"

Crystal nodded. As usual, the other girls followed. Even though I couldn't have eaten more than a peanut without throwing up, I ordered a plate of pancakes, hoping the carbs would relax my stomach.

"Eww, I can't believe you just did that," Tara said once the waitress walked away.

"Did what?" I asked.

"Ordered pancakes. Those things are loaded with calories, and there's only five days 'til the festival."

"Ah, so that's why you all ordered cottage cheese plates," I said, trying not to laugh.

"The festival isn't just another school project, you know. There's going to be a red carpet and everything," said Sammy.

"I posted a recommended diet on Pop this morning to help everyone prepare," said Crys.

"Oh, sorry," I said. "Hard for us nonmembers to keep up with the latest dietary restrictions."

Crystal folded her arms across the table.

"Look, we all feel bad about what happened to you," Sammy said. "But that's no reason to take it out on us. It's not like we are responsible for your termination. We all told you to stay away from Brandon."

"I'm not so sure he's the problem," I said, biting my tongue after I said it. I was supposed to be on best behavior, yet here I was acting like a jerk. Even though they deserved it, I knew running my mouth would cause more trouble than it was worth. So I took a deep breath and opened my eyes a little wider.

"But, I am willing to listen," I said.

"Finally, something reasonable," said Tara. "Now I believe it's time for Sammy to explain what really happened."

I nodded and Sammy began, just as the food arrived. Ten minutes later, everyone's plates were still untouched. Most of her story sounded like what I'd seen unfold on the video, only Sammy chose to leave out her drunkenness. And instead of her being the temptress, she painted herself an injured little lamb that big bad B-Dash had sought out to slaughter. According to Sammy, B-Dash was giving her the eye, leaning in over her, hugging her as soon as she lost her balance. And it was he who leaned in for the second kiss. The kiss on the cheek had been nothing, just Sammy's typical way of saying goodbye.

The story would have made sense. Except that it didn't look that way in the video. Not to mention that by the end of her account, Sammy was crying into her napkin and snorting through her nose.

And that gave it all away.

Because Sammy didn't cry. Not even when her

grandma died. When Sammy was really upset, she just burrowed into bed with dry eyes and a frozen frown. Meaning today's tears were nothing more than an act to cover her transgressions. But, still not wanting to be an outcast for the next two years of high school, I let her tell her story and even handed her a clump of clean napkins when hers got soggy. And then, employing equal acting skills, told her that I forgave her for whatever small part she'd played in the incident and promised to have a serious talk with Brandon.

"It sounds like you both weren't thinking clearly. I know nobody wanted it to happen," I said.

Sammy dotted her eyes with her sleeve. "So will you end it with B-Dash?"

I shook my head. "If there's anything this whole termination thing has taught me, it's that we all deserve second chances, right?"

An awkward silence fell over the table. Tara grimaced while Sammy stared down at her empty water glass. Crystal was the first to talk.

"You're right. And I'm sorry for giving you such a hard time. Of course we understand if you and Dash wanna work things out. We all make mistakes."

Sammy nodded, her eyes now dry. "I just couldn't stand the thought of you being mad at me. I'd never do anything to hurt you."

"You know I could never stay mad," I said, looking away.

"Thank God," said Sammy, leaning over the table for a hug. "Why don't we get out of this place. You need a ride home?"

Tara shot Sammy a look as she grabbed her jacket. She was upset about something, but I didn't care enough to ask.

"No, I'm all set. I told my mom we'd be done by 1:00. She's probably outside already."

"Okay, well then we'll catch you later, Livs," said Crystal as Tara and Sammy walked away.

As soon as Crys and I were alone, she grabbed my arm. "Before you leave, I can't believe I forgot to tell you. We've been doing the math and we think we've got enough votes to get you back into Populatti."

"Really? Why didn't you tell me earlier?" I asked, my heart jumping.

"Because I'm losing my mind."

I stared back in silence.

She sighed. "Look, I'm sorry Livs. About everything. Populatti, the other night. Everything. I know you're right about the Sammy thing. I looked over the video a few times and she was definitely wrong. Drunk too. But I don't think she likes Brandon. She was just lonely and pissed off and hates that you're so happy with him."

"Yeah, I know. And I'm over it. Or at least done fighting."

"Sorry for not sticking up for you," she said.

"As long as you know Brandon's innocent."

"Yeah. And I meant what I said about Pop. We might even be able to get you back in before the film festival, which would mean you could come to the Oscars-themed after party."

"Really?" All of a sudden I was pleased I'd spent so much time picking the perfect dress. As angry as I was at Tara and Sammy, the idea of being side-lined for more events was even more devastating. As long as Populatti existed, I needed to be in it.

"When's my nomination going to be?" I asked, my voice creeping higher.

"I'll post it tonight, voting will commence tomorrow, and then you'll have three days to get 13 votes. And then, no more excuses about not knowing 'bout the five-day party diet," Crystal said, trying to sound upbeat.

"You got it," I said, spotting Mom's car. "Though I'm not giving up my pancakes. Or my pizza and fries and ice cream."

As I headed across the parking lot, everything seemed more vivid than when I'd entered the diner just an hour earlier. The lopsided pine trees bordering the strip mall looked like an Alpine forest. The faded red paint on the Beast was shining in the sun, decades of wear and tear stripped away. I watched Sammy and Tara jump inside before opening the passenger door to Mom's car.

"You want to drive?" Mom asked.

"Sure," I said.

I marveled at the dancing sunlight as we

switched places and I envisioned myself reclaiming my rightful place in the Populatti hierarchy. In just three days I would be back. And while I knew Val had insisted I break ties with Tara, from the sound of it, Crys had gotten enough votes without her help. I was pretty sure once I explained everything to Val, I'd win her over too. Because it was hard to deny that I was more valuable to everyone as a member of Populatti. Feeling lighter than I had in weeks, I let myself smile as I thought of the upcoming weekend. Not only was my group going to rock the festival, but now I could actually celebrate the success afterwards.

Mom seemed to sense my happiness as she asked if I wouldn't mind a trip to the grocery store. Although I usually gave Mom a hard time about stopping, this time I just smiled.

"Can we go to the Stop & Shop over by the train station?" I asked as I turned onto the Post Road. "There's a tanning salon over there. I could run in for a quick spray after we get the food. A tan would really go with that dress."

If the film festival was now going to be a coming out party, then I needed to look my best.

"That's fine," Mom said as she punched out an email on her phone. "I need to get back to the hospital by 3:00 so why don't you take care of that while I get the groceries."

"You don't mind?"

"Not at all."

The tanning salon was hopping, filled with girls all waiting for their chance to get airbrushed with the latest mix of skin coloring chemicals meant to mimic a real, sun-kissed tan. Eying the line, I frowned, wondering if I'd have time to squeeze in a session before Mom needed to leave for the hospital. Lucky for me, I'd been a frequent tanner at Sun Spray for years and knew most of the staff by name.

"Oh Livi, hey. You here for the usual?" asked Mira, the tangerine receptionist who'd graduated from Golden Hill a few years earlier. Mira had been known to show up uninvited to more than a few of our parties, but despite the breach in protocol we usually let her stay, if only because it got us out of jams like the one I was in now. No appointment and no time to spare. Thank God Mira was working.

"Yeah, just a quick spray," I said. "Nothing too dramatic."

Mira plucked down a pot of coconut moisturizer and led me to the back. "You're lucky, this room was booked but the girl is running late."

I locked the door behind me and undressed. Then I jumped into the stall and pressed the green button that told Mira I was ready to go. A few minutes later I was done, my skin transformed from pale to sunkissed, all without a single UV ray.

As I jumped out of the stall and got dressed, I heard a familiar voice coming from a few rooms over. It was Tara, sounding upset.

So this must be why she didn't want Sammy to drive me home, I thought, as Tara's voice seeped through the slits in the wooden door. They might have wanted my forgiveness, but apparently they weren't ready to let me crash their tanning appointment. Something was wrong, and it went a lot deeper than Sammy's kiss.

I placed my ear against the door and waited.

"I can't believe Mira is making us share a room," Sammy said. "We were only ten minutes late."

"Whatever. We can always come back tomorrow if they don't come out right," Tara said.

"Don't we have to help Crys round the troops for Livi's vote tomorrow?"

"I'm pretty sure that's wrapped up. Coop says he's got four votes and with what we have, that should make 13."

I breathed a sigh of relief at Tara's confident tone. But just as I started to relax, the conversation changed directions.

"Do you think Livs will help us out?" asked Sammy. "You know, once she's back in?"

"Of course she will," said Tara. "We're her best friends. She has to."

"But how much clout do you think she really has? I mean, she tried to help Eva, but she still got suspended," said Sammy.

Tara sighed. "Well, she got a shorter suspension than originally recommended. But cheating is a whole different thing. We just skipped class. It's a much smaller offense."

I placed my hand over my mouth to muffle my scream as the words sunk in. Sammy and Tara were in trouble. And wanted me to bail them out.

"True, but aren't they gonna write us up on leaving campus too? It's the driving during school hours that worries me," said Sammy.

"They can't prove it," said Tara. "Mr. Henkle only saw me holding the keys, not driving. So we should be safe on that one. Unless Val says anything."

"Ugh. Why did she have to be in the parking lot?"

"I know. Bad timing. But I don't think she'll cause any trouble," said Tara. "And if she does, we'll just vote her out. Which wouldn't be a bad idea anyway, seeing as she knows about my talks with Eva."

"I forgot about that, I still can't believe Eva told her. We're lucky Livi and Val aren't close. So when do you think the case will make it to honor council? Next week?"

"Might even be the week after. Livi said they're really busy."

I reminded myself to breathe as my head began spinning.

"Well at least we have a plan," said Sammy. "Once we get Livs back into Pop she'll owe us."

"Yeah. I just want things to go back to normal,"

said Tara. "I still can't believe Eva took that Nick story so badly. I never meant for things to spiral so far out of control."

"I know, though I guess I didn't help matters kissing Brandon," Sammy said.

"Whatever, it's not like you meant to do it. You were drunk. And once Livs gets back into Populatti she'll be so thrilled she won't even remember..."

As if I could ever forget.

The humming of the spray machines grew louder, drowning out their conversation. So I gathered my purse and ran out to the parking lot. With my legs shaking, I asked Mom to take over driving duty for the short ride home. As soon as we reached the house, I booked it to my room and collapsed onto my bed. After locking my door, I drew a bubble bath and eased myself into the scalding water, hoping it would help relax my prickly skin. But all it did was burn the remnants of last week's scrapes as my salty tears mixed with the soap. So I lifted myself out of the tub, grabbed my robe, and turned on some music to drown out my whimpers. Then I retreated to my bedroom and pulled out my old journal.

While I hadn't written in it regularly since middle school, my mind was swirling with a sea of emotions that threatened to pull me under if I didn't sort everything out. A list of bullets poured out of me as I started recounting everything that had happened. But instead of bringing clarity, all

294 jackie nastri bardenwerper

the list showed was how little I knew. One minute I had been singing to the radio and dreaming about my reentry to Populatti. The next I was overhearing Tara and Sammy admitting their transgressions and saying they wanted me back in Pop so they could use my position on honor council. And to help terminate Val. A shiver ran down my spine as my wet hair dripped down my back. When the bullet points crawled onto a second page of the journal, I knew I had to talk to Val. But after five rings, her phone went to voicemail.

My phone buzzed before I put it down. Hoping it was Val, I snapped it open and said hello. Brandon's voice greeted me back.

"You up for getting food? Thought you could use some cheering up after that lunch."

I felt my stomach rumble. So much for the pre-Oscars diet.

"Yeah, sure," I said.

"Great, I'll pick you up in a few."

"Oh and do you think we can stop by Val's afterwards? I really need to talk to her."

"We're actually just finishing up practice next to the softball team," he said. "Their practice should be over in a minute. I'll ask her to tag along."

After finalizing our plans, I hung up the phone and got dressed. Then I tried to focus on my new copy of *Vanity Fair,* but my eyes kept darting to my phone. So instead I headed to Populatti, hoping to find some helpful ammunition for my next battle.

populatti.com

BrandontheGreat: 84%

Approved Members: 23
Pending Applications: 1
Access Denied: 49

POP REPORT: hey popsters, I am proud to announce the nomination of LIVI STANLEY for membership!!! Voting starts tomorrow so don't forget to vote early so we can celebrate her return on fridayyyy ~Crys

COMMENTS:

Jake *posted at 3:01 p.m. ET June 1*: thank god maybe now crys can stop acting all depressed

Tarable *posted at 3:00 p.m. ET June 1*: mine too, sammy

BiancaA *posted at 2:56 p.m. ET June 1*: intriguing

celebSAMmy *posted at 2:45 p.m. ET June 1*: livi's got my vote ☺

BrandontheGreat *posted at 2:35 p.m. ET June 1*: can't wait to cast my vote. vote for livi!

EvaBeautiful *posted at 2:28 p.m. ET June 1*: seems a little soon for another vote *sigh*

CHAPTER SEVENTEEN

"So let me get this straight. They got caught skipping class and Val saw them. So now they want you to go easy on them in honor council, but then also terminate Val?" asked Brandon, taking a sip of Coke.

"I don't think voting out Val is the goal. It sounded more like they were gonna use it as a threat so she doesn't talk. I guess she saw them driving back in Tara's car or something. But then they did say something about voting her out anyway," I said.

"Why would they be angry with Val?" asked Brandon.

"They're not. I just don't think they want her

around since she knows about Eva and Tara's relationship. They know Matt will break up with Eva soon enough and she'll lose her membership. So really they just don't want anyone around who could fill me in on why I was terminated."

"But you already know."

"Yes, but Tara and Sammy don't know that."

"God, you girls are crazy."

"Hey, don't group me with them. I'm just collateral damage."

"Livs, believe me. You are anything but damage."

I looked at him and smiled. We were sitting in a back booth at Rojo Casa, a local Mexican joint known for their overstuffed burritos and mile-high nachos. The food was good, though after eating pancakes at the diner it hadn't been my first choice. But it was close to the high school, making it convenient for Brandon.

And Val, who arrived minutes later.

"So what's the new crisis," she said, shuffling over to our table with Bianca in tow.

I scooted into the booth so Bianca could slide in. "Don't worry, there's not much to tell," I said, before diving into the story.

Not wanting to completely trash my so-called friends, I left out Sammy's lukewarm apology and made it sound like she'd begged for forgiveness. And I built up the news about my reapplication to Populatti so that it sounded like things were looking up. My fake enthusiasm seemed to work, as Bianca patted my back, excited by the prospect of celebrating a potential film festival win at the Pop Oscars after party. Only Val looked suspicious, as if she expected there to be a catch. Which of course, there was.

As I reached the climax, Val just nodded slowly, as if she'd been expecting the outcome.

"So they really want me out," she said, her voice drifting.

I frowned. "If this whole skipping class thing blows over, they'll probably drop it."

"Except that's not going away," said Val. "Mr. Henkle cornered me on my way in. I'd been out there grabbing a textbook and I saw Tara and Val drive up in her Prius. I couldn't lie."

"Great. So now they're gonna want me to bend the rules at honor council and help vote you out of Populatti."

Val shrugged. "Maybe, but who cares? You're not the only voice on council, so tell them you tried but got outvoted. And if they want to vote me out of Pop, then let them. It's not like they can take away my real friends."

I nodded as she spoke, wishing I could have that kind of strength. Even if part of me had started to see Populatti as unnecessary, the other part knew that without it, I was just another sophomore trying to survive difficult classes, annoying little brothers, and the hectic schedules of my parents. I didn't have any friends except those in Populatti. Without it, I sat home on the couch unless Brandon took me out. And that wasn't always an option. Meaning without Populatti there was a lot of alone time. Just like back in middle school. The thought of Val becoming Golden Hill's Drumstick made me shudder. As did the realization that I could have contributed to hurting others, not just Val. Feeling a little sick, I promised myself that no matter what happened, I couldn't let Val get hurt. If I could save her, maybe in time I could learn how to help others as well.

Luckily, Bianca seemed to feel the same way. "But Val, we need you," she said, her voice wavering. "You're the one that got me into Pop in the first place. Without you, the softball contingent will seriously dwindle. And you know that ever since Pop started, our softball parties haven't been so well attended."

Val nodded. "I hate that I'm a slave to the site."

"I know. I just wish it would all go away," I said.

"Well, as far as I can tell it's not going anywhere," said Val. "So maybe we start our own termination vote against Tara, like we've been talking about. You know, give her a little of her own medicine? What do you say, Livi? Will you support her termination once you're back in?"

I folded my fingers into a ball to keep from biting my nails. It was the same question I'd been grappling with for weeks. "Tara and I have a lot of history. I'd like to try to work things out with her if possible."

Val shook her head. "Livs, I understand how you feel, but they're using you. Didn't you hear what you said? They want you to break your honor code and give them a more lenient punishment. And they want to vote me out just because I happen to know some information. And this is all after Tara tried to steal Coop from me and sold you out to Eva. I don't think there's much of a friendship to save."

I signaled to the waitress to refill our pitcher of Coke. "I know you're right. I just don't feel comfortable turning on her like that."

"What if we just start campaigning for Val now then?" asked Bianca. "I'm sure we could get the necessary votes to keep you in."

"But that would require Livi to support me, which would not fly with Tara," Val said.

"Oh. Right. Then what if we started our own Populatti? Or just planned our own parties?" asked Bianca.

"We don't have the computer skills or the time," Val said. "And our parties could never compete with Sammy's. She treats party planning like a full-time job. It's amazing she even has time to sleep."

"She doesn't sleep much," I said.

"Too bad. It might be a better use of time. Her dark circles are pretty scary."

"You think? I've never noticed," I said.

"Ladies, there's a guy here, remember," said Brandon.

"Oh yeah, right. Well we better get going," said Val. "Bianca's parents were expecting us after practice. I'll call you if I think of anything else, Livi, but as far as I'm concerned, I would just let this go. If Tara and Sammy want me out, there's not much we can do to stop it."

I frowned. "Well, we're not going down without a fight."

She smiled, mouthing 'thank you' as she and Bianca disappeared out the door.

Brandon dropped me back at home an hour later before we could reach a resolution about what to do about Tara and Sammy. I spent the rest of the night trying to hatch a plan that could let me vote my conscience on honor council while saving Val from the humiliation I knew too well. Because even if she didn't think getting kicked out was a big deal, and even if I wished things were different and that Populatti didn't exist, the reality remained that Populatti was real. And being excluded was painful. Just wait until your first Friday without Coop and Bianca and everyone else, I thought, thinking back to the emptiness I'd felt during the night of Jake's birthday party.

Lucky for me, regardless of Sammy and Tara's motives, my emptiness was almost a thing of the past. Because when I signed into Brandon's Pop account Monday morning, I found that Crystal had indeed posted my application. According to the screen, Crystal, Sammy, and Tara had already cast their votes, bringing me just ten votes away from redemption.

"You need to go vote now," I said to Brandon when he met me by my locker later that morning.

"With what? I thought phones were banned during school hours," he said, trying not to laugh.

"Come on, I know you have it."

This time, he did laugh, as he pulled it out of his pocket and got swiping.

"All right, it's done," he said a minute later. "Though what are you so eager for anyway? I thought you agreed with Val when she said Populatti was no big deal."

"I do. It's not. But that doesn't mean being voted out doesn't still totally suck."

"Well then, I'm glad I could help," he said, before heading off to class.

Time slowed to a crawl as I fought my way through my morning classes, willing the clock to hit noon. When lunch finally came, I bolted to the cafeteria, which was buzzing with energy. The film festival was on Friday. Everywhere I turned groups were discussing their projects. Girls talked about their dresses, and popsters speculated as to what Sammy had up her sleeve for the Oscars after party. Rumor had it there might be a pre-party too. This was to be her biggest bash yet. My stomach jumped as I reached my usual table. My new application to Pop had come just in time. Now all I needed was enough votes. I tried not to think about it as I pulled out my Dijon turkey sandwich.

"So do you really think there will be a pre-party too?" asked Brandon, grabbing the chair between me and Tara.

Tara laughed, her smug look burning my retinas. "Guess you'll have to wait until Sammy reveals the plans on Friday."

This time, I chuckled. "Okay, Tara, because I'm sure Sammy won't tell us. Though I have to ask, do you think a pre-party is the best idea? Shouldn't we save the celebration until after we finish the schoolwork?"

"All we're doing is watching videos. Not much work in that."

I bit my tongue, guessing she wasn't the spokesperson for her group. Nor did she care about those, like me, who would need the hours before the event to practice.

Silence enveloped the table as more regulars piled in. Jake, Sammy, Matt. Even Eva slid over a chair, having joined our table sometime during my days spent skipping lunch. The only one missing was Crystal. Who, as the one who saw vote numbers in real time, was the only person I wanted to see. I kept my eyes on the cafeteria entryway as I ate my sandwich.

As I moved onto the second half of my roll, I

caught sight of her yellow and brown messenger bag, jostling in the crowd.

"Okay, popsters please rise," she said, skipping over to our table. She waved her iPhone like an orchestra conductor motioning everyone at our table to stand.

Reaching the empty chair we'd saved for her arrival, Crys jumped onto the seat, her tiny frame looking even smaller as it looked down on us, her disciples.

"All right, now this is a monumental occasion," she said, lifting her voice. "It is with great pleasure that I announce that Olivia Stanley is once again a member of Populatti!"

Crystal then squealed and began clapping her hands, encouraging the rest of the table to do the same. Out of the corner of my eye I saw Tara shoot Sammy a look. As much as I wanted to scream at her, to yell that she couldn't control me – especially now that I had a lot more popster friends than before – I refrained. The relief coursing through my veins was way too great for me to care about their petty schemes.

So instead I took a step forward, then fell back into my chair. The lonely nightmare was over. I was a member of Populatti only six hours after voting had opened. I knew that had to be a record, but decided not to comment, seeing as the speed of my termination had been unprecedented too.

"Thank God," yelled Sammy, throwing her arms

around me. "I knew we'd get you back!" She bent down, a sparkly headband in hand, and placed it on the top of my head. "I wanted to bring in our crown but Tara told me it'd be too much."

"Good call, Tarable," I said, hugging Sammy as I pulled my hair through the band.

For a moment all the hatred and pain and anger I'd felt over Sammy's kiss with Brandon was gone. She'd been stupid, but now we were moving on. She'd gone out of her way and brought me a headband. So what if she and Tara wanted help with their latest dilemma. Of course I would help if they asked. Wasn't that what friends were for? I found myself breathing deeper as I sat amongst my friends. I was back in Populatti. Everything was falling into place.

Yet the feeling was short lived. Because as soon as I glanced over at Tara, I was reminded that things were far from okay. Sitting just one seat away, my so-called best friend was still staring into space, her expression unchanged. Happy but annoyed. Excited yet bored. Only Tara could convey two contradictory emotions so perfectly, as she sat there twirling her hair and munching on a piece of organic celery.

"Tarable, aren't you happy for me?" I said, trying my best not to sound too condescending.

"Of course, girl. We're all stoked," she said, her eyes cast down.

"Does that mean I can sit with you in study

hall?"

"I never said you couldn't."

"But now it won't be breaking any rules. Though I was thinking I may need to test out my user ID in the computer lab…"

"Oh, that won't be up 'til tonight," said Crystal, cutting in. "The administrator features don't load on my phone, but I'll set up your account as soon as I get home."

I nodded. "So who voted me back in anyway? I can't believe we got all 13 so fast."

"Girl, you got more than 13. By the time I checked, you had 22," said Crystal.

"Who voted no? I bet it was Val," said Tara, making a face.

"No. Val was a yes," said Crystal.

"Weird," said Jake. "Why would she have seconded Livi's termination if she was just gonna vote her back in?"

"Who knows, she's strange," said Sammy, trying to change the topic.

But Brandon wasn't about to let it go. "Maybe she realized whatever she heard about Livi wasn't true."

Tara's cheeks reddened. One of the drawbacks of her fair skin was her inability to hide her emotions. She mumbled something about running to the bathroom before class, then left the table. And I couldn't help but grin as I watched her skitter away.

By the time I met Tara in study hall, her expression had softened. She pulled out a list of all the different film festival groups and started gossiping about each one. Which groups were fighting throughout filming. Which hadn't started filming at all. And which were real contenders to win the competition. Talking about the film festival was a good diversion and I bought into it willingly, relieved that Tara was acting a little more like herself. It was much easier to play along with her than acknowledge that the foundation of our friendship was crumbling.

"So are you excited to be unveiling your video on the school dress code?" I asked as she finished describing her dress. "Sammy says it's going to be scandalous."

Tara feigned a laugh. "I guess. Really though I'm excited for the party. You know, I'm finally talking more with Christian."

"Oh great," I said, hoping I sounded convincing. "You must be happy he doesn't seem that into Val."

She sighed. "I am, though I have to say, I did see them hanging out at Jake's party. They seemed to be getting along. I'm trying my best to make sure it doesn't become anything serious."

"I'm sure they're just friends."

"But that could lead to more."

"Well then it's good you're talking to him too," I said, still shocked that Tara was so caught up in Coop. It was hard to believe so much of this drama had been about a guy I had pretty much tagged as a spoiled brat.

Tara took a big breath and opened her mouth to speak, then closed it as she caught sight of someone in the distance. I looked up to see Sammy weaving towards our table. Her eyes looked tired, her nerves frazzled. It was like she'd had a full costume change since lunch.

"You okay?" I asked.

"Yeah, just stressed," she said.

"Uh-huh," I said.

"You know, the whole Val thing has really gotten me upset," she said, sitting down.

I opened my mouth to speak, then closed it. This was obviously the ambush they'd been planning at the tanning salon.

"We were all so angry when she helped vote you out," Sammy continued, "and now on top of that she's been spreading rumors about me and Tara."

"Rumors? About what?" I asked, playing dumb.

"Oh geez, you're not filling her in about the Val thing now, are you?" said Tara. "It's her first day back in Populatti. Can't we just celebrate?"

"Not yet. This is important. Val's been trying to get us suspended, Livi. We need her out of Pop now so that she'll back off."

"Sounds serious. What happened?" I asked.

Sammy sighed. "Well, it started last week when Tara and I ran out to her car to grab some books. She apparently told Mr. Henkle we'd been driving around or something. That we'd left campus during school hours."

I tried to look surprised as Tara and Sammy shook their heads in disgust.

"I really didn't want to bother you with this," said Tara, eying Sammy, "but Mr. Henkle did give us citations for skipping and leaving school."

I shook my head. "But if you weren't skipping, couldn't they just check with your teacher? What class were you in?"'

"That's the problem," said Sammy. "It was in Spanish, but we had a sub. And the sub didn't take attendance and doesn't remember who was there."

"Which is also why we didn't have a hall pass," said Tara. "She didn't know where the forms were."

Their story sounded convincing, but deep down I knew it was just that. A story. Sammy and Tara had been known to duck out of classes before, especially when there was a sub. Something told me this time had been no different. But here they were trying to punish Val for telling the truth. All of a sudden it was a lot less surprising that Tara had betrayed me for intel on Coop. It seemed she would hurt anyone to get what she wanted.

"Well I don't know if I can help you with Val yet," I said, "just because as a new member I need some time to reestablish myself. But you know I always try to be fair at honor council."

"Well, why don't we drum up some votes against Val so yours doesn't stand out, okay? And thanks for hearing us out about the whole skipping thing," said Sammy. "I know you'll do the right thing."

I nodded, wishing I didn't have to.

"You still up for mani pedis?" Sammy asked as the bell rang overhead.

"Yeah, sure," I said, not wanting to look suspicious breaking the plans we'd made at lunch.

"Good, because we do need to celebrate."

"And let's not give another thought to Val," said Tara. "If all goes well, we'll have her out of Populatti in no time, okay?"

"Yeah, sure," I said, fighting a wave of dizziness. "But why don't we wait 'til after the film festival? I'd hate for your big party to suffer because we're campaigning for termination votes."

"Now you're talking, girl," said Sammy. "And I agree. This week is all about the festival. What do you think, Tarable?"

"If that's what you guys want," she said, her voice stiffening.

"Then let's do it," said Sammy. "No more Val talk until next week. All I want to hear about is manis, pedis, dresses, and parties."

I nodded, before pulling out my phone and sending Val the text I'd been writing in my head all week.

"Populatti has to end."

populatti.com

<u>lululivi : 97%</u>

Approved Members: 24
Pending Applications: 0
Access Denied: 49

POP REPORT: so popsters, after wks of waiting, the festival is only hrs away…good luck to tonite's presenters and to all the films. May the best one win! oh and don't forget to GET READY TO PARTY!!!!!! ~Crys

COMMENTS:

celebSAMmy *posted at 3:31 p.m. ET June 6*: come on jake, I sent the invite out this morning. It's right after the festival ends!!!

Jake *posted at 3:09 p.m. ET June 6*: hey sammy, what time does this party start again?

EvaBeautiful *posted at 3:04 p.m. ET June 6*: time 2 get gorgeousss!!!!!!

ValieGal *posted at 2:56 p.m. ET June 6*: ahhhh can't wait to see all the videos ;)

Coop007 *posted at 2:49 p.m. ET June 6*: do presenters really have to wear suits to this thing??

Tarable *posted at 2:45 p.m. ET June 6*: time to get beautiful with my girls!!

CHAPTER EIGHTEEN

"Livi, let's go! It's getting late," yelled Crystal from the bathroom doorway.

Brandon was coming to my house to pick up the girls and me for the festival at 4:30 sharp, giving us just a half hour to finish prepping. It hadn't been my idea to invite over Crys, Sammy, and Tara, but in the end, I was glad Crys had insisted we put the bad feelings behind us and adhere to tradition. The electric energy of blow dryers whirring and mindless banter was helping me keep down my early dinner. A real accomplishment seeing as I was the spokesperson for our video. I looked down again at my summary blurb before waving my wand of mascara over my eyelashes for the second time.

"OhmiGod, emergency, I need cover-up now! I can feel a pimple forming," yelled Tara, breaking my concentration. She was dressed in a black sheath dress that was supposed to be trendy but was so narrow at the hem she could hardly walk.

"Here ya go," I said, handing her a jar of concealer.

"Thanks," she said, inspecting my outfit. "Cool dress."

I smiled wide in the mirror, inspecting my teeth. "I was going for Old Hollywood."

"I like it," said Sammy, barging through the door.

"Yours is great too," I said, pulling on her bubblegum pink skirt.

"Ladies, come on, we have to get going," said Crystal.

I grabbed my school bag as well as my fancy wristlet as Crystal threw on a sparkly shawl, positioning it so that it fell off the shoulder of her red and black beaded dress. Tara and Sammy emerged from the bathroom and did the same, leaving me the only one with bare shoulders. Though for once I was happy not to belong. The shawls looked too sparkly for daytime, and not very Hollywood at all. I swallowed my laughter before grabbing my black cardigan that matched the neckline of my dress.

Downstairs, we had just enough time for Mom to snap off a few pictures before Brandon arrived with Jake. It was time to head over to the school. Given the 5:00 festival start time, Sammy had nixed the idea of a pre-party, a good thing seeing as I still needed to meet with Bianca beforehand to go over my lines.

Though as soon as I saw B-Dash, I knew that concentrating was going to be a problem. He was wearing a simple black suit with a grey and blue tie, covered in tiny dolphins that matched the color of my dress. He looked better than I'd ever seen him.

Apparently he thought the same about me.

"You look incredible," he said, low enough that Mom couldn't hear.

"So do you," I whispered back.

Everyone seemed excited as we piled into two cars and headed over to school, Jake and the girls in the Beast, and me with Brandon. Even though I was relieved to be riding with Brandon over the girls, I couldn't help but feel my back stiffen. No matter how I turned and fidgeted, I couldn't get comfortable. Nor could I concentrate on anything but the butterflies kicking the sides of my stomach.

"So are you ready for tonight?" Brandon asked, his brow raised as he watched me twist and turn in my seat.

I tried to smile, but my expression fell flat. "I'm all right. Just scared."

He nodded. "You know I talked to Val last night. I know something's up."

I looked at him, my eyes wide. "Nothing's up," I said. "I'm just nervous, especially since the Board of Ed is going to be there. I really want them to like our video and take the problems seriously."

Brandon shook his head. "Then why did you shoot a new video?"

"New video?"

"About Populatti?"

A chill ran down my spine. "What did Val tell you?"

"Just that you and Bianca are going to use your film spot to take down the site."

I breathed in deep. "And you believe her?"

"I don't know. Should I?"

I hesitated, then opened my mouth. "Well, we're not taking it down. Just educating people on its existence."

"And when did you have time to do this?"

"Last night," I said. "The video's really short. We just used a lot of footage from the, uh, kiss video and threw in some screen shots from the site. We cut out the kiss though, of course."

"God. I was hoping Val was wrong. Are you actually going to show it?"

I hugged my legs, unable to control my shaking knees. "I don't know. I think I have to."

Brandon sighed. "Livs, you do know this could get the entire sophomore class in some serious trouble. Not to mention your whole group."

"Well not Jake and Matt. They don't know what

we're doing and Bianca and I will vouch for that."

"Still Livs. I know you're pissed at Tara and Sammy, but is exposing Populatti the best way to deal with it?"

"Probably not," I said, "but I think a lot of the problems I've had with the girls are because of the site. And if I've had problems because of it, I'm sure other girls have too. Like Eva. And isn't this project supposed to be about telling stories about real issues that need addressing? What could be more serious?"

"And scandalous."

"Believe me, it's not like I'm looking forward to this. Especially since I really thought our project on the building could change things for the better. Not to mention maybe win this thing."

"Then show that one," said Brandon. "Wow the Board of Ed, then deal with Populatti later, in another way. You know I'd help you boycott parties or throw our own or something."

"Thanks," I said, knowing by now that Brandon meant it. "It really means a lot that you want to help, but as long as there's a Populatti, there's going to be all this drama. The site just makes it too easy. Populatti has to die."

Brandon shook his head as we turned into the parking lot. "I can't say I'll really miss the site. But I wish you didn't have to be so involved."

"I know. Hopefully the honor council will go easy on me," I said, trying to smile.

Brandon tried to smile back. "Well then, if there's nothing I can do to change your mind, I guess this is good luck."

We stepped out of the parked car and toward the red carpet.

As advertised, Ms. Tilfry had gone all out for the occasion, with not only a red carpet but one of those large screens with a photographer snapping pictures of arriving students. Emblazoned with the words Golden Hill Film Festival, the screen looked straight out of a premiere night, especially when behind groups of posing students. Sequins and satins in neon pinks and greens and purples brightened the school's scuffed beige walls, while the clicking of heels added an air of importance. With the lights on and scores of faculty in attendance, the night felt much different from a dimly lit school dance. But then, part of that difference could have been me. With my whole body shaking, the night would've felt different no matter where we'd been.

"Hey Livs, over here," said Bianca, waving through the crowd gathered by the entrance. True to her word, she was in an emerald green dress with three quarter sleeves and a pointed collar. It was much more businesslike than Hollywood, but somehow it seemed well suited to the occasion.

I waved back, then began weaving through the crowd as quickly as I could, trying to work in as many 'hellos' along the way.

Matt stopped me halfway to Bianca. "Hey Livi, I was looking for you," he said, breathless.

"What's up?" I said, my eyes still on Bianca.

"It's our video. I cleaned up a few more of those choppy cuts. I have the final version right here," he said, handing over a black USB drive.

"Oh, thanks. I'll be sure to use this one then," I said, throwing it into my dangling wristlet. "Well I better go check in backstage. Maybe get in a little last-minute rehearsing."

Matt nodded. "Good luck. We're all rooting for you. Can't wait to hear what the Board of Ed thinks."

"Thanks," I said, "for all of this. I know you've put in a ton of time." Then I continued on toward Bianca, my heart sinking at the thought that Ms. Tilfry and everyone else would never see Matt's amazing production skills.

When I reached Bianca, she looked just as nervous as me, her arms shaking, as I reached out and squeezed her hand.

"Are you ready to do this?" I asked, steering her toward the side hallway that would bring us to the auditorium's stage entrance.

Despite its run-in with the killer mold, the auditorium had reopened that past fall, giving us the perfect venue for the festival. Yet not all was forgotten. Already I'd spotted two guys carrying gas masks as props. Something told me it was going to be a busy week of festival cleanup in honor council.

That is, if I was still there to do the cleaning.

Bianca breathed in deep, then handed me a thumb drive, identical to the one from Matt. Again I opened my wristlet, though this time I was sure to place the drive in the purse's side pocket, separating it from the other.

"What did Matt want?" Bianca asked as I secured the drive.

"He made more changes to our group video. Cleaned some more cuts."

"I thought we already submitted the final one for approval?" said Bianca.

"That was still a draft. Ms. Tilfry said it was okay to make some final changes."

Bianca frowned. "Poor Matt."

"And Jake."

"We have to make sure they don't get in trouble."

"The good thing is that Ms. Tilfry knows another video does exist," I said, happy that at least we'd handed in an early draft. Although the students would be viewing the films for the first time, Ms. Tilfry and her panel of faculty judges had already taken a sneak peek. In fact, something told me they probably had favorites in mind. I wondered what would happen now that ours would be out of the running.

"I wish there was a way we could show the video anonymously," said Bianca.

"I know. We're going to be the most hated peeps

at Golden Hill High," I said.

Bianca shook her head. "Maybe, maybe not. Though there will definitely be some angry popsters."

"Yeah. The only one I really feel for is Crystal," I said, folding my arms.

In the past twenty-four hours, I'd gone from hating to loving to again hating Populatti. And after careful consideration, I'd decided my hatred was stronger than any love I may have harbored for the site. Yet still I couldn't help but think of Crystal. When she'd first told us about Populatti, she'd been beaming, saying she'd come up with the perfect way for us to plan parties and stay in touch while avoiding more public sites that were often monitored by parents. Then she had poured countless hours into creating a website to make our lives better, yet all it had done was tear friendships apart and pit popsters against those who couldn't get voted into the group. And as much as she drove me crazy with her insistence that we girls forgive and forget, I had to give her credit for trying to keep our friendships intact. Something told me after tonight she wouldn't be trying so hard to repair any damage.

Yet as Ms. Tilfry had taught us, there were times when you just had to act. Even if it's not popular to be the messenger, it's the messenger who can bring awareness to big issues that need fixing.

"I know this is going to be pretty terrible," said

Bianca, "but we're helping more people than hurting. Think of Val. And you. And even Eva. She might have been a jerk but it's because they used her too."

"It's the power of the site," I said. "The parties, approval ratings, termination votes..." My voice trailed off as Ms. Tilfry's boomed over the loudspeaker. The night was about to begin. It was time to take our seats. So I parted with Bianca as I went to join the rest of the group spokespeople in the room backstage.

The one drawback of being the group spokesperson – well, besides the obvious one of speaking and presenting to the entire auditorium – was that from backstage we couldn't watch the films, which would have been a welcome distraction. While most of my peers used this time to practice their speeches, I found myself pacing back and forth and around piles of castoff costumes and props left over from the Drama Club's spring performance. The films had been broken into four flights of five films. We were the first film in the second set.

So for another hour, I relived the past two years in my head, from the day Crys told us about her idea for Populatti to that awful realization at the tanning salon that my friends were voting me back in solely for their own benefit. I thought of Brandon, of the parties, of laughing with Sammy over wardrobe selections and party favors and themes. And I thought of Val and Bianca, girls I'd never known be-

322 ☙ jackie nastri bardenwerper

fore but who had been there for me in a way few
had ever since my termination. Last I thought of
Eva. For months I'd blamed her for the mess that
Tara had created. Whether Tarable would've acted
this way if Populatti didn't exist was a mystery. But
what Bianca had said earlier rang true. Eva, like
me, was a victim.

"All right, Livi, you're up in three minutes," said
Ms. Tilfry, breaking my concentration.

Looking up, I smiled.

"Go get 'em," she said. "I think the students are
really gonna like yours."

"I think so too," I said. Then I steadied my
hands on my wristlet and walked onto the stage.

The clicking of my heels echoed throughout the
room as I reached the podium, eying the laptop
which would project our video onto the massive
screen behind me. Taking a deep breath, I opened
my wristlet and pulled out Bianca's USB from the
side pocket. As I waited for our video to load, I
grabbed the microphone and began talking.

"Now, this next video should hit a little closer to
home than say, problems in the country, or Connecticut or even our town. Because our group chose
to focus on issues affecting every one of us at Gold-
en Hill High."

I stopped, paused, cleared my throat.

"By exposing one of Golden Hill's greatest se-
crets."

I turned to the computer, our Populatti exposé

loaded on the screen. All I had to do was push Play and the site would be gone forever.

I grabbed the mouse in my hand.

Moved the curser over the button.

Then stopped.

Reached for my wristlet.

And kept talking.

"Some say high school is a volatile time. Friendships are made and broken, first loves won then lost, and in the midst of this turbulence, we are tasked with learning, growing, and shaping the unknown futures that lie before us," I said, remembering the speech I'd written during the week.

"There are a lot of great aspects of Golden Hill High that continue to help us on this challenging journey. Yet, there are a few that are troubling. That some would say make it difficult for students to achieve success. And while not all of these are in the school's control, we believe they need addressing."

As I spoke, I scanned the crowd for familiar faces. Yet all I could make out was a sea of black. I wondered if Bianca knew what I was doing. Or if anyone else was suspicious of my behavior. With no way of knowing, I continued on, switching USBs beneath the podium.

"So over the next ten minutes, you will all learn about the issues holding our school back," I said. "Specifically, you will hear interviews from students and faculty members about issues such as overcrowding, air filtration, and of course, the ever-popular mold fiasco. We hope that you find this video to be fun and informative, as for the first time we put real voices behind the issues that so often get pushed under the table."

My piece finished, I hit Play on the laptop and walked off stage. Without sticking around to hear the reaction to our film, I ran off to the girls' restroom, Bianca's USB in hand. Then I laid the drive down on the Formica counter and smashed my wristlet on top of it, shielding my eyes as shards of plastic went flying.

In silence, I collected the pieces and flushed them down the toilet. My shoulders sank as our exposé floated away.

Deep down, I knew Populatti shouldn't exist. But the truth was, it did. Crystal had created the site and it had run our lives for the past two years. And that was the problem. Not the site exactly, but the way we used it. Populatti had become our lives, had taken over our friendships and outfits and parties and transformed our self-worth into numerical approval ratings that moved with as much predictability as the wind.

Exposing the site wasn't going to solve the problem. Because who was to say another site wouldn't take its place? For all I knew, there was some freshman ready to launch an even better site next week. No, the answer wasn't destruction, but education. I needed to learn to live with the new reality. The world where Populatti existed, but other things did too. Tangible, real-world things, like my secret spot on the beach. My relationship with Brandon. And the problems with Golden Hill High that we'd just shown to the Board of Ed. It was time to focus more on those things instead of wasting so much time trying to please girls who cared only about themselves. Whatever role Populatti would play in that was still to be determined. But for the first time, it seemed within my control. I would use Populatti for good. I wouldn't be its slave.

Feeling calmer than I had in weeks, I swung open the stall door, almost running into Val on my way out.

"What happened?" she asked, hands waving. "I thought you were going to play your video. The one on Populatti. Didn't Bianca give you the drive?"

"Yeah, she did," I said, "but I was having trouble getting it to work so I had to abort."

Val pursed her lips but didn't question me. Instead she stood silent for a long time.

"Well, maybe that's for the better," she said a minute later.

"Yeah, maybe," I said. "Not that I want Tara or Sammy to get away with being so destructive. But maybe it's better I'm not the one to ruin them."

"Or us in the process," said Bianca, swinging open the door.

I turned to her, eyes wide. "You're not mad?"

"No. Actually a little relived," she said. "I wasn't

looking forward to getting kicked off the softball team right before States."

Val laughed. "Neither was I."

"Well, thanks to Livs, the season is safe. And our real video won third place."

"Third? Really?" I said. "Any feedback yet from the Board of Ed?"

Bianca smiled. "Not yet, but there was a lot of clapping after ours, probably the most. There's no way it didn't make an impression."

"Then I'm really glad we showed it," I said. "The school's problems do need addressing."

"You know, you're right," said Val. "You can never underestimate the power of air purification."

I laughed. "So who took first? And second?"

"Some of the lacrosse guys won," said Bianca. "They did this hilarious piece on why they need a new practice field. Not much of an exposé but fun to watch. You'll like it. The second place one was weirder. Something about the dangers of organic farming?"

"I thought organic farming was good."

"I know. It was weird."

"I wish we could've watched them backstage," I said, breathing deep as the weight of exposing Populatti lifted. I felt free. Relaxed. And happy.

"Yeah, it was fun to see them all," said Val.

"Hmm, I wonder if Crys has posted the winning videos on Populatti yet," I said.

Bianca pulled out her phone to check. "Not yet,

but I'm sure they'll be up soon. You know how quick Crys is."

"Yeah, she'll definitely have them up before the party," I said.

"Speaking of which, we should get back out there, Livs," said Bianca. "Ms. Tilfry wants to congratulate the winners backstage. Jake and Matt are already on their way."

"Well, then I guess we better go."

I smiled as Bianca extended her hand.

Grabbing it, I let her pull me out of the bathroom and down the hall.

"I can't believe we won third," I said, laughing. "Tonight we have to celebrate."

"For sure," said Bianca, breaking into a run. "Oscars after party here we come."

Reaching the stage door, I jumped as Brandon caught my arm. He was there waiting, a single flower in hand.

"I would've gotten more, but I didn't know how this would go," he said, kissing my cheek. "But I'm glad it turned out the way it did."

"Yeah, me too," I said. "Though thanks for supporting me either way."

He smiled as Bianca pulled me backstage.

And I found myself wanting nothing more than to be lost in his arms on Sammy's dance floor. Sure, there was still business to sort through with the girls, and I knew my relationship with Eva would always be a little weird. But these were things I could handle in time. Tonight I just wanted to celebrate what I had. A good English grade. New friends. A pretty amazing boyfriend.

So I closed my eyes and let myself smile wide. Tonight was going to be fabulous. I could already hear the music. And taste the Cherry Coke.

Acknowledgements

Writing a second book has been a very different experience from writing the first. Instead of wondering if there will be readers, I have spent hours hoping that those who fell in love with Piper will enjoy reading about Livi as well. To those faithful readers of *On the Line*, I hope that I have succeeded, because it is your enthusiasm for Piper's story that has motivated me to keep writing and not give up on an idea I first had over four years ago.

To my family, I am forever indebted to you for your help throughout each step of the writing process. To my mother, Violet Nastri, your critical eye and ability to focus on each detail, no matter how small, has made Populatti infinitely better – as has your willingness to read countless versions. To my father, Mark Nastri, your unwavering belief in my abilities continues to guide me every step of the way. And to my brother, Mark Nastri, not only are you one of my biggest fans, but one of my best promoters as well! Your sincere excitement in sharing my work with everyone you meet means the world to me.

To my grandparents, Dolores Nastri, and Elizabeth and Andras Repasi, and to my aunts, uncles and cousins who encourage me through all my endeavors, thank you. You all continue to amaze me with your support, from attending book signings to handing out copies to everyone you know.

To the entire Bardenwerper clan – Walter, Patricia, Will, Nelly and Patrick (and Nora!), Annie and Matt, and Buddy – thank you for reading, reviewing, and championing my work. And to Patricia and Annie, thank you for your knack at finding missing words and books! Without your help, the final proof would still be lost in the mail.

To my fellow writers, Nina Mansfield Haberli, Jeff Faville, and Mary Warner McGrade, thank you for your critiques and all the help along the way.

To my dear friends – Heather Higgins, Lauren Neustat, Danielle Higgins, Christie Petrella, Fabi Mitnick, Julie Fraser, Aarti France, Jennifer McCauliffe, Ashley Cohen, and Kirsten Snyder – thank you for your support and for helping influence much of this story.

To my village – Shanae, Arley, Sara, Jaclyn, Sara, Naddya, Stephanie, Danielle, Kera, Julie, Jai, and all the stroller moms – thank you for inspiring me each day to keep reaching for my goals.

Lastly, to my husband, Tad, and our beautiful daughter, Cecilia, thank you. Words cannot express how lucky I am to have you both in my life. Ceci, you are my happiness. The joy and love you give me each day is the fuel that allows me to keep writing long after the point of sleep deprivation. And Tad, you are my first reader, most dedicated editor, and above all else, my best friend. I cannot thank you enough for always believing in me and in this story.

About the Author

Jackie Nastri Bardenwerper is the author of the young adult novel On the Line, an honorable mention recipient in the Writer's Digest Self-Published eBook Awards. She graduated from Cornell University and lives in Stamford, CT with her husband Tad and daughter Cecilia. For more, visit www.jnbwrite.com.

42034311R10209

Made in the USA
Lexington, KY
05 June 2015